REAL ESTATE

A Novel

REAL ESTATE

A Novel

Kathryn Holzman

Second edition. 2023
Cover photo courtesy of Deposit Photos.
ISBN-13:9798987221747 (paperback)

Visit kathrynholzman.com for author information.

Santa Clara Valley

Santa Clara Valley, 1962

On a cloudless Saturday afternoon in May 1962, Harriet Jackson rode her brother's battered blue Schwinn bicycle along Mariana Avenue, alert for passing cars. She inhaled the delicate spring scent of newly budding manzanita blooms, delighted that her mother had sent her to the store for a quart of milk. As she pedaled, she sang "Johnny Angel," mouthing the words as sung on her favorite 45 by Shelly Fabares.

Harriet let the breeze carry the lead but provided the chorus's echo under her breath. The popular song complemented the sense of possibility in the crisp morning air. The rotation of her bike tires provided the backbeat. *Together we will see how lovely heaven will be.* She tilted the bike automatically into a left turn at the Shell gas station on the corner of Foothill Boulevard, pausing for a bright red Mustang about to pull away from the gas pump.

Boom! A roar as loud as her father's F95 Panther breaking the sound barrier filled the air. An explosion followed by a sharp crack, a lightning bolt announcing an arriving thunderstorm despite the tranquil blue of the storm-less California sky. In only seconds, flames consumed the gas station's underground storage tank engulfing the idling Mustang in a ball of fire. An enormous plume of black smoke shot high into the sky.

The flash silenced her song. Harriet fled the flames, pedaling with all the might her skinny ten-year-old legs could provide. She raced back down Mariani Avenue, abandoning her chores and heading for the safety of home. The houses and yards she passed dissolved into a colorless blur. She did not notice her neighbor, Bobby Hopkins, watching from his bedroom window. She turned into her driveway, tossed her brother's bike to the pavement, and tugged at the locked front door, pounding with her fists.

***

Bobby Hopkins lay belly down on his bed, reading *A Wrinkle in Time.* Transported by travel through time and space, the voracious reader attributed the seismic rumble of earth beneath his bedroom floor to *Terrerat, the* strange force described by Mrs. Whatsit, the most human of the three Mrs. W's—at least before she turned into a winged centaur. Then, he realized that his bed was actually shaking.

Bobby didn't panic. He adjusted his glasses, smudging already dirty lenses, and sat up on his knees to look out his bedroom window. Scrutinizing the foothills on the horizon, he registered a cloud of dark smoke climbing the sky. He dismissed the girl from next door frantically pedaling by on her bicycle as an irrelevant distraction.

After some consideration, he postulated four theories to explain the event:

1) An earthquake. High in the Santa Cruz Mountains, Bobby's sixth-grade class had recently visited Crystal Springs Reservoir. At vista points in the park, Bobby had straddled fence posts, analyzing the plates that realigned in response to the accumulated strain.

2) An explosion of an orbiting spaceship. On *Lost in Space,* the Robinson family's spaceship careened into a meteor storm. An engineering malfunction was blamed, but

later the family learned that Dr. Zachary Smith's sabotage caused the robot to accelerate the ship into overdrive.

3) A nuclear missile attack from Cuba. Having survived a dry run of this event in class, Bobby knew that any nuclear attack required you to crouch underneath your desk with hands held tightly over your head.

4) A car crash on Foothill Boulevard, the busy thoroughfare two blocks away.

Bobby didn't leave his bedroom to test his theories. He didn't go outside or put himself at risk. Instead, he trusted that observation and his superior intelligence were sufficient to understand the forces that caused the tremor. It would take more than an explosion to interrupt his reading.

1990-1

The law offices of Silicon Valley's LaFleur and Associates sparkled clean, with bright upholstery and framed architectural prints. The stylized blueprints on the pristine white walls portrayed the vision of an unworldly building, a headquarters for Santa Clara Valley's most successful computer company. A mile around, the illuminated circumference glowed, a gleaming halo for the Valley.

Harriet arrived late for the closing, tucking her starched white blouse into gray slacks as she exited the elevator. She apologized to the receptionist for her tardy arrival as she opened the suite's glass doors. For the occasion, she wore high-heeled black pumps, the ones she had squirreled away in a dark corner of her closet when she swore off men. She raked her short, mousy brown hair with trembling fingers and looked over at her sister Kat. How dare Kat sit there, cool as a cucumber, as if today was like any other day? Not a hair out of place. Her eyeliner flawless. Her lips frosted pink. Still, despite the knot in her stomach, Harriet was relieved to see a familiar face in the sterile office.

Why would her sister share her apprehension? She knew Harriet would come through for them. Hadn't that always been their story?

Harriet paused in the doorway, as if waiting for them to invite her in.

Ignoring her, Kat and Mike continued to flip through magazines. Although they barely acknowledged her entrance, her nephew Eddie, who towered over both of his parents, made room for his aunt.

"Hi, Harry." He tapped the seat beside him.

"Look, Hon." Kat held open a People magazine for her sister's perusal. "Bobby Hopkins was on the Smothers Brothers last month."

Bobby, the tech icon who had grown up next door to Harriet and Kat, was now a large man with a mischievous grin and a graying beard . "Richer than God," Kat said, "Listen to this." The article described Bobby dancing to Pump up the Jam by the Techtronics. "I would have loved to see that," Kat laughed. The article reported that their former neighbor was heavy on his feet, stumbling more than once, but that his delighted smile had charmed the audience.

"Figures. With enough money," Kat concluded, "anyone can be a celebrity. Harriet, do you remember what a dork Bobby used to be?"

Harriet, conscious of her nephew Eddie waiting for her to reply, chose her words carefully. "The Hopkins family never had much to do with us, but Bobby was always kind to me."

Mike put his arm around Kat as he read over his shoulder. When she had finished the article, he nuzzled his wife's neck. The two of them, inseparable even today. Was it any wonder that they seemed oblivious to what was being asked of her? Probably Kat didn't even remember the night she had come between Harriet and Bobby. Her sister had never accepted responsibility for her actions. She wasn't about to now.

✳✳✳

The receptionist looked up. "Are we all here?"

Patty Hopkins waited at the end of a long walnut table. Behind her, picture windows looked out on the busy Sunnyvale crossroads. Taking a sip from her Starbucks cup, she stood up and shook Harriet's hand.

"Hi Patty," Kat said. "Been a while."

Harriet, overwhelmed by the formality of the room, shook the lawyer's hand. "We appreciate your agreeing to represent us today. I know the sale of the house is below your pay grade, but the lawsuit..." Harriet fumbled for the right words, "is a little more complicated. My realtor's lawyer suggested I find someone with litigation experience."

"It's my pleasure," Patty gestured to the chair at her side. "It's good to see you again after all this time.

"Patty is Bobby Hopkins' sister," Harriet said to Eddie, unable to resist an urge to impress her nephew.

Patty rolled her eyes. "Younger sister. The bane of my existence."

"You already know Kat," Harriet said, "Have you met her husband, Mike?"

"We used to play together when we were kids," Kat told Mike. "Patty had the best dress-up clothes on the block."

"I can't believe you're selling the house after all these years," Patty said.

Impatient with his mother's walk down memory lane, Eddie introduced himself. ""I'm Kat's son," he said. ""Pleased to meet you."" Patty shook his hand, examining the athlete with the cocky smile. Although Harriet had filled Patty in on what she called this "nonsense lawsuit," Eddie appeared unfazed. He exuded an air of unrepentant confidence.

"This won't take long," Patty said. She straightened the color-coded file folders on the table in front of her and added, "By the time we have gone over the paperwork, the buyers will be here, and we should be set." Patty, with her blond-streaked hair and California tan, smiled at Harriet as if to reassure her she had this all under control.

Eddie requested a glass of water. The receptionist fetched a chilled bottle of Shasta Spring Water. Patty opened the folder in front of her.

"I've itemized the transaction here." She removed a sheet outlining the sales agreement and associated distributions. After the realtor's commission, taxes, and lawyers' fees, the balance Harriet would receive for the sale of her childhood home was $322,250 .

"Nice offer," she said. "I don't think my parents got half as much."

Harriet blinked her eyes as the digits blurred. She studied the address: 1319 Picaflor Court. An address more familiar than her own aging face.

"Do you want to look this over?" she asked Kat, sliding the folder over to her. Neither Kat nor Mike had asked to see the closing settlement. Kat pushed the paperwork back towards her without looking at it. Like Harriet, she seemed out of place in the swanky office. Only Eddie seemed at ease. He took a long swallow of water, followed by a satisfied burp.

"And my money?" he asked. "Is that here?" He appeared calm; he could take it or leave it. As if nothing hung in the balance. He cracked his knuckles. The popular Aikido teacher knew how to intimidate his sparring partners; he would never show his fear. This's what he taught his students. A calm facade gave nothing away. Only Harriet could see the little boy hiding behind his steely facade. Looking at him, Harriet knew he would never reveal to the lawyer how much this transaction meant to him. Let her know that his future depended on it.

That was why they were here. Why she was giving it all away.

From the proceeds, Harriet had agreed to transfer $300,000 to the firm's holding account to be disbursed by the attorney Patty had selected to handle her nephew's case. The money was to be used to satisfy all pending claims against him . In exchange, the parents of the children who had accused him of abuse had agreed to drop all charges. Both Eddie and his beloved dojo would be cleared of all allegations.

Patty tapped another manila file on the table. "Once the real estate transaction is complete, I'll finish that paperwork. With Harriet's consent, we'll wire the funds by the end of the day."

1959

Bobby peered out the side window of the Hopkins family's metallic blue Kings Chevelle station wagon. He watched the construction workers who climbed the roofs of stores being built on a strip mall on Foothill Boulevard, pounding nails into the asphalt shingles. *Opening Soon*, a banner in the window of the Safeway Store announced. A block further on, his father turned onto Mariani Avenue, entering a subdivision with houses in various stages of construction.

During the drive down Highway 101, his father had once again recited the familiar tale: developers had carved out sixteen hundred lots from acres of abandoned apricot orchards. Buyers had a choice of twenty floor plans, each offering three bedrooms and two bathrooms, as well as a long list of modern conveniences: two-car garages and state-of-the-art appliances. "If desired," his mother read the promotional brochure out loud, "every sparkling new kitchen will be equipped with a giant Frigidaire and a Wedgewood Griddle Middle-Top Gas Range. A fully automatic laundry with a Frigidaire Imperial Automatic Clothes Washer and a Filtramatic Clothes Dryer will also be available."

At Picaflor Court, his father pulled up to the curb of a vacant lot. The dirt, flattened by bulldozers, resembled an erased blackboard. At the edge of the newly cleared lot, a solitary apricot tree remained, a relic of the orchards now being replaced by the suburban subdivision.

Sunnyvale was, as the name implied, always sunny. Low, wooded mountains loomed on the horizon. The neighborhood basked in a balmy Mediterranean climate under a sun that shined almost every week of the year. In such a mild climate, a house didn't need to have a basement. Today, their builder would pour a cement slab, the footprint of the house to come.

Bobby's father lit a cigarette and examined the week's progress. He returned his matchbook to the pocket of his short-sleeved plaid shirt, patted the pack of cigarettes in his carefully creased pants. As he smoked, he ran a hand through the bristles of his crew cut and squinted through thick eyeglasses. Bobby watched his father check that the concrete forms were in place. The cement trucks were due any minute.

Alice, his mother, opened the car door and stretched. She walked the perimeter of the house-to-be and examined the forms.

"The living room will be here," Alice said, pointing to a rectangle that paralleled the newly paved street. "The kitchen faces the street." She paced the length of each room, comparing her measurements to the architectural drawings which she held in her left hand.

Bobby couldn't wait for the trucks to arrive. The previous week, he had checked out every book on construction he could find in the elementary school library. Now, he considered himself an expert on the process.

"They're called mixers," he explained to his sister Patty, who had heard it all before. Patty asked where they had taken the rest of the apricot trees.

"I don't know," he answered, fixated on the cement trucks.

"I can still smell fruit on the breeze," Patty said.

"All I smell is dust," Bobby said.

The Hopkins had made the drive to Sunnyvale every Sunday since the night his parents announced at the dinner table that they would be moving soon. Most of Bobby's life, he had lived in a rented house in San Bruno, an established suburb of San Francisco in the shadow of the San Francisco Airport. The move to Sunnyvale was progress in every way. The house would be bigger. The school, his parents assured him, better. During the weekly drive south on 101, the sky opened; the dense suburbs sprouted open space, and the Bay sparkled. In Sunnyvale, his mother assured them, everything would be new.

Alice liked things new. In her house, everything would shine. They would eat in the modern new kitchen with its brand-new appliances, watch TV (color!) in the family room, and sleep in bedrooms that no one else in the world had ever slept in.

"I see it!" Bobby pointed at the concrete mixer lumbering around the corner. He jumped up and down, unable to contain his glee, mesmerized by the truck's swirling drum. The driver hopped out of the cab and saluted the family as he positioned the truck so that the chutes could be directed into the waiting forms. Soon, viscous concrete began to flow.

"Like cake batter," Patty said. "They're baking our house."

Bobby, used to his sister's foolishness, snorted. "It's chemistry."

Patty, accustomed to being dismissed, ignored him.

The truck rumbled noisily as the workmen repeatedly repositioned the chute, pouring a slab beneath each of the rooms. Bobby paid close attention when they poured the foundation for the smaller room in the back which would soon be his. Patty's bedroom would face the street. Each time the man moved the chute, the children redirected their gazes.

"Now?" Bobby asked his father.

"Not yet," his father replied. "Wait until they're done with the garage." His father lit another cigarette as he squinted at the workmen. An engineer, he clearly reveled in the process. The very concreteness of it appeared to please him. He fondly tousled his son's sandy-blond hair. Bobby immediately smoothed the wayward locks. He hated his cowlick.

Finally, the garage floor was poured. The cement men watched as Bobby carefully placed his hand into the already setting concrete. His father bent down beside him and, with a stick from the yard, dated the impression: 6-10-59.

$$***$$

One of life's greatest joys was shopping at Moffett Field.

Harriet, the oldest Jackson daughter, led the way, pushing a metal shopping cart while her pregnant mother, Hiroko, selected cereal boxes, cans of Spaghetti-Os and blocks of American cheese. Behind her, five-year-old Kevin propelled a smaller cart like a scooter, racing through the aisles as he scooped up cookies, loaves of bread, and cartons of ice cream. Kat, seven, pushed Chrissie in an over-sized stroller, her younger sister's limp legs covered with a plaid blanket.

The military commissary had aisles and aisles of packaged food, pyramids of cans, frosty freezers filled with TV dinners and ice cream, rolls of toilet paper stacked six feet high. Everything in mass quantities. Everything cheap and tax-free.

The catch was, you had to be, or have been, in the service to gain access to this abundance. The Jacksons took it for granted that this was part of their privilege as the family of a navy pilot.

This Sunday was more exciting than usual. Their father, Joe, told the children that he had a surprise. As they stood in line to check out their mountain of groceries, they tried to guess what their father, so seldom home, had planned.

"A movie?" Harriet asked, sucking a lock of her mousy brown hair.

"A bicycle?" Kevin asked. For the energetic boy, life was all about motion.

"A new dress?" Kat, adjusting Chrissie's blanket so that the other shoppers wouldn't stare, loved any opportunity to dress up.

Moffett Field, located at the southern end of San Francisco Bay, had been home to the family for as long as the kids could remember. Built on a 1000-acre parcel of farmland purchased by the town of Sunnyvale in 1932 and then sold to the U.S. Government for one dollar, the active military airbase was sheltered from the San Francisco fog by the Coastal Range to its west. As toddlers, the Jackson children had played in the shadow of its three over-sized hangars. Constructed by the Navy during World War II as a part of its coastal defense plan, the hulking structures were large enough to have their own weather. Moffett Field had served as Joe's squadron's fighter base for a decade; the base was home to F95 Panther and FJ3 Fury jets that the children could proudly identify as their father flew overhead, a flash of silver in the deep blue sky. Joe captained maritime patrol aircraft along the Pacific coastline.

This was their world, divided in half by a runway system which extended almost the length of the base property. Their father's flight training operations took place on the east side of the runways. They lived in base housing, located on the west side, and only a walk away from the commissary.

Today, their father was loading their groceries into the back of their red station wagon. Hiroko, Joe's Japanese-born wife, pregnant once again, shifted uncomfortably in the front passenger seat. Joe, in civilian clothes, draped a tanned, muscular arm over the back of the front seat as he turned to the kids crammed in the back. Only Chrissie was allotted a full seat. The other kids doubled up or climbed in back with the groceries. "Ready," their father said. "Blast off!"

The kids jostled for position as he drove west, through the small Sunnyvale downtown, along the expressway and past acres and acres of verdant orchards. A half an hour later he turned into a recently built subdivision, slowing down to 25 miles per hour, letting them take it all in. "Almost there," he answered their endless stream of questions, before turning right into a cul-de-sac with six newly built homes. He stopped in front of an unoccupied house with a "Sold" sign rooted in its uncultivated front yard.

"Welcome home!" he ignored their flabbergasted silence. "Grab those bags. We're stocking up the homestead."

The Navy was transitioning to larger aircraft, recognizing the need for longer runways. His squadron, their father explained, was being transferred to NAS Miramar in San Diego where they would be reassigned to the F-8 Crusader.

"So, I decided, rather than move you all to another Navy base, I would buy you a house," Joe said. "For the first time in your lives, you kids will not be military brats." Joe beamed as he made his announcement. Harriet had never lived off-base, never heard the term "military brat." She looked over at her mother who continued to look down, her face expressionless.

Joe threw open the front door of the vacant house, explaining that the model was an "Eichler." The house, like nothing they had ever seen, had a flat roof and 2-inch pattern wood siding, skylights, and floor to ceiling windows looking out onto a central courtyard.

"Like living outside," he said, setting the bags of groceries on the kitchen counter and opening the brand-new refrigerator. Hiroko examined the wooden cabinets. Everything was empty.

"Dinner in the dining room tonight," he almost sang as his wife began to unpack the grocery bags. "Look, Hon," he hugged Hiroko from behind, "a backyard for the kids to play in." Hiroko smiled patiently but continued to arrange boxes on the kitchen shelves. When Joe failed to get her attention, he turned once again to the children. "The school is right around the block. A park too."

The Jacksons moved into the house that week. Their quarters on the base had already been re-assigned. Moving vans delivered boxes of their belongings and the few pieces of furniture they owned. Their well-used kitchen table looked shabby on the shiny, new linoleum. The plaid tweed of the couch faded in the invasive sunshine of the living room windows. Clothes, packed into boxes, were stacked in the entry hallway of the empty house.

After the moving vans disappeared down Mariani Avenue, Harriet watched her father, in uniform and erect as the soldier he was, chop through the trunk of the remaining apricot tree in the backyard. With one well-intentioned swing of the ax, he felled the tree, carpeting the backyard with blossoms. "Too sloppy," he said. "I don't have time to rake up rotten fruit."

Harriet remained in the back yard after he had stacked the logs formed from the decimated trunk. Without the tree's shade, the yard was barren and lifeless. She listened to children playing on the other side of the wooden fence, hearing the swish of a shuffleboard puck.

"I win!" a young boy cried.

"Not fair," his sister replied.

That night, Harriet inhaled the sweet aroma of the floral arrangement her mother created from the delicate blossoms she had collected from the fallen tree.

"Help your mother," Harriet's father instructed her when he packed his bag before leaving for San Diego. "I want you to go with her when she sees the Navy doctor. Anything important, let me know. I'm counting on you to be my eyes and ears on the ground."

Two weeks after moving into the new house, Joe deployed to the Indian Ocean. He told Harriet that he would be gone for six months. Harriet, barefoot on the fresh black tar of the circular driveway, watched her father's car turn the corner. Her mother didn't leave the house to kiss her husband good-bye. Except for weekly trips to the base, Hiroko hadn't left the house since they moved in. Boxes (many still unpacked) barricaded the entryway.

Her father hadn't even stayed long enough to seed the lawn.

1960

Down the hallway, Elvis crooned: *Will you kiss away my cares and woe?* Harriet joined in, singing softly, swaying in time to the music: *I gotta know, gotta know, gotta know.* Her eyes closed. Every word came from deep inside, the dreamy singer giving voice to the unspoken longings only Elvis would understand.

Harriet laid out eight pieces of Wonder bread. Chrissie, strapped in her highchair, looked absently out the kitchen window. Hiroko slathered mayonnaise on the bread and then placed a slice of American cheese on every other one.

"Let me do that, mom," Harriet said.

Her mother stared at her blankly.

"Let me help you," Harriet repeated.

"You good girl," her mother said and continued wrapping the sandwiches.

Chrissie's diaper needed changing.

Harriet knew not to ask her mother what was wrong. That was one of the few things she did know about her mother.

Hiroko had been born in Tokyo. Joe liked to tell his children that the Navy men had been told not to fraternize with Japanese women, "but your mom...," he would wink, "was a beauty. I couldn't take my eyes off her. Yes, siree, she swept me off my feet. Captain of her high school basketball team, she ran circles around the other girls."

It was hard to see that now. Harriet's mom seldom put on makeup and, when she did, the effect was strange. She would pluck her eyebrows off and pencil them an inch higher. Or worse yet, leave her eyes strangely undressed, plucked plain. It had been weeks since Hiroko had worn anything other than the stained housedress she was wearing now. Her belly, swollen from her recent pregnancy, threatened to topple her slight frame.

At the base, Harriet had watched her mother when she met up with other Japanese-born wives. Harriet was so used to her mother's silences that she had been surprised to hear the women chattering away even though they spoke in a language Harriet could not understand. At home, Hiroko seldom spoke. The only time Harriet had seen her mother communicate with similar animation was one evening when she had entered her parents' bedroom without knocking. Her mother had been sitting at her desk, wrapped in a terry-cloth robe, engrossed in writing a letter on tissue-like blue paper. As she wrote, she smiled as if greeting a friend. Her mouth formed incomprehensible Japanese words as she wrote with great ferocity, her expression that of a young girl, almost unrecognizable. Harriet coughed to announce her presence, and her mother had quickly covered the page, protecting the letter from her daughter's prying eyes.

"What are you writing?" Harriet asked.

"A letter to my family," Hiroko answered. Harriet thought her mother's family was here, in the house on Picaflor Court, but of course her mother meant her other family, the one in Japan.

Soon after, Harriet had asked her father to tell her the story of how he had married her mother.

"I fought for her," her Dad had replied. "I proposed to your mother in Tokyo soon after we met but we had to wait for the War Brides Act in 1945 before I was allowed to bring her home." For the first two years of their marriage, Hiroko lived with her parents in Tokyo. "Her father was dying, and I was forbidden to enter their house," Harriet's father chuckled.

Chrissie was getting heavier all the time. Harriet lifted her sister out of the highchair. The young girl's legs dangled to the ground. Harriet knew how to support Chrissie's weight by sliding her arms under her armpits, but sometimes, despite her best efforts, Chrissie's legs dragged limply along the floor. Fortunately, it didn't matter. Her sister couldn't feel anything below her waist. The doctors called what Chrissie had spina bifida.

After Chrissie's birth, Harriet's mother came home from the hospital without a baby. Chrissie had multiple surgeries to close the hole in her spine before she too was finally discharged from the hospital. Now, every two months, she returned to the hospital to have a needle inserted into the soft spot of her skull to drain excessive fluid.

At least the newest baby, Joey, was healthy.

Hiroko hung up the dish towel with a sigh and left the kitchen without speaking.

Harriet understood why her mother couldn't find time to finish unpacking the boxes in the front hallway. Since Joey was born, her mom spent most of her time attending to the newborn. Despite her best efforts, the baby kept the family up most of the night.

After changing Chrissie's diaper, Harriet kissed her sister on the forehead and left her lying contentedly on Kevin's bed, watching Captain Kangaroo on the TV. Taking advantage of the peaceful interlude, she slipped into the bedroom she shared with her sister, Kat, and flopped down on the floor next to the two twin beds. Flipping through the stack of 78s in front of Kat's prized Dansette record player, she discarded Kat's favorite of the moment—"Itsy Bitsy Teenie Weenie Yellow Polka Dot Bikini"—for being too silly. Instead, Harriet once again placed Elvis's "Gotta Know" on the turntable and carefully positioned the needle in the first groove. She knew every word by heart.

"Pu-leez," Kat said, swinging open the door. "We can hear your howling in the living room. The neighborhood dogs will be barking at our door any moment now."

Startled from her reverie, Harriet picked up the needle off the record too quickly. The speaker emitted a jarring screech.

"Sorry." She examined the disk.

"You better not have scratched it," Kat turned to the mirror, examining her long, black hair for split ends. "You know, your voice stinks."

Elvis, however, had done his job. As Harriet changed into her nightgown, she continued to hum silently to herself, taking care her sister could not hear. "Will you kiss away my cares and woe?" She imagined Elvis, his bedroom eyes fixed on her, his curly pompadour and thick lips. He held out his hand, saying "Baby, I know times are hard but I'm here for you whenever you need me."

Kat might think she was tone-deaf, but Harriet heard every note of his song as clearly as the voice of Captain Kangaroo broadcast from her brother's bedroom next door.

✳✳✳

Next door, Bobby was perfecting the art of pie-throwing, or more precisely, the knack of having a pie thrown in his face. Pie-throwing, he was learning, was an important circus skill. Studying the library book open on his bed, he mimicked the recommended tilt of his neck, shutting his eyes at precisely the right moment. He'd been practicing for hours.

While Bobby practiced his circus skills, Patty, followed her mother as Alice did her daily chores. Through his open bedroom door, Bobby could see his sister perched on top of the brand-new white Sears refrigerator watching her mother slice potatoes and carrots. As long as Patty's sneakers didn't scuff the appliance's gleaming surface, his mother didn't complain. Patty looked so hopeful. Even as Bobby prepared for incoming pastries, he wished he could make them both disappear.

He had heard his mother's litany before. The linoleum counters had to be kept spotless, not a single stain. When his father spilled his morning coffee, his mother sniped, "Good god, Jack. Can't you do anything right?" Alice angrily scrubbed up the coffee stains before they could sully the table's veneer.

This was their new start. The pastel-painted walls were flawless, not a scuff, not a scratch. The colors matched the paint chips that his mother had spent months choosing during construction, paint swatches spread out on the kitchen table of their rented house—the imperfect house where Alice declared that she would die if she couldn't get away from the stink of other people's possessions. This was their chance. The oven, pre-warmed to 350 degrees, wafted the aroma of roasting beef. Sunday's dinner was to be served at exactly at one p.m., not six o'clock which was when dinner was served on weekdays, exactly twenty minutes after her Dad drove in the driveway after work.

Last night his family had watched the World of Disney on TV, the story of a perfect family assembled for Thanksgiving dinner. Around a dining room table covered with a cloth trimmed in lace, candles burning warmly, the TV father proclaimed that family was everything, that family loved you no matter what, that you loved your family no matter what.

Bobby emerged from his bedroom and watched Patty set the dining room table, the napkins folded in perfect triangles, the silverware precisely straightened. They might be able to pull it off, that perfect meal.

And then his father entered the kitchen. His mother exploded. "What the hell did you get on your pants now?

How many times have I asked you to take off your filthy shoes in the garage? Goddamnit, look at the floor."

His dad cowered. Mom was on her knees with the sponge, scrubbing the linoleum furiously.

Patty put the water glasses exactly three inches above the forks.

His father sat sheepishly at the end of the kitchen table. Bobby sat down reluctantly, tilting his head at the right angle. Following his lead, Patty aimed an invisible pie, rotating it exactly the prescribed quarter turn (for suction), and launched the secret projectile. Bobby inhaled, flinched, and blew out.

At least his sister was a cooperative student, the perfect foil.

"What the hell is wrong with you kids?" His mom asked as she set the salad on the table. Beside the wooden bowl, she placed a platter with sliced white bread.

Giggling was never a good idea.

Dad sliced the roast beef, not too thick, thin but not so thin that it fell apart. The meat and vegetables were soft and succulent. Patty looked relieved. Everything smelled delicious.

"It would have been nice if you had changed your filthy clothes before eating," Alice snapped at Jack. "Bobby, put your napkin in your lap."

"C'mon, Alice, can't we eat in peace for once? This roast is delicious."

Mom set down her fork and lit a cigarette. "I suppose."

Mom wasn't much for eating. She watched her figure.

"Dad," Bobby said. He took a bite of roast beef and chewed it thoroughly. His mother hated it when he talked with his mouth open. "I know you are an engineer. But what exactly do you do?"

His father answered: I am a cyberneticist."

"A what?"

"A cyberneticist. I work with computers."

Cyber - net - icist. He liked the word, the sound of this.

"What's a computer?" Patty asked.

"A big machine that thinks. My company put me in charge of using this machine that can think for them."

"Cool," Bobby said.

Dad and Bobby each took a piece of bread and mopped up the thick, onion-y gravy.

"I work in the home," his mother added. "Thank you for asking. Damn it, Jack, close your mouth when you chew."

Dad flinched when his mother spoke.

"After all my work putting dinner on the table, you would think you could at least eat in a civilized manner." Alice pushed back her chair in exasperation, stood up. As she passed the kitchen counter, she scooped up her black leather purse and headed out the door. They watched her go.

"Goddamnit, Alice," Jack said to the back of the door, the freshly painted surface blank in reply.

The three of them sat around the kitchen table wordlessly. Bobby started practicing again. His sister watched for cues. He inhaled, blinked, flinched, and then exhaled. Over and over.

Family. They loved each other no matter what. A lot of good crying would do. So much for the family's fresh start. For a moment, Bobby considered taking Patty with him when he left for the circus, but the last thing he needed was a weepy sister clinging to him while he mastered the circus arts.

He didn't say a word. What was the point? He went outside to the backyard to practice, leaving Patty to help clear the abandoned dinner table.

Out on the patio, Bobby progressed to the art of spitting, chapter two, a necessary precursor to fire eating. Spitting was a lot harder than he had imagined. Like being on the receiving end of a pie, the skill began with taking a deep breath, but this time you had to completely fill your lungs. Spitting had to be explosive. The more forceful the explosion, the more successful the trick. When it came to eating fire, spitting was the only way to keep from getting burned.

Bobby sat on the new yellow mesh lawn-chairs that his parents had purchased for the freshly poured concrete patio, under the clear blue California sky. That night, like almost every night, there was not a cloud in sight.

***

None of the landscaped front yards had any shade. In summer, the sun burned brighter than ever. Kat headed outside as Harriet cleaned the sink after the boys' breakfast, humming under her breath with a contented smile on her face. How dare her sister say she was tone deaf? As she prepared a snappy retort, Kat burst through the front door with an unexpected request.

"Harriet, do you think Mom would mind if Patty and I played dress-up in her room?"

Harriet knew that the best clothes for dress-up were in Hiroko's closet—not only the forbidden kimono but elaborate dancing outfits her mother had worn as a teen in Tokyo, slips with built-in hoops to be worn with full circle skirts, and brightly colored floral and gingham dresses. Kat's favorite was a pink, sleeveless sundress with a sweetheart neckline, black straps and velvet trim, a tiny belted waistline, and a full skirt embossed with a repeating pattern of black pumps. In a corner of the closet, there was a shoebox containing pumps, including black velvet slip-ons with three-inch heels.

Harriet hesitated for a moment. Would her mother mind? The kitchen was relatively clean. Hiroko was resting in the boys' bedroom with the baby. Her mother had never objected when they invited playmates home when they lived on the base. Besides, Harriet had to admit, she was curious to meet the blond-haired girl who had been her sister's first friend in the neighborhood.

"Sure, but we'll have to keep it down. Joey is taking a nap."

Kat threw open the front door. Patty Hopkins blew into the house like a breath of fresh air. "Cool house," she announced, her eyes darting from room to room.

Who knows what Patty had heard about the family next door? The two neighboring families had had very little contact. Through the slats of the backyard fence, Harriet had watched Mr. and Mrs. Hopkins relax in chaise lounges on their patio drinking cocktails on Saturday afternoons while the kids played croquet on their manicured lawn. Those moments of leisure were as foreign to Harriet as the Jacksons must seem to the family next door.

Only Kat, who had struck up a friendship with Patty, had dared to enter the Hopkins' tidy house. Returning home, she'd described a spotless kitchen and color-coordinated living room which children were not allowed to enter.

Patty's hesitation disappeared immediately when Kat showed her Hiroko's treasure trove of fancy dresses. Kat and Patty tried on one outfit after another. Harriet held up Hiroko's kimono proudly. "My mom is from Tokyo, you know," she told Patty. "We're not allowed to play with this one."

"Wow," Patty said, "your mother must have so many stories to tell you."

"Maybe," Kat snickered. "But if she tried, we wouldn't understand."

Patty looked up. Her blue eyes behind thick glasses asked for an explanation.

"My mom's English is pretty bad. On the base, she hung out with the other Japanese wives. Since we moved, it seems like she doesn't have the energy to learn English." In her mother's defense, Harriet added: "When she needs to, she gets her point across."

Patty stroked the kimono. White flowers on a dark blue background with a wide red sash.

"This is beautiful," she said.

Kat tried on the pink dancing dress and matching black pumps. "Let's play Spin the Bottle," she said. Nothing made Kat happier than inventing her own versions of popular games.

Patty pushed her eyeglasses up her freckled nose and opened her eyes wide. Harriet was thrilled to be included in the girls' game. Sitting on the bedroom floor surrounded by clothes Hiroko had worn in a different life, Kat, Patty, and Harriet dressed up in as many layers as they could pull on, hoop skirts, taffeta cocktail dresses, and boas.

Once they had emptied the box of cast-off clothes, they took turns spinning the Coca-Cola bottle that Kat retrieved from the kitchen garbage can. If the bottle pointed at you, you had to remove one piece of clothing. The winner of Spin the Bottle was supposed to be the last girl to remain clothed but long before the final round, the girls giggled in response to the slow titillation, the first blouse removed, the first shock of white underpants revealed.

As the finery piled up in the corner of their mother's bedroom, Harriet blushed, self-conscious about the paleness of her nearly naked body. She listened for baby Joey's cry, her mother's slow steps, the drag of Chrissie pulling herself across the floor. All was quiet. Then Kat shrieked.

"Kevin, get out of here!"

Kevin and several of the neighborhood boys, including Bobby from next door, were jostling outside the bedroom window, hoping for a glimpse of the girls.

Patty giggled, holding her arms over her flat chest. Only Harriet, at ten, had a suspicion of breasts. She quickly grabbed a flowered shawl. Harriet could feel the boys' eyes on her, especially Bobby's. Bobby was the smartest kid in her fifth-grade class, the teacher's pet. In school, he never gave her the time of day.

Kat began to whistle "The Stripper."

"Kat!" Harriet cried out in dismay.

"Harriet, what happen in there?" Hiroko's inquired from the other side of the bedroom wall.

"You guys had better clean up. Fast." Harriet frantically pulled on her pedal pushers and t-shirt. Running her fingers through her disheveled hair, she closed the bedroom shade. Embarrassed by the excitement that her beating heart revealed, she rushed to her mother's side.

"Chrissie hungry." Her mother sat on Kevin's single bed with baby Joey fast asleep in her arms. Fortunately, her mother had not been able to get up when she heard the scuffle in the adjoining room.

"I'll take care of it, Mom." Harriet slipped her hands under Chrissie's arms, taking charge of her sister's care. Struggling to support her sister's weight, she soon forgot the California sun, shining as always outside the darkened room.

Later that night, Harriet picked up the toys from the Jacksons' chaotic living room.

Kevin was insistent: he wanted to watch the Cassius Clay fight. For weeks, he had been fascinated by the Summer Olympics. "Clay's going to win the gold medal," he said, feinting at Kat who simply rolled her eyes.

Harriet preferred to watch the news.

"We always watch what you want to watch," Kat whined. "The news is so boring. Can't we watch the Andy Griffith show? At least it's funny."

"We can watch Opie after the Huntley-Brinkley report."

"Harriet's in love with John Kennedy," Kat announced. Her sister was right about that. The presidential candidate was almost as handsome as her father.

Chrissie had recently had a catheter inserted into her bladder. Instead of changing diapers, now Harriet kept an eye on her urine bag which needed to be emptied regularly. If she forgot, the plastic bag was inevitably spilled by Kat or Kevin as they jockeyed about on the floor, unable to sit still for even a second.

Harriet wasn't about to tell her sister why she watched the news. She worried about her father, flying over the distant ocean. Every night there was another story about an air disaster. In August, there had been a fiery collision over New York City. A United Airlines DC-8 and TWA Super Constellation had collided mid-air, killing all 128 passengers on board.

Harriet knew her father had flown all his life, but she depended more and more on her father coming home. Even fantasies about Elvis couldn't relieve her concern.

Tone-deaf. Harriet was still smarting at her sister's stinging critique of her voice. When she was sure that Kat was not watching, Harriet had looked the term up in the

Webster dictionary her father had bought so that Hiroko could work on her English.

Tone-deaf: 1: relatively insensitive to differences in musical pitch; 2: having or showing an obtuse insensitivity or lack of perception particularly in matters of public sentiment, opinion, or taste

What a crock! No one was more sensitive than she was. Among her siblings, only Harriet was attuned to the subtle variations in her mother's moods. Only she perceived the vacuum left by her father's absence. The swell of emotion that she experienced every time she listened to one of Elvis's songs was undeniable evidence of her ability to hear the music behind his lyrics. Certainly, sensitivity to pitch was a part of that.

Harriet insisted they watch the nightly news. Kat couldn't care less about public sentiment, opinion, or taste. (Except, of course, if the opinion was about her.) If anyone in the family was tone-deaf, Kat matched the dictionary definition.

Nevertheless, Harriet resolved to be more careful in the future. She would avoid singing in front her of her sister. One could always mouth the words to popular songs. In the fall, Harriet would start sixth grade. The last thing she wanted was to call attention to herself.

Kat and Kevin continued to fight over the channel. Kevin grabbed Kat's wrist and twisted her arm behind her.

"Make him stop," Kat screamed looking up at her older sister.

Hiroko, nursing Joey in the armchair by the window, didn't notice. Chrissie curled up at Harriet's feet watched her siblings as if they were the entertainment.

Kevin won the struggle and the whole family watched the Olympics. Eighteen-year-old Cassius Clay didn't seem to have a chance at first. Despite fancy footwork, Clay lost the first round against his opponent, a Polish fighter built like a truck. But in the second round, he held his own. In the end, Clay finished big, striking from both sides and drawing blood.

"He got the gold! He got the gold!" Kevin danced around the living room. Kat didn't have a chance. To avoid his blows, she left the room, slamming the door of the girls' room behind her.

Harriet didn't have much sympathy. When she closed her eyes, she still saw Kat in the pink sundress and black pumps, her waist-length black hair straight and shiny, her eyes flashing with excitement. Despite having concluded that it was her sister who was tone-deaf, Harriet would have given anything to climb into her sister's skin. Instead, she began the evening's chores. The dinner dishes needed to be washed. Despite her resolution, she began to hum as she picked up the dirty drinking glasses that her sister had left behind. This time the tune that came to mind was *Shake, Rattle, and Roll.* She turned up the faucet to let the water run hard enough to muffle the words, but not so hard as to drown out the music in her head. Before drying her hands, after checking to be sure that none of her siblings could see, she even did a brief rendition of the twist in time to the beat. She adored the newest dance sensation and had been practicing the moves in her free time.

✳✳✳

Alice stood at the kitchen counter preparing breakfast as if she hadn't stormed out the night before. The kitchen smelled of hot coffee, bacon, and toast. Bobby entered warily, avoiding his mother's eyes. He had decided that the circus life wasn't his destiny. Last night, he had dreamed that he lived on a submarine, far below the ocean's surface. Through the boat's circular windows, colorful fish appeared and disappeared in the waving seaweed. With scientific detachment, he studied the aquatic creatures as they prowled for nourishment on the ocean floor and identified patterns in the seemingly chaotic patterns of their gelatinous fluttering.

"You need to get out of the house more," his mother said when he described his magical dream to her. On Tuesdays, Bobby knew, his mother cleaned bedrooms. Until school started up in the fall, the "kids" were in her way. "You can't read all day," she said. "Get out and get some fresh air and sunshine. You should ride your bike for a change."

Bobby hated outside. His forays outside his bedroom inevitably resulted in embarrassment, like the afternoon he had joined a cluster of neighborhood boys peeking into Harriet Jackson's bedroom window. He had nothing in common with boys who were content to ride their bicycles for hours in endless circles around the cul-de-sac. He preferred the safety of his own bedroom where he could watch *Marshall Dillon, Dragnet,* and *Have Gun Will Travel* on the small TV his parents had given him when they bought the more elaborate console for the new living room. He cherished his collection of superhero comic books which he stored in a box underneath his bed and never tired of playing with his plastic brigade of army men, lining the good guys up against the bad guys. The good guys won every time, but not until fierce battles ensued. When the earth was infiltrated with alien warriors, the Flash joined forces with the Justice League to save the planet.

Standing awkwardly on the front porch, he felt like a fish out of water, unable to move on land.

"Hey, Glasses," Kevin rode past on his bike, the leader of a pack of four neighborhood boys.

Kevin Jackson called the Hopkins the "Glasses," right to their faces. Bobby could understand why. His whole family wore eyeglasses. His father, legally blind, had not even been able to serve in World War II. Legally blind didn't mean that he couldn't see. Only that he wore glasses with thick lenses that made his eyes look strangely magnified.

Bobby hated being singled out. He wasn't about to counter and point out the scrawny kid's own shortcomings. It wouldn't be right. Besides, what would be the point? It was a random occurrence that the Jacksons' lived next door. The two families had nothing in common.

Kevin skidded to a stop and grinned. "Hey, Glasses, wanna ride with us?" The boy was breathless; his invitation seemed sincere.

Bobby's hadn't ridden his bike since they moved in. It was suspended on the garage wall by two large, red hooks. Under Kevin's watchful eye, he took it down and wiped the dust off the handlebars.

What did he have to lose? He wheeled his bike into the cul-de-sac and kicked off, concentrating on maintaining his balance as the other boys rode their bikes around him in disorganized circles, hooting and mocking him with delighted grins. Kevin was practicing wheelies. Bobby didn't even try. Several of the other boys did, but none of them with Kevin's finesse.

Slowly, Bobby gained confidence. He smiled shyly, pushing the cowlick out of his eyes. He began to get comfortable, balanced without thinking about falling. The other boys quickly became bored with the novelty of Glasses having joined their loose-knit gang. He felt himself blending in, pedaled at their pace as the circles widened.

"You want to have some real fun?" Kevin asked. The other boys smiled, called him Glasses as if it were his real name, an affectionate nickname not a slight. He rode among them now effortlessly, his arms relaxed on the handlebars, trying on the possibility of becoming one of the gang.

"Let's ride to Artie's," Kevin suggested.

Artie's, the local pharmacy, was located in the strip mall right next to the Safeway. Sometimes, while his mother did her grocery shopping, Bobby wandered into Artie's where, up front by the cash register, there were racks and racks of candy bars, sweets with names like Heath Bar, Almond Joy, multicolored M&Ms, bags of butterscotch sucking candies, treats that his mother called "garbage." Sometimes he dreamed about Almond Joys, a chewy coconut bar with a crunchy nut in the middle, coated with dark chocolate. Bobby liked to examine the bags of candy and pretend to select his favorite. His choice varied from one day to the next.

The boys on bikes stopped circling. They headed up Mariani Avenue. Bobby fell into the procession easily. He had this now. He kept pace, his legs gaining strength by the block. The row of tidy houses and blooming gardens disappeared as the boys approached the gas station on Foothill Boulevard. They leaned left and turned as one, unfazed by the heavier traffic on the thoroughfare. Riding on the left side of the street (the wrong side, his mother would say), they reached the row of stores and abandoned their bikes in a heap of tangled metal at the end of the stores' sidewalk. Bobby's on top as if it belonged there.

Kevin threw open the door of Artie's Pharmacy. His friends followed, pushing and shoving. When Kevin banged Bobby's shoulder with a thud, Bobby accepted the jolt with a smile, imitating the other boys' ease. Was friendship really this easy?

In the store, the boys paged through magazines. Bobby picked up his favorite comic, explaining the complex plot to the other boys. They listened with rapt attention.

"The good guys always win in the end," he told them. Snickering, they asked him if he wanted to be a superhero.

"Of course!"

When Kevin farted, he laughed with the others, although he didn't really get what was funny.

"I'm hungry," Kevin said, rubbing his belly. It was nowhere near lunch time.

"Me too," the next boy said. "I'm so hungry. How about you, Glasses?"

"I..." It was obvious there was a right answer. Bobby, used to knowing every right answer, stumbled.

"Boy, I sure would like some candy," the third boy said.

"Hey, Glasses, you like candy?" Kevin asked.

That was easy. "Of course, M&Ms are my favorite. When I go trick or treating, I always save the M&Ms for last."

"Mmmm. M&Ms," the boys said, looking at him expectantly.

"Why wait for Halloween?" Kevin asked. "Artie stocks them all year long."

Their smiles brightened. His new friends looked over at the counter, unmanned at that moment.

Kevin walked over, nonchalantly grinning back at his crew. Without a blink of his guileless brown eyes, he slipped a bag of M&M's into his pocket and sauntered back. He raised his eyebrows, inviting his friends to follow suit.

One by one the boys strolled by the counter while their friends flipped through comic books. Bobby realized that not one of them was reading. They weren't interested in the content, superheroes or not.

In the parade of bikes riding to the store, Bobby had brought up the rear. Now he was the last to approach the counter.

His heart pounded. He could taste the almond in the candy bar's center, craved the sugary shock of dark chocolate. The boys continued to flip through their comic books but he knew they were watching him.

They were waiting for a magic trick. They were asking him to be a friend.

With clammy hands, he set down Superman and walked towards the counter, convinced that his pounding heart could be heard all the way the back of the store where Artie was filling a prescription. He looked down at the bags of M&M's; he tasted chocolate melting on his tongue, felt the crisp crunch of the sugar coating even though it was only ten o'clock in the morning, too early in the day for any good boy to be eating chocolate.

He was so tired of his mother's rules.

Looking once more to the back of the store, he grabbed the bag of candy and prepared to scurry back to the gang watching him with obvious amusement.

"Boy," a man's voice bellowed, "what do you think you are doing?"

Bobby froze.

His so-called friends ran from the store, giggling and jostling one other as they grabbed their bikes, leaving Bobby standing alone, the bag of candy in his hand.

"You kids," the burly pharmacist said. "It's time you learn right from wrong."

Ignoring Bobby's protest that he would pay, Artie dialed the police, never releasing Bobby's arm which he held like a vise. He held onto Bobby's sleeve until a local cop responded, a red light flashing on the roof of his patrol car as he parked in front of the pharmacy.

Bobby knew better. He wanted to return the bag of candy to the shelf and didn't deny his crime. Regardless, Artie insisted that the policeman drive the sniffling boy home. "Tell his parents," he instructed the cop. "This time," the shop owner said, "they're not getting away with stealing my merchandise. I've had it up to here," he extended a fat finger in front of his chin.

The policeman wrote down Bobby's name and address. When asked, Bobby gave all the correct answers.

When the patrol car pulled up to the curb in front of the Hopkins' house, the Jacksons watched from next door, Kevin hopping from foot to foot, unable to control himself. "Bobby's in big trouble," he said to anyone who would listen. In front of his audience, Kevin recounted the story, words tumbling out of his mouth as he acted out the scene in the pharmacy: Bobby taking the candy, Artie catching him red-handed.

The cop strode up the Hopkins' front walk, solemnly shook Bobby's father's hand. Bobby covered his eyes. He crouched beneath the car window, refusing to look at his parents or the cluster of kids ogling from the sidewalk.

Bobby's mother came to the front door, looking curiously at the police cruiser parked at the curb. As the neighbors watched, she spotted Bobby slumped in the back seat, sullen and silent.

"Bobby is so busted," Kevin crowed.

After a solemn discussion with Bobby's parents, the policeman opened the back door of the car and released the red-faced criminal. Head down, Bobby walked up his front walk, through his front door. He said nothing to his stunned parents who reassure the policeman that this would never happen again.

"Bet he's gonna get a whupping now," Kevin said.

But Bobby knew better. For a Hopkins, humiliation was punishment in its own right. Bobby's mother's white face, the disappointment of her pursed lips was worse than any imaginable physical retribution. Bobby hid under his bed for the rest of the afternoon.

Outside his door, Patty waited, wondering what her parents would do. Her father told her that Bobby didn't need to be punished. "I think your brother has learned his lesson."

Bobby, curled in a fetal ball in the dusty dark beneath his bed, heard every word. Eventually, his mother's tone softened. His father began to cajole him to come out when Bobby skipped dinner. He couldn't believe he had been so stupid. By evening, Bobby's parents began blaming the neighbors. "That Kevin is a hoodlum," his mother said. A bad element. The Jacksons let their children run wild."

His bedroom began to darken. The sun set but he didn't turn on his bedside light. Before dozing off, he wondered what had happened to his abandoned bike but soon decided that he didn't care. Bobby would have no use for the bike in the future. Regardless of who was to blame, he would never play with the boys on the cul-de-sac again.

He did, however, spend the next week's allowance on a bag of Almond Joys, bought, not at Artie's but at the Safeway next door. The treasured bag was the first of many, the beginning of a stash of candy at the back of his desk drawer.

***

Watching the commotion next door, Harriet thought of her father. Joe took great pride in giving Kevin a "licking," Harriet couldn't imagine Bobby's dad raising his voice. Harriet's father believed boys needed discipline. They had to be reined in like wild horses. Once Kevin had broken a dinner plate when he was fooling around in the kitchen. Joe had made him stand in the corner at attention for the rest of the evening.

"Son," he said, his voice meant to be overheard "it's my life's work to enforce the military code of justice. You will have a real advantage when you go out into the hard, cruel world. You'll thank me later."

Joe insisted that discipline was a sign of his love.

Harriet never got in trouble. She wouldn't dare. Kat knew when to smile to soften her father's ire. Chrissie, of course, never had a chance to challenge her father's rules. No matter how hard Harriet tried to imagine what was going on that evening in the Hopkins' household, she had no idea. Bobby's family had a whole other set of rules, and she had no clue what that they might be.

1962

Chrissie was mobile.

After breakfast, Harriet carefully wheeled Chrissie's new wheelchair backward down the front porch stairs and positioned it in the circular driveway. Kevin was riding his bike around the cul-de-sac. Patty Hopkins, who had been watching from her front porch, came over to see the new addition to the Jackson family fleet.

"Hey, Chrissie. New wheels?"

Harriet released the brake and Chrissie demonstrated her mobility, rolling first forward towards the street and then back towards the front walkway. She turned right, then left. A rare smile broke out on her face.

"Neat."

With a stick of blue chalk, Kevin drew roads on the street. With only six homes along its perimeter, the cul-de-sac was frequently used by the children as a playground. Kevin completed a labyrinth with stop signs and intersections.

Chrissie sat up eagerly in her wheelchair as the other children tinkled their bikes' bells. They cruised through intersections and accelerated into straight stretches before screeching to a halt at the stop signs. "Whoa," Chrissie said, "you'd better watch out."

Bobby emerged from the Hopkins' front door, holding a model plane up in the air, testing the breeze with his finger.

"Hey, Bobby, look! Chrissie has a new wheelchair."

Harriet flinched at Patty's enthusiasm. She avoided Bobby's eyes as he looked up, clearly annoyed that his sister had interrupted his important investigation.

"Chrissie, do you want a ride?" Patty asked.

Harriet watched Chrissie react. Her sister's baffled expression said *yes*, said *no*, said, as it always said, *I can't*. She put a protective hand on her sister's shoulder. The poor thing didn't know what was happening.

"Don't mess with her," Harriet said to Patty.

"I would never," Patty said. Harriet watched as Patty, at first cautiously and then, once she got the swing of it, with more confidence, pushed Chrissie along the road that Kevin had drawn. At the stop signs, she stopped short, along the straight-aways she skipped. On the curves, she lifted one side of the wheelchair.

Bobby's plane flew okay the first time he threw it but then dive-bombed onto the lawn.

"Harriet, look at me," Chrissie called, waving as she passed, her smile as bright as the sun overhead. Even when Kevin yelled, "Beep, beep!" and passed her by, unable to hold himself back to accommodate his sister's plodding journey, she beamed and laughed uncontrollably.

"She's on a roller-coaster," Patty sang out, raising first the chair's front wheels, then the back. "Raise your hands," Kevin instructed Chrissie, and she did, stretching her pasty white arms into the air, imitating the children she had seen in TV ads for Disneyland.

Everything was in motion. Chrissie in her chair and Bobby flying his plane. Harriet watched both of them with vicarious fascination, her sister's fleeting moment of independence and Bobby's complete concentration on his project. First, he shaved slivers off the wooden wings with a surgeon's delicacy and then he repositioned its tail with patience and persistence.

By the time Hiroko called the children in for lunch, Bobby was flying his plane the full length of his yard and Patty was flushed with her success at making Chrissie smile. "Let's play again soon," she chirped as Harriet awkwardly worked her sister's new wheelchair back up the front steps.

Once inside, Harriet closed the heavy wooden door behind them. The house was dark. The kitchen quiet. Setting the sandwiches her mother had prepared on the table as the others washed their hands, the reality of the morning's exuberance seemed as far-fetched as Chrissie riding the ups and downs of an amusement park roller coaster.

***

Bobby watched Kevin Jackson scoop up the rusty bicycle that he had dropped haphazardly on his driveway the previous evening. In one move, Kevin kicked up the kickstand and headed in the direction of the park. Right behind him, Kat skipped down the street, her arm through that of a leggy, red-headed girl that Bobby recognized from school. Harriet was the last Jackson to leave, intently reviewing a shopping list in her hand as she carefully pushed off on her bicycle. Harriet was the only Jackson who looked up at the Hopkins' house as she passed.

Patty was already planning her next outing with Chrissie. "Maybe I can take her to the new park," she announced to no one in particular. Bobby ignored her. He opened the morning's newspaper to the comic pages and began laughing at Charlie Brown's dry humor as Alice scrubbed the kitchen counter.

Patty didn't even notice, and Bobby wasn't about to tell her, that the Jacksons had all deserted her. She wasn't going to be able to ask Chrissie out to play.

Bobby looked out the window as he finished his cereal. An unfamiliar man parked on the cul-de-sac. Dressed in a gray suit and tie, he walked to the back of his blue sedan, opened his trunk, and took out a leather suitcase. Opening it, he examined the contents before walking up the front walk of the Jacksons' house.

"Who is that?" Patty asked her mother.

"Probably a salesman," Bobby said.

Alice looked up from the sink where she was rinsing the breakfast dishes. "He certainly picked the wrong house if he intends to make a sale."

"Maybe it's the Fuller Brush man," Patty's said, instantly transferring her enthusiasm to the new arrival. Bobby never did understand his sister's excitement at the appearance of the Fuller Brush "man," any of a fleet of salesmen who regularly knocked on their door hawking not only brushes (all with a lifetime guarantee!) but cleaning products (Alice's favorites) and toiletries. The salesman who spread out an array of samples on the coffee table in the living room and chatted with Alice. He shared her mission of keeping the house forever clean.

Bobby couldn't imagine the silent Japanese woman next door chatting with the Fuller Brush man. He watched curiously as the salesman knocked on the Jacksons' front door. At first, there was no response. The man stepped back, examined his watch and knocked again. He was picking up his suitcase and beginning to turn away when Hiroko answered the door.

Bobby couldn't see either of their faces.

At the window, Patty strained to get a better look at the salesman. "He's shaking her hand," she reported. "Hiroko won't talk to him. He won't be able to sell a thing. I bet she doesn't even invite him in." What a waste. She won't even see the quality of the Fuller merchandise.

Patty could be so stupid. Bobby listened to his sister's chatting with increasing annoyance. The neighbors were, after all, none of her business. She was getting carried away after her success entertaining the crippled girl next door.

"Do you think he's going through his whole presentation and doesn't realize that she can't understand his pitch?" Patty asked her mother. Bobby sidled out of the room to escape her pointless prattle. "Do you think Hiroko is trying to explain to him that she is not interested in what he has to sell?"

No one in Bobby's family had a clue. It was pointless to imagine their neighbor's response. The Japanese woman would remain a mystery to them. Bobby, who was frequently embarrassed by his sister's lack of restraint, opened a Superman comic and tried to ignore the chatter from the kitchen.

Finally, Bobby heard the salesman click open the trunk of his nondescript car. That's when he heard the scream—Hiroko's scream.

Alice and Patty ran out the front door. Bobby followed them and spotted Harriet turning the corner on her bike, a brown bag of groceries in the front basket. He watched as she jumped off the bike, grabbed the bag of groceries and sprinted into the house. He heard her cry out, "Mom, what happened!"

Alice held Patty back, a firm grip on her arm. "If Harriet needs us, she will see that we are here."

Five minutes later an ambulance turned the corner, lights flashing, sirens wailing. A police car followed close behind. They watched as Harriet opened the door for the emergency medical technicians. The policeman stood outside for a moment, taking in the disarray of the Jacksons' driveway, and then followed the medics inside.

"It's not polite to stare," Alice said. Nevertheless, they continued to watch as the medics carried Chrissie out on a stretcher. The young girl's face was calm, but her body was covered by a white sheet. In the Jacksons' doorway, Hiroko and Harriet stood beside the policeman. Harriet did all the talking, gesturing frantically as tears ran down her face. The policeman wrote notes in his black leather notebook and pulled his hat down over his eyes to shield them from the intrusive sun.

✲✲✲

"I asked Harriet what happened," Patty was breathing heavily. Pausing for dramatic effect, she asked her mother for a glass of water.

She sipped the water, enjoying the attention that her neighbor's crisis evoked.

"Harriet said that Chrissie got burnt," she said at last. "Her mom was warming the bathwater when the salesman knocked on the door. She forgot to turn off the hot water. Chrissie's legs are covered with blisters."

"Is Chrissie okay?" Alice asked, her horror at the mother's neglect apparent, her lips pursed with disapproval, her eyes wide.

"Harriet said she couldn't feel a thing."

Blue chalk marks still brightened the empty pavement. From his bedroom window, Bobby studied the intricate map that Kevin had drawn. The imaginary streets that led nowhere. Did it help that Chrissie couldn't feel the pain? Under the medic's white sheets, the young girl's legs had once again caused her to lie flat on her back. In his opinion, it was obvious that none of them, not her family, not Patty, not even the medics, could do anything that would ameliorate the damage. Chrissie's birth defect had taken its toll even before she was born.

What troubled him was why. Neither luck nor science, certainly not religion, provided a satisfactory explanation. Nothing dispelled the shiver of horror he experienced watching the young girl carried out on a stretcher, taken away from her home by ambulance. The vision of Harriet Jackson standing in the open door trying to explain the situation to the policeman unsettled him. No matter how hard he tried, he could not determine who was to blame. There was no textbook he could read that would alleviate his neighbor's despair.

✳✳✳

At eight o'clock on Saturday night in California, it was six a.m. in Vietnam. Whenever Joe was able, this was the time he called his family.

Harriet dreaded his call as much as she anticipated hearing his voice.

Hiroko answered the phone.

"Joe. Hello. Joe?"

The other children clustered around, listening for their father's voice, hoping for news of his return. Hearing only Hiroko's side of the conversation, they tried to reconstruct the conversation.

"You okay?"

"Yes, fine..." After a long pause, "A man knocked on the door." Their mother was crying now.

"Don't yell at me. I try, Joe. I try."

Harriet stood at her mother's side, waiting for her mother to hand her the phone. The more her mother cried, the less sympathy she felt. Her father needed her to be strong. The family, he frequently reminded her, depended on her. She was one of his most dedicated officers.

When her mother finally handed her the receiver, their eyes met, her mother's pleading, Harriet's full of resolve.

"Hi, Dad. How are the Vietnamese?" She turned her back to her mother.

"A holy mess. What the hell is going on over there?"

"We're OK. Chrissie is fine. She never felt a thing."

Her father's voice traveled through a long tunnel. "Why wasn't someone watching her? I count on you to be sure that accidents don't happen."

"I know, Daddy. I know."

"Your mother needs help. She can't do this on her own."

Her father's familiar voice strengthened her determination. Harriet could almost see Joe, standing tall in his uniform, in charge. She wanted nothing more than to please him, to be the rock that he asked her to be. "But there is good news, too, Daddy, the doctors at the hospital asked the March of Dimes to feature Chrissie as the Fall poster child. They are fitting her for braces."

"Braces?"

"Daddy, when you come home, maybe Chrissie will be walking."

"I'm not sure I'm crazy about your sister's picture plastered all over town. We don't need their charity. I hope the doctors know what they're doing."

"It's a good thing. Mom said it's OK."

"Your mother would. You should have called me..."

"We never know how to reach you. I wish you were here." Harriet hated the tremble in her voice. She hoped her father couldn't hear.

"Hang in there, sweetheart. Let me say hi to Kat and Kevin."

The kids passed the phone around. Even Joey said "Daddy" at the sound of his father's voice. No one thought to take the phone to Chrissie who was sitting up in her bed as Hiroko combed her straggly hair, singing softly in Japanese.

After the kids said hello to Joe, Harriet handed the phone to her mother who said as she did at the end of every phone call, "Good-bye, my husband. Be safe." Hiroko handed the phone back to her daughter and continued to sing a song that Harriet could not understand. The tune, though soft, was soothing. The words, though foreign, were sung with clarity. Harriet listened closely, wishing she had inherited her mother's musical talent.

Joey toddled in and plopped down in his mother's lap. To Harriet's surprise, the toddler began to sing along, stroking his mother's arm as he sang.

In the living room, Kat and Kevin were once again arguing over TV shows.

"C'mon Joey," Harriet said. "It's time for bed." Her father would be so proud of her when he returned and saw the little boy. He was a delight, this latest one, happy and well-cared for. Her father would see. The family was doing fine.

1990-2

Harriet signed, page after page, following a fan of post-it notes instructing her to *Sign Here and Signature required.* Mike offered Kat an unlit cigarette, but his wife waved his gesture away. Harriet felt her sister watching. Even as Kat applied more gloss to her already shiny lips, Harriet felt her sister's intense scrutiny, her undivided attention as Harriet signed document after document.

Each time Harriet wrote her name, she recalled the prior transactions. The occasions when these mortgages had been refinanced, always with her father at her side: Joe's gift to Mike—the gas station he had funded when Mike agreed to marry Kat, the startup money for Kevin's racing career, the account set aside for the purchase of Eddie's dojo. These pages, these numbers, calculated her family's story, once and for all to see. The celebrations, the heartbreaks and now one final family rescue. When she reached the last sheet, she handed the folder to Kat who signed as the witness. With shaking hands, Harriet relinquished the house keys, setting the familiar key ring, a Christmas gift from her father, on the polished wood of the conference table.

The closing was over. Eddie, Kat, and Mike, already on their feet, made no attempt to cover up their relief. Kat refreshed her lipstick, peering into a pocket mirror as she headed towards the door.

In the waiting room, the buyers were now sitting on the couch where the Jacksons had perched only moments before: a young Asian man, his diminutive wife, and two giggling children. "This will be the first home for the young computer engineer, Mr. Nguyen, and his pregnant wife," Patty whispered to Harriet as she walked her to the door. "The young couple couldn't be more thrilled. He's accepted a job at a new company named Cisco."

The Jacksons rode down the one-floor elevator together. Kat and Mike hurried off to check on their gas station which they had left under the oversight of an inexperienced employee. They waved a cursory goodbye, lighting cigarettes as they walked away already deep in intimate conversation. Eddie headed to the parking lot, his powerful stride energized with relief, his long legs carrying him into a brighter future. It took a moment before Harriet realized that her nephew, already out of earshot, had forgotten that he had promised her a ride. Before she could call out to him, he disappeared around the corner. She was stranded, standing alone at the busy intersection.

On her right, the atrium of the lawyers' office opened onto a recently opened Starbucks where young people sipped expensive coffee drinks as they read the financial pages of the *New York Times*. To the left, there was a Merrill Lynch "wealth management" storefront with a purposeful air of exclusive elegance. Across the street, the Hewlett Packard campus was obscured by carefully manicured landscaping. Harriet had been left behind, homeless, without a ride. The day was hot, and she was overdressed. She stood on the familiar corner waiting for someone to return for her.

And then she remembered.

As cars poured by, some honking impatiently, making last minute turns into Mike and Kat's busy Shell station on the other side of the six-lane expressway that Foothill Boulevard had become, she recalled the day she had watched an exploding gas tank set fire to a red Mustang. The plume of black smoke that had engulfed the station. The heat and terror which had sent her fleeing back to the safety of home.

Now she had no home. Harriet stood on the corner and recalled those distant flames. Eddie had left. He no longer needed her. Her mother, her siblings, the family who had always depended on her, were gone. At last, the smoke began to clear. Kat and Mike had built a life from that rubble. Eddie had no need of safety. Her family had moved on. She was what they had left behind. She watched the Nguyens exit the building, hand in hand, and she knew that she no longer belonged here.

The Valley she loved and the family that she cherished had left her behind. Only successful entrepreneurs like Bobby belonged here now.

Harriet could not remember who had been hurt in that long-ago explosion nor how badly. She remembered only dark smoke and panic. She had once asked Bobby what had lit the flames, what science explained it. Bobby had answered with his normal objectivity. He had adopted the pedantic tone he used when speaking with classmates who lacked his own intelligence. "Some things are too complicated for a non-scientist to understand." Even then, in the aftermath of the explosion, Bobby had more important things on his mind.

Harriet turned her back to the station and ran through the glass lobby of the office building, climbing the flight of stairs to Patty's office two at a time. She hoped that she was not too late. This time she would not leave without insisting on an answer.

1963

The best thing about Sunday morning was waffles. Bacon, too. On Sundays, Bobby's mother went all out. The worst thing about Sunday was church. But here he was in the back of the station wagon dressed in his itchiest clothes.

"I wish those Jacksons would sweep their driveway," Alice complained as the family climbed into the car, off to church. "Their house is an eyesore."

Ever since Jacqueline Kennedy guided television viewers on a tour of the White House, Bobby's mom had displayed a new confidence. Alice had started to smile more and wear pink lipstick. This morning, she wore a pillbox hat with a veil that resembled that worn by Jackie in *Time* magazine. She had even redecorated their living room to match the Kennedy's more contemporary tastes. The young President exuded high hopes, and Alice was an avid fan. Bobby watched his mom light a cigarette as she surveyed their neighborhood from the side window of the car. He was encouraged by her optimism. After all, his father shared the name of the handsome president as well as an eye on the future. Jack's company had recently promoted him to Systems Administrator. Computers, it turned out, were an integral part of the future that the President envisioned.

For that matter, the entire Santa Clara Valley seemed primed for progress. California was the place to be, a continent away from the old rules, a place of new beginnings, invention unsaddled by convention. By 1960 one million people had settled in the county. Housing prices were going through the roof.

The image of the President's daughter Caroline hiding under her father's desk in the Oval Office had been on the cover of *Time* magazine. Patty bragged that her size nine feet were as large as Jacqueline's. Alice let her daughter wear new black high-heeled pumps to church. His sister's breasts were beginning to swell in her training bra. Bobby had been selected for the exclusive Stanford Advanced Mathematics Study Program. Kevin Jackson might continue to call the family the Glasses, but Alice was right, the Jackson house was a neighborhood eyesore.

As his father backed the station wagon out of the driveway, Bobby watched Harriet in her bathrobe, carrying a bag of garbage to her garage.

"Joe Jackson is never home," Alice observed, her carefully colored lips threatening to settle into their usual look of prissy disapproval.

"He's stationed in Vietnam. The Navy is advising the insurgents," Bobby said as if that explained the neighbors' windows, each with a blind drawn.

"I hear Chrissie has been selected as the March of Dimes poster child for 1963," Alice said. "Maybe that poor child will finally get the attention she deserves. Her mother certainly doesn't have a clue."

Ever since Alice had watched the EMTs carry Chrissie out on a stretcher, she made it clear that she disapproved of the next-door neighbors.

"It's always something with that family," Alice said as she lit another cigarette.

Bobby sighed. His dress pants were tight and uncomfortable. Despite his declaration at the dinner table that he was now an atheist, his parents insisted that he go to church until he was confirmed in June.

He wasn't about to disturb the family's equanimity by speaking up in the Jacksons' defense. Besides, they were on their way to church where Alice had volunteered to man the coffee table after the service. As Episcopalians, Alice had explained to the family that they weren't quite Catholic like the Kennedys, but that her new suit was almost as chic as the first lady's. He was willing to accept her prognosis: the world was changing for the better.

✷✷✷

Harriet sidled into in the back of the classroom where she hoped Mrs. Landon wouldn't notice her. She had missed two weeks of class during Chrissie's hospitalization and, although she had caught up on her homework, she had barely started to read *A Tale of Two Cities*.

Bobby, in the front row, was debating the finer points of the French revolution with the teacher when the overhead speaker crackled. After a few painful screeches and more static, the principal's voice interrupted the class. Bobby, intent on making his point clear, spoke louder over the unwelcome announcement.

"Shortly after noon today," the rumble of the principal's baritone competed with Bobby's adolescent pedantry, "President Kennedy was shot as he rode in a motorcade through Dealey Plaza in downtown Dallas, Texas."

Even Bobby was quiet now.

Mrs. Landon collapsed into the chair behind her desk, her legs refusing to support her. The teacher's face was white.

"As soon as we receive updated information, we will pass it along. We hope and pray that President Kennedy will be alright."

None of the children spoke.

Mrs. Landon pushed a strand of ash blond hair off her forehead. Shaking her head, she kept repeating "Oh my God."

Bobby never resumed his spirited argument. The other students watched their teacher, waiting for her to model what to do next. When she, finally, regained her composure, Mrs. Landon suggested that the students read quietly on their own. Harriet flipped through her novel without interest. She had lugged the book each night to the hospital when she had visited Chrissie. The perky nurse who had dressed her sister's wounds said she had read Dickens in middle school. Harriet hadn't read past the first chapter and didn't expect to get any further now.

Five minutes passed. The speaker crackled again. This time silence muffled the classroom. The air itself went dead.

"President Kennedy died today at 12:30 p.m.

"After consultation with the district office, we have decided to allow students to return home to be with their families at this time. Students who are unable to go home are asked to report to the auditorium where counselors will assist them.

"God bless the President. God bless the U.S.A."

"No." Pamela Goodman cried. "I can't believe this."

Mrs. Landon mumbled to herself, "He was so young, so healthy."

Harriet thought, *another school day lost.* Life wouldn't give her a break. She picked up her notebook, slid her pen into its plastic sleeve and stood up. The last place she wanted to go was home.

"He was such an inspiration," Bobby said as they walked out of the classroom. "My mother called him a breath of fresh air."

The playground was empty. The students seemed disoriented. Some of the boys pulled out transistor radios. Silent students clustered around them, listening to the news.

The announcer said Jackie had been at the President's side when he was shot.

Bobby continued to walk beside Harriet. They passed the boys on the corner, the ones who were talking about a conspiracy. The ones who were ecstatic at the unexpected departure from their routine.

"Maybe it was the Cubans," Bobby said. Harriet had no idea what he was talking about. Lately, Kevin had dictated the evening selection of TV shows. With their Dad in Vietnam where a coup d'état was taking place, Harriet had decided they were better off not watching the evening news.

"The President had enemies," Bobby said.

"What do you mean?" Harriet asked. Bobby smelled shower-fresh. His brown hair had a slight wave, and an errant lock fell across his forehead. When he pushed his glasses up on his freckled nose, she noticed that his eyes were as blue as Patty's.

"I guess Johnson is President now." Bobby looked at her like he knew she would understand. "Lots of people disagreed with Kennedy's stand on the Bay of Pigs. Not to mention his support for civil rights. Who knows who wanted him dead? It could have been the mob."

Until that moment, Harriet could not have imagined any circumstance where she and Bobby would be walking home together. They had lived next door for most of their lives, but they had almost nothing in common. His house with its meticulous gardens might as well have been in another universe from hers—a universe with an orderly succession. Now she listened attentively thinking about how much she had to learn.

The president had been assassinated and Bobby was walking her home. Even Kevin wouldn't be caught dead at his sister's side when he was with his classmates, but Bobby didn't seem to care.

Later that night, watching endless replays of Jackie in her blood-stained suit holding the dying president in her arms, Harriet was careful to shield a smile from her sisters and brother. Not that they ever would have noticed. As far as her siblings were concerned, she was like a piece of living room furniture. Always there when they needed her, reliable but invisible. Today, the tragic day that the President was assassinated, Bobby had seen her.

Tomorrow she would ask Bobby if he thought there was a lone gunman. Tired of the repetitive loop of the commentator's speculation, she opened *A Tale of Two Cities.* "It was the best of times. It was the worst of times..."

Chrissie was home now. The doctors at the hospital had assured her mother that there were new medical treatments on the horizon, that the family should not give up hope.

Harriet couldn't wait for school to resume. She read late into the night, swept up in the poverty of the French peasantry and the vivid descriptions of the opulent life of the aristocracy.

When the French Revolution occurred, everything changed. Until the day Kennedy died, Harriet's life had seemed predictable, her choices limited. But reading Dickens, she began to wonder. Dickens' story showed her that sometimes there are events that change everything, break down the rules as we have come to know them. Bobby seemed to understand this; walking beside him, she, too, wanted to have an opportunity for change. Maybe for her, Kennedy's death would be like the French Revolution. An event that triggered a fundamental shift in her relation to the world around her. If so, Harriet wasn't about to miss that opportunity. At Bobby's side, she'd had a vision of a world larger than the Jackson household, larger even than Picaflor Court. She had so many questions that she wanted to ask the boy next door. The whole country was in mourning, but that night Harriet felt truly alive.

"Can't you leave me alone?"

Since President Kennedy had been assassinated, Bobby had spent most of his time at home in his bedroom with the door closed. Whenever his mom or Patty knocked on the door, he snapped, "Go away." Time after time, he asked them to leave, telling them he was reading (he sometimes was), studying (which he didn't do often since his classwork was moronically easy), or that he needed quiet in order to think.

Reading *Great Expectations* for his English class, it occurred to him that his mother had a lot in common with Miss Havisham who lived in a "large and dismal house barricaded against robbers." His mother's distaste for the Jacksons and the chaos next door was unfair. Bobby was working on an essay, of which he was extremely proud, which explored the issues of class in Dickens, comparing mid-nineteenth century London to the current American South and the brewing struggle for civil rights.

Theories about the Kennedy assassination continued to fascinate him. He devoured every issue of *Time* and *Life*, certain that if he read the articles carefully enough, he would be able to discern the actual truth of the assassination and the events that followed. He dismissed his classmates' emotional responses, especially the girls who teared up at any mention of Jackie, Caroline or John John. He had resolved to live his life based on science, observation, and objectivity. On the other side of his bedroom wall, Patty played the Beatles "*Love, love me do*" over and over until he swore he heard the insipid tune in his dreams. His parents preferred show tunes which they proudly played on their brand-new GE coffee table stereo. Alice would sing along with Gigi as she vacuumed. Patty countered with "Thank heaven for little girls" as if the tune were written specifically to praise her.

"Pop music is mindless pap," he declared at the dinner table after an excruciating afternoon of Maurice Chevalier. Jack chuckled when his son informed the family that from that point on he intended to listen only to jazz. To prove his point, the next day Bobby spent his allowance on albums by John Coltrane and Mingus. He lost himself in *The Black Saint and the Sinner Lady*. Behind his closed door, he stared at the white ceiling of his bedroom with his head in his hands, letting the wail of Coltrane's sax filling the vacuous air. He sensed that something was amiss in his orderly life.

At 13, being a brain wasn't enough. Things were brewing underground in the world and in his life. Patty's endless chatter was driving him up a wall. The humiliation he had experienced that afternoon in the cop car resided like a lump in his throat. The memory of the boys laughing at him. He knew life was not a laughing matter.

If only his sister was more like Harriet next door, calm, quiet, and responsible. Recently he had begun to picture his neighbor at the oddest times—Harriet's serene expression, the vaguely foreign tilt of her brown eyes, the plastic barrette that held her straight black hair away from the smooth curve of her golden neck. Harriet was everything his family was not.

No one in his life listened to him with her rapt attention. No one else understood him.

With pianist Duke Ellington, John Coltrane played *In a Sentimental Mood*, stirring emotions that Bobby had never known existed. Outside his bedroom window, he heard the neighborhood kids playing, but the ruckus faded into the distance as the improvisations increased in volume, rhythmically and methodically.

He aspired to the heavenly reach of the music that surrounded him, but, in truth, he kept picturing the girl next door.

Christmas 1963

Harriet wondered if her father would notice her new maturity. So many things had changed since she had last seen him.

"What does Daddy look like?" The last time Joe was at home, Joey Jr. was a baby.

"Like a superhero," Kevin said.

Chrissie wore the outfit she had been given for the March of Dimes photo shoot. A frilly plaid dress with red bows and a matching cardigan sweater with a white fake-fur collar. Matching white tights covered her spindly legs. Despite Harriet's best efforts, she had not been able to duplicate the Shirley Temple ringlets that the professional photographer's assistant had achieved, but for once Chrissie's hair had been professionally cut. She sat upright in her wheelchair, eager to share her new fame with her returning father.

Hiroko inspected the girls.

Harriet knew that Kat was bound to catch her father's eye. Over the past year, Kat had become a beauty who looked much older than eleven. Her glossy black hair and the subtle Asian tilt to her chestnut eyes gave her an exotic appearance. Her legs were long. For her father's return, she had chosen a turtleneck sweater that hinted at the changes taking place in her slender body.

Harriet was dressed in a neat, pleated skirt and white blouse. She was determined to show her father that she deserved his respect. She had tied her unruly hair into a ponytail. Nothing frivolous for her.

Hiroko had plucked her eyebrows and painted new ones higher on her brow. She wore the red lipstick that her husband liked and for once had dressed up in a pretty blue dress she had purchased from the commissary.

Kevin, all twitches and impatience, complained loudly about having to wear a white dress shirt. While Harriet was dressing Chrissie, he practiced taking the chain on and off his bike, a skill he was dying to show his Dad, but which had resulted in a collection of greasy stains on the neatly pressed shirt.

"Dad is so tall," he told Joey. "A Commander."

When Joe's 1961 Impala turned the corner, Kevin let out a hoot. The whole family headed out to the driveway to greet the returning hero. They cheered when he swept Hiroko up into his arms.

"Dad, look what I can do," Kevin tugged on his father's arm but unable to get his attention.

"Chrissie, my love," Joe kissed his daughter on the head.

"Kat," he looked her over, "Wow. You've grown."

Harriet extended her hand. Joe chuckled. "Hey, Kiddo."

"And who is this?" he asked scooping up little Joey, who flinched at his touch.

Harriet hoped the Hopkins were watching. She wanted Bobby to know that she, too, had a happy family.

✳✳✳

"Defense Secretary McNamara was very clear," Joe told the boys as they looked under the hood of his Impala. "The U.S. will not accept a Communist victory. We will do whatever is necessary to ensure the Commies' defeat."

Joe had changed out of his uniform, but his khakis were as stiff and neatly ironed as his uniform pants. He demonstrated the V8 engine, revving the motor for his sons' admiration while talking nonstop about the battles to come.

He had already promised the boys to take them on a ride in his Lockheed NF-104A Starfighter over the weekend but for now, they settled on a trip to the supermarket in the back seat of his car to buy beer for an afternoon of watching football. Kat came along, comfortable to be one of the boys, flipping her thick mane of hair every time they passed one of her classmates.

Kevin tugged at his father's sleeve, asked again for a chance to show off his mechanical skills. When Dad was home, he had trouble getting a word in.

Harriet watched from the kitchen window. Her mom wore an apron over her new dress. After Joe's initial embrace, he had hardly spoken to either of them. Instead, he lavished his attention on the boys and Kat. When he was home, the house smelled differently; the air crackled with masculine energy.

Over dinner, Joe described his exploits at the USO club where the officers played cards late into the night. He painted a picture of the lush jungles of Vietnam, the busy streets of the cities.

"In Saigon, everybody gets around on cyclos." He directed his comment to Kevin, who looked up hopefully. "Bikes are everywhere."

Turning to Harriet, "One of the oldest buildings in the city is Our Lady's Basilica. They say mass in French and English."

Harriet wondered if her father knew that the family no longer attended mass.

"On the Saigon River, there is a Memorial to the Trung Sisters, heroines of the Vietnamese struggle for independence 2,000 years ago. They say that their faces resemble Madame Nhu, the first lady of the Republic of Vietnam, but Hiroko, she reminds me of you."

Hiroko blushed, obviously pleased by the comparison.

Between sentences, Joe ate enthusiastically, holding court. Hiroko made sure the serving dishes were full.

After dinner, Joe asked Harriet to join him on a walk around the block. Despite feeling guilty about leaving her mother to empty the sink full of dishes, Harriet pulled a cardigan over her white blouse as her father lit a cigarette.

"Your brothers and sisters look well," he said as they turned the corner. He blew out a stream of blue smoke and raised his eyebrows, asking a question. "The boys are growing up so fast and Kat is gorgeous."

Harriet tried to ignore a pang of jealousy. She pulled her sweater tighter around her.

"It's been a hard year." Harriet wanted her father to know that she, too, was maturing, shaped by the assassination and changing world around her.

"Chrissie looks good."

"They are fitting her for braces in January. She likes the attention."

"Kat is..."

Harriet didn't know what to tell him. Kat came and went as she pleased. "She's popular."

"No surprise there."

Harriet looked down as they walked. Her father's shoes were so shiny that she could see a reflection of the sky in their leather.

"You know you will always be my favorite. The one I have always depended on to keep things together."

"Mom is doing her best."

"I know, I know, but your Mom is...

"Daddy, can I ask you something?"

"Anything, Sugar."

"Did you marry Mom because you had to?" Blushing, Harriet added, "You know, 'cause of me?"

Joe looked surprised. He took another drag on his cigarette, squinting his eyes against the smoke.

"You are growing up," he said. She couldn't help but smile at the acknowledgment.

"Mom seems so lonely sometimes," she said.

Her father took another drag on his cigarette. She watched him thinking through what to say.

"Your mother's dad was very ill when I met her. She wasn't much older than you are now." Joe looked at his daughter; she stood taller as if to demonstrate his point. "Even then, Hiroko seemed sad. The Japanese believe in 'Taisho.' They hold things inside. Your mother never talked about her father's cancer. When she invited me into their home, her mother never mentioned her husband's health. Instead, she always made an elaborate dinner. At the old man's funeral, your mother hardly cried; her mother encouraged her to smile, as was appropriate."

Harriet waited. He had not answered her question.

"When your mother informed me that she was pregnant, it was the same thing. A few tears covered with a smile. I have never been able to tell if your mother is happy, but I have always done the right thing by her." His words became more vehement. "I love your mother. I love all of you. I will always do my duty. That is why I need you to be my eyes and ears." He put an arm around her shoulder.

"You are my life." She didn't know if he meant her or the family, but his words made it all worthwhile, gave her life—as difficult as it sometimes was—meaning.

"Daddy, you know you can count on me."

"I know, Sweetheart."

He was walking faster now.

"As soon as we push those damn Commies out of South Vietnam, I'm coming home."

They were almost back to the house. Kevin rode his bike up to greet them.

"Hang in there a while longer," her father said.

"Dad, do you want to see me change my bicycle chain?" Kevin asked for the one-hundredth time.

As they passed Bobby's house, Harriet was almost certain she could see his mother peeking out through the kitchen blinds. How handsome her father must look, in contrast to Mr. Hopkins with his thick glasses, plaid shirts and gardening pants, his limp blue windbreaker. No one stood taller than her father. The image of Joe towering over the neighbor made her smile.

That night, all the children knew that their mother's bedroom was off limits. Dad was home at last.

Tomorrow they would buy a Christmas tree.

1964

Bobby sneered when Alice insisted that the whole family climb into their blue Belair station wagon to see the Beatles. The popular band was on their first visit to the United States. The *San Jose Mercury News* reported that the mop-tops from Liverpool were staying at a luxury hotel near the freeway. From the moment they made the turn off of 101, Bobby could see the hotel's circular drive, crowded with masses of teenage girls bearing signs saying, "Paul, we love you."

Bobby was there under protest.

As always, his mom had a plan.

"Mom," Bobby said, "the Beatles aren't going to be able to pass through this mob."

"You're right," Alice said. She directed their father to drive to an unmarked rear entrance of the hotel. Amenable, Jack snaked the car through an alley used by maintenance men and hotel employees and parked next to garbage dumpsters at the rear of the hotel. Patty said she hoped that they had the inside track. Two other cars followed, evidently hoping that the family had knowledge they did not.

The excursion was a waste of time. Patty said that stalking the Beatles was way more exciting than their usual after-dinner fieldtrips, but Bobby had no use for the mop-tops' music. He preferred to stay home and watch TV. But instead, like most nights that summer, after his mother had loaded the dinner dishes into the dishwasher, he was forced into the station wagon while the family went to ogle the ashes of train wrecks, house fires, or plane crashes. Now that the day's headlines were unremarkable, his mother was trolling for something new to give her life meaning. Often his father would park the car beneath the runways at the San Jose airport, waiting for calamity but settling for the thunder of landing gear being lowered and reversed engines bringing the massive vehicle to a vehement halt.

"One thing you have to admit about your mother," Jack liked to say. "She makes life interesting."

Bobby didn't see the point.

"You can't lock yourself up in your room for the rest of your life," his mother said, giving him no option.

Tonight, Jack drove, as usual following Alice's directions. He held his cigarette outside the car window, content to go along for the ride.

The crowd was growing fast. From her perch in the backseat, Patty craned to see the band, every muscle taut with anticipation. Bobby could almost feel the heat of the mass of the bodies crushing against each other. His skin crawled.

"God, this is embarrassing."

They waited. At some point the roar of the crowd filled the air, intermixed with the wail of police sirens. A crescendo shook the ground, rattling the metal of the malodorous dumpsters. It was happening. The arrival of the Beatles in America was a big, big deal. They were there.

Or as close as they would ever be.

All summer, as most summers, wildfires had burned in the foothills of the Santa Cruz Mountains. On their evening drives, the family got as close to the disaster as the police allowed, finding dirt roads to bypass roadblocks. Smoke signaled the highest flames. The sky darkened and the acrid smell filled their nostrils. They tracked the progress of the fires, gauging who was winning, the flames or the fire squads. Sometimes they could feel the heat, even from the distance. Patty spread her hands on the car's window. She could almost touch the approaching fever.

"Never a dull day in the life of the Hopkins," their father said. "These are days you will remember."

Bobby hoped not.

When Jack took his hands off the steering wheel to light his cigarette, the car careened, hitting the curb before he gained control. "Dad!" Patty and Bobby called out in unison, afraid of crashing down the steep embankment as the car radio played "*Close your eyes and I'll kiss you.*"

Bobby watched Patty. She closed her eyes and sang along with the car radio as if she, too, were at the Beatles concert, surrounded by her peers on the vanguard of a world that was ripe for change. With a minor revision, he could see that history was being made. It all added up.

Even his silly sister knew that the world as they knew it would never be the same.

✳✳✳

El Camino Real was gridlocked again. Each year new highways opened but there were never enough. The newly completed eight-lane I-280 Freeway, with its six-lane extension to Cupertino had only brought more traffic to the area. The recently opened 5.5-mile Route 85 freeway between Cupertino and US 101 in Mountain View came to a dead stop during rush hour. As Harriet and her mother drove to the Commissary, the air was redolent with car exhaust.

The subdivision where the Jackson and Hopkins families lived was only one of many that had been built during the 1950s. The population of Santa Clara County had doubled in the last ten years. Many of the new fathers were engineers like Mr. Hopkins. Looking out the car window, Harriet spotted the semiconductor manufacturer Fairchild on Borregas Avenue, National Semiconductor on Kifer Road, and Ampex Industries on San Aleso, all within five miles of the Moffett Field. The companies filled industrial parks that lined the streets of Sunnyvale with buildings designed to look like college campuses in imitation of the modern Stanford Industrial Park. The new companies followed strict building codes which included concealment of smokestacks, generators, transformers, cuts, storage tanks, and air conditioning equipment. The whole area buzzed with prosperity.

At least Moffett Field looked the same. The Navy had recently discontinued fighter aircraft sorties departing from the base, but Moffett remained the home of the Navy's principal Pacific Fleet, in addition to housing NASA activities and the California Air National Guard. As Hiroko turned into the base, Harriet observed the familiar geography: runways which disappeared into the bay, the large spectral hangars and faceless institutional office spaces, the low huddle of barracks, housing she had once called home.

Nowadays, when Kevin rode his bike along Foothill Boulevard, his favorite route took him to the construction site for the new high school. Her brother was mesmerized by the construction vehicles and the endless brickwork. He reported the building's progress nightly over the dinner table. Although her brother wasn't old enough yet to attend the expansive two-story brick school with its central plaza and football field, Harriet would be a member of the first class to attend the new state-of-the-art school whose students would come from many of the surrounding subdivisions, including some of the wealthier suburbs in the foothills.

Her mother had promised to buy her new clothes for the first day of school. At the commissary, Harriet flipped through rack after rack of back-to-school clothes while her mother searched for familiar faces. With each visit, fewer of the women her mother knew were living at the Base. Harriet hadn't a clue what to buy. She chewed on her split ends until tendrils of wet hair stuck limply to her face. If only Kat were there to help her pick out an appropriate outfit. Harriet had no idea what high school kids wore, and Hiroko was, as usual, no help at all.

✳✳✳

In the parking lot, waiting for the High School bus to arrive, Harriet adjusted the velvet headband that she had selected to match her navy-blue skirt. Self-consciously, she applied the lip gloss that she had borrowed from her younger sister after she had ironed her new white blouse twice.

Beside her, Bobby was sitting on a post, engrossed in the third volume of Asimov's Foundation Trilogy. Harriet lingered beside him for five minutes before he finally looked up, but when he did, he smiled. She was the only Jackson child on the bus. For once in her life, she was not the older sister of the poster child. Her classmates would not identify her with the house with the broken-down cars in front. She would not be trailed by Kevin on his bicycle nor overshadowed by Kat's good looks.

"Good summer, Bobby?"

"OK." Her neighbor had grown taller over the summer. She suddenly wished she had a book to read so that they could sit together on the bus, reading silently side by side. Ever since the day that Kennedy was assassinated, Harriet felt drawn to her studious neighbor. Bobby was serious. While the other kids prattled on and on about their summer vacations, she was perfectly content to sit quietly. With him near, she didn't feel like an outsider.

Bobby's companionship was welcome. Everything else in the new school was different.

At the opening day assembly, Mr. Ito greeted the new students warmly, encouraging them to participate in student government. Harriet was surprised to see that the vice principal was Japanese. She wondered if he spoke his native language. She studied his smiling face, noted the familiar slant of his eyes. If she were to pass him in the hallway, would she have the nerve to speak to him? Would he see in her a familiarity?

She couldn't imagine joining the student government but was thinking of trying out for the chorus.

All day long teachers handed out textbooks. Between classes, she lined them up in her locker. The books were new, their spines stiff.

Between eleven and one, the students took turns eating lunch outside in the sunshine of the central quadrangle. Harriet, who had always gone home to make lunch for her siblings, sat on the brick wall, outside of the chaos. The more popular boys trolled the pavement, and the confident girls smiled back. Harriet pretended to be reading her history textbook.

She looked for Bobby, but he was nowhere to be seen.

By early afternoon, she missed home with a gnawing in her stomach like hunger. She wondered if her mother was keeping an eye on Chrissie. She clung to her textbooks even though her teacher had not assigned any homework.

When Bobby sat down next to her on the bus home, she opened her algebra book.

"Algebra I?" he asked.

"Yeah." He was taking geometry.

Bobby shuffled his feet and marked his place in his book with a finger and cleared his throat. "My family is going to see the new Beatles movie at the Monte Vista drive-in on Friday."

"Neat."

"It's probably pretty trite. Have you seen it?"

"No." Kat played the Beatles all day long on her record player, but Harriet hadn't paid much attention. She still preferred Elvis, but Kat said that every girl she knew had a favorite Beatle and that, if she had to pick, she supposed that hers was George.

"It's actually supposed to be pretty funny. A typical day in the life of the band."

Harriet had never been to a drive-in movie.

"Want to come along?"

Go to the movies in the Hopkins' shiny new station wagon? With Bobby? Her mother would never allow it. Kat would say she was crazy. She wished she had listened more closely when Kat played the Beatles records in their room. What could she wear? She couldn't possibly.

"That'd be cool," she said, taking care to keep her voice calm despite the pounding of her heart. The bus pulled into the elementary school parking lot and kids began to disperse.

"What's Asimov like?" she asked as they walked home together side by side. Once Bobby got started, he didn't stop talking. He liked Asimov that much.

✳✳✳

Harriet knocked on the Hopkins door at exactly 7:30 on Friday night. She had memorized every word of the song *A Hard Day's Night,* mouthing the words after Kat fell asleep at night. The movie wasn't scheduled to start until nine, but Bobby was tasked with buying the family refreshments before the show began. From what Harriet could discern, this was his favorite part of the evening.

"Hey, Harriet," Patty greeted her.

"Sweetheart, did you bring a jacket?" Alice asked.

Harriet looked down self-consciously at her clean jeans and baby blue blouse. Kat, who was blown away that her older sister had a date, had looked her over and snorted her disapproval.

"At least put on some earrings, for God's sake," she'd said, but Harriet had not.

Hiroko had lent her one of her sweaters—a cardigan with appliqued flowers that smelled vaguely of mothballs. When Harriet left the house, Hiroko had handed her a package of commissary cookies from the kitchen cupboard and said "For our generous neighbors. Don't forget to say thank you."

Harriet was nervous enough without any of their advice. However, under Alice's scrutiny, she was glad that she had agreed to wear the sweater. It had never occurred to her that she would be squeezed into the back seat of the Hopkins' station wagon with Bobby on one side and Patty on the other, their legs packed together like six hot dogs shrink-wrapped in plastic.

"You've never seen a movie at the drive-in theater?" Patty asked incredulously. Bobby's sister was in middle school now, a little chubby. She wore a strap around her head attached to a contraption that was supposed to make her teeth straight.

"George is my favorite Beatle," Harriet answered, happy to change the subject.

"I like John. He's cerebral." Close up, Patty's face was covered with blackheads. Along with the extra pounds and the silver braces on her teeth, she was a bit of a mess.

"But George is the spiritual one," Harriet answered. That was what Kat always said.

Bobby snorted. In the front seat, Jack and Alice smoked cigarettes, blowing streams of smoke out the open windows of the car. Harriet liked the way Bobby seemed to be above it all. Beside his talkative sister, she tried to mimic his composure. She couldn't stop thinking of his leg next to hers.

Jack parked the car in the middle of a gigantic parking lot. All the cars faced a giant movie screen. Bobby jumped out of the car to buy candy from the concession stand.

"Get some Bonbons too," Patty said.

"Just what you don't need," her mother commented.

"Mom!" Patty protested, rolling her eyes.

Harriet accompanied him to the refreshment stand. "Don't mind Patty," Bobby said. "She's a pain." He studied the candy counter with impressive concentration. The boxes of chocolate were enormous, each enough to feed an entire family.

"Popcorn would be great," Harriet said. "Thank you." In truth, she found Patty's enthusiasm a welcome relief. It took the attention off her. She envied the ease with which Patty bantered with her brother. The unspoken intimacy of the family which, for the moment at least, included her.

Bobby chose Almond Joys. "My favorite," he said, opening the gigantic box of chocolate as they walked back to the car. Harriet, afraid of talking with her mouth full, said: "No, thanks." Her stomach was tight, and she wasn't sure she could eat in such strange surroundings.

After they climbed back into the station wagon, Jack removed speakers from a pole next to the car and hung them off the car's front windows. Previews of coming attractions played out on the large screen; the soundtrack blared from the speakers. In addition to popcorn and chocolate, Bobby had purchased cardboard cups of coffee for his parents. Harriet watched as Jack added whiskey to the hot drinks.

"We used to wear our pajamas when we came to the drive-in," Patty said. "I'd fall asleep in the back before the movie was over."

Bobby didn't stop laughing once the movie started. The Beatles were playing cards in a moving train under the gaze of adoring fans. Harriet could barely follow the fast-paced dialog, especially given the band's Liverpudlian accents. Crammed in the back seat, cozily enveloped by the frivolity, she tried to laugh at the right places.

Bobby and Patty took turns imitating the Beatles. "A li'l," Bobby said instead of little. They never got it quite right, but that didn't seem to bother them at all. Even their parents laughed at their attempts to sound British.

Ringo reminded Harriet of her brother Kevin, droll and understated but basically well-meaning. When Paul's grandfather, a "real king mixer" convinced him to go outside and experience life rather than reading books, Patty pointed at Bobby who protested vehemently.

"I DO go outside," he said, and his sister laughed.

"Only when Mom makes you."

Next thing Harriet knew, the whole band was looking for Ringo, who for some reason that she didn't understand, had been arrested by the police. They found the errant band member in time to play drums for their evening concert.

The movie ended with the band in a helicopter, leaving behind a horde of screaming fans waving good-bye.

"We almost saw the Beatles once," Patty was laughing so hard tears ran down on her cheeks.

"Let it go, Patty," Bobby said.

"We saw a garbage dumpster instead."

Jack and Alice laughed harder than either of their kids. Harriet couldn't help wondering if Bobby's parents were drunk or if this was how happy families got along.

"Never a dull day in the life of the Hopkins," Jack said, his favorite line.

On the drive home, Bobby kept rehashing his favorite scenes. Harriet was already imagining saying to the other kids on the school bus, "When Bobby and I went to the movies..." When the Hopkins dropped her off, she thanked Bobby's parents profusely.

"Anytime," Alice said.

Hiroko was waiting for her at the front door. "I said thanks, Mom," Harriet assured her. Tomorrow, she would take the cookies out from behind the bush where she had stashed them. She could hide them in the trash.

1965

Harriet dreaded her mother's words: "Chrissie sick." The two words could puncture any good mood, turn any good day into bad.

Chrissie's health was closely monitored by the doctors at the Stanford Medical Center. Not only were braces being fitted for her sister's spindly legs, but the doctors regularly checked the shunt that drained excess fluid from her brain.

Kevin was determined that his sister would walk. Each morning before school, he insisted that Harriet strap the metal braces onto his sister's flaccid legs. With Harriet supporting Chrissie's weight, Kevin attached crutches with padded strap-on bands to Chrissie's slender arms. Willing, Chrissie attempted to swing her legs forward, balancing on the crutches as best she could.

"You can do it!" Kevin cheered her on.

Chrissie wrinkled up her nose and clenched her teeth; the effort required everything of her. Harriet watched as the color drained out of her sister's face and tears appeared in the corners of her trusting brown eyes.

"You can do it!" Kevin insisted.

Sometimes there was a minuscule movement, at most an intention. The morning sessions were torture.

Fortunately, Kevin's attention span was short. The basketball courts of the school playground opened before the morning bell rang. He wanted to be the first one on the courts, bouncing his ball and waiting for a challenge.

"Tomorrow, Chrissie. I know you will do it tomorrow," he grabbed his brown bag lunch from Harriet and headed out the door.

Every morning, after her brother had left, Chrissie begged Harriet to let her go back to bed.

Since Harriet had started high school, Chrissie had been losing weight. Her normally thin frame appeared increasingly fragile. Her skin color looked unnatural. Harriet wondered if her sister was suffering under her mother's care, but Hiroko assured her that she faithfully drove her daughter to medical appointments and reported that the doctors were doing everything they could.

In March, a surgeon replaced her shunt. After the brief hospitalization, Kevin no longer mentioned the braces which had been stowed away in the coat closet where their uselessness no longer betrayed the family's good intentions.

"We are doing everything we can to improve her quality of life." The March of Dimes had paid for a social worker, Stephanie, to visit the Jacksons' home. Hiroko's valiant efforts to clean up the chaos did not prevent the cheerful young woman from taking notes on a clipboard when she looked in the kitchen cabinets. During Stephanie's visit, Chrissie shrunk a little more. Despite the social worker's bright smile, Harriet knew that the assessment she made was not encouraging. Her sister was clearly an invalid in the eyes of the world.

Chrissie's impaired bladder function required a stent. Four times a day Harriet emptied the bags of urine. Although Chrissie's lack of sensation kept her from feeling the persistent irritation of the stents, she started to get urinary tract infections on a regular basis. The Jackson kitchen counter began to resemble a pharmacy, with bottle after bottle of her required medications.

In early May, Harriet arrived home from school to find her mother in tears.

"Chrissie sick," Hiroko said.

Chrissie had, once again, been admitted to the medical center.

"She can't pee again?" Kevin asked. He was at that age when boys relish the opportunity to discuss bodily functions without censure.

"Her kidneys no work," Hiroko said, looking at him darkly.

After dinner, the whole family drove to the sprawling Stanford Hospital Center. Visitors' passes in hand they rode the glass-sided elevator out of the massive lobby and up to the children's ward where Chrissie lay in a sterile bed, swathed in white sheets, her face strangely aged in the room's fluorescent light.

"We've done everything we can to preserve her renal function," Dr. Wright told the family, clearly uncomfortable in delivering his diagnosis.

"We could put her on dialysis, but..." he looked over at the social worker, "I suggest you discuss the alternatives with Stephanie. This is not a decision we take lightly."

Dr. Wright spoke directly to Harriet and waited while she took notes that she could pass this information on to her father. Hiroko watched his lips as if to read them. Stephanie's smile was muted.

"Let's sit down in my office," the social worker said.

Kat offered to stay with her sister. Kevin had spotted a pool table in the patient's lounge. For years now, he had considered the frequent visits to the hospital an opportunity to play with the well-funded medical center's toys.

Stephanie ushered Hiroko and Harriet into a room with a round walnut table polished to a perfect sheen surrounded by four upholstered chairs. She asked them to sit down.

"Would you like some tea?" she asked Hiroko.

Harriet watched Stephanie turn on an electric hot plate and set out two mugs and a box of tea bags.

"Chrissie's," the social worker said, "quality of life is not good." Wisps of steam escaped from the cups she filled with water.

Harriet wanted to tell Stephanie about Chrissie's wheelchair rides around the block. About Patty's amusement park game. But Stephanie didn't give her a chance.

"She has never gone to school. She will never live a normal life."

Hiroko's gaze never left the young woman's face. Harriet had no idea if her mother understood what was being said.

"I know you are both exhausted. Harriet, you barely attended school enough days last year to pass."

How did she know? Harriet wondered.

"Her father is never home."

Harriet had heard enough. She came to Joe's defense. "We take good care of Chrissie. I take good care of her."

"I'm not saying that you don't."

"She's going to be able to walk with braces soon," Harriet reminded the social worker.

"Sweetheart," Stephanie took Harriet's hand in hers. "Chrissie will never be able to walk." Swallowing so hard that Harriet could see the movement in her throat, Stephanie continued. "At best, your sister will live the rest of her life in an institution where..."

"No," Hiroko interrupted the social worker. "She stay with family. She always stay with family. My husband say."

Harriet had never seen her mother so upset. Nor so determined.

"We take my girl home now," Hiroko stood up defiantly.

Stephanie was not smiling now. She nodded her head, a sad, but unarguable no.

"You don't want this for your child."

Stephanie reached for Hiroko's hand, gestured for her to sit back down. "You need to let her go."

Taisho, her father had called it. The curtain that settled over her mother's face as she sat down in defeat. The stoic lack of expression, the gentle smile which she offered as she poured herself another cup of steaming tea.

"The doctor does not recommend dialysis," Stephanie said softly. "We will do everything possible to keep your daughter comfortable, but it is highly unlikely that Chrissie will ever go home."

Harriet watched her mother sip her tea, her dark eyes fixed on the distance. "What are you saying?" she asked the social worker. "Of course, Chrissie is coming home."

"No, sweetheart. Not this time."

The steam from the teapot engulfed her. She was warm, too warm. She searched her mother's face, challenged the all too familiar mask of resignation.

"Mommy!" she cried out. "Is Chrissie going to die?"

The social worker stepped away. "Take all the time you need."

As Harriet wept, the deep, strangling sobs of a young child who has been abandoned, Hiroko stroked her back gently, ran her fingers over her quaking arms. Harriet, sure she would never be able to stop crying, clung to her mother, inhaled the milky scent of her, timed her gasps for air to the slow, jagged sighs which were the only sign of Hiroko's silent grief.

Harriet closed her eyes and saw her sister, jubilant, arms in the air. "No, Mommy. No. It's not fair."

Hiroko didn't speak. They rocked together. Their shared grief slowly sinking in as the sun set outside the conference room window.

How, Harriet wondered, would she ever tell her father? Releasing her mother's grasp, she accepted a tissue from Stephanie who had returned to her side. This was all her fault; Harriet had let him down and Chrissie was paying the price. If only she had tried harder. If she had not been distracted by school, by the neighbors, by the endless demands of her brothers and sisters. If only she had not gone to the movies. She would never be able to make this up to him. He would never trust her again.

Hiroko nodded "no." She could read her daughter's thoughts and wanted to tell her that this was not her fault. Or maybe her mother understood because the guilt was what they shared, the glue that joined them.

Chrissie was asleep when Harriet kissed her sister. After one look at that their mother's stony face, Kevin and Kat put on their jackets and prepared to leave. This late at night, the hospital corridors were quiet except for the muffled footsteps of the nurses and the occasional whimper of a suffering child.

****

Joe came home for Chrissie's funeral, but, as always, duty called him back to Vietnam. He had hardly taken his uniform off before he hugged Harriet, saluted the others, and returned to his assignment in the Central Highlands of South Vietnam.

In the months that followed, Hiroko withdrew completely. During the day, Harriet's mother cooked and cleaned in her bathrobe, wandering from room to room with Joey toddling behind her. Once a week she shopped at the commissary, but in the evening, she retreated to her bedroom where she wrote endless letters in Japanese. Every morning, she sealed thin blue-tissue paper international letters and put them in the mailbox, raising the red flag to signal to the postman that there was outgoing mail.

Kat rarely came home until supper time. Sometimes later. Kevin lived on his bike, ogling the construction of the newest corporate park or racing classmates around the block at top speed pretending they were competing in drag races. His father had left him a wreck of a car with the promise that if Kevin could make it run, it was his. Her brother hadn't started tinkering with it yet, but he spent hours detailing his plans and ambitions.

During his visit, her father had barely spoken to Harriet. Bobby was the only person who asked Harriet how she was doing.

Bobby got straight A's. He told Harriet casually that it was no big deal.

Harriet and Bobby walked home from the school bus stop together. With Bobby beside her, Harriet felt calm, freed from the obligation to hurry home to care for her younger siblings. Grown up, almost pretty. The other girls watched them. Bobby listened when she spoke.

After Joe had returned to Vietnam, Bobby suggested that they go to the Sunnyvale library one day after school. Harriet had never visited the expansive library with its shelves and shelves of books and sunny, central garden. She liked the silence that resulted from the obligation to whisper, the reverence that the patrons showed for the written word. Bobby, who had visited the library once a week for years, showed her how to search the card catalog. Together, they wrote down the Dewey Decimal numbers that told them where to locate books on the recent advances in the treatment of congenital disorders. Among the periodicals, they searched for articles on spina bifida. They took notes, recording outcomes and life expectancies. Bobby explained the graphs to her, the treatment trends. As they sat together in the garden, he assured her that nothing else could have been done for her sister.

Bobby believed in science, that there was an explanation for everything if you looked hard enough. He was patient as he explained to her that there was nothing else she could have done.

"One day soon they will come up with better treatment modalities," he assured her, his words like those of a doctor except he had the time and patience to explain the research to her. He never condescended. "You know that Chrissie had the best care available."

Bobby was logical, unemotional and always considerate, holding doors for her and carrying her heavier textbooks as they walked home.

They began to do their homework together, sitting on Bobby's bed. He had his own room! The Hopkins' home couldn't have been more different from Harriet's. Alice's meticulous housecleaning meant that everything was in its place. The sunshine glimmered through crystal clear windows.

Even though Bobby aced AP English and loved physics, he never made Harriet feel stupid when she struggled with her algebra problems. Sitting on his bed, solving for X made sense.

The order of the house reassured Harriet. The light that poured through the windows gave her hope.

"My mom," she told Bobby, "has been so sad since Chrissie died."

"Give her time," he said. Harriet knew that Bobby lived a sheltered life, with a father and mother who were always there for him. His life couldn't have been more different from hers, but this was the attraction. She knew that all the time in the world might never bring her sister back but in Bobby's presence she believed that time, and science, could heal all wounds.

When they finished their homework early, Bobby and Harriet tinkered with the guitar that Bobby had received from his parents for his birthday. At first, Bobby attempted to learn simplified Spanish classical tunes, studying the finger charts in books that he purchased from the Music Store in downtown Sunnyvale. Harriet loved the way he scrunched up his face when he was concentrating. She watched him place his fingers methodically on the fretboard, move them mathematically from string to string. Then he allowed her to hold the instrument, walking her through the placement of her fingers, explaining the resonance of chords. They never did quite get the songs right.

When Harriet discovered a Beatles songbook among the sheet music Bobby had purchased with his allowance, she asked Bobby to teach her the familiar songs. At first, he struggled with the unfamiliar fingerings, but after he picked up speed, Harriet got up the nerve to sing along, careful to keep her voice softer than his, comfortable enough to join in on the familiar choruses.

Unlike her sister, Bobby did not criticize her voice. Although she had never followed up on her plans to audition for the high school chorus, chickening out when she saw the long line of students stretching from the high school auditorium door, she loved singing duets with Bobby. His range easily accommodated her more tentative notes. They sounded, if not good, at least reasonably in tune. She treasured the opportunity to share the songs that she had come to love.

Some afternoons Bobby, Harriet, and Patty played Spades in the family room while Alice nursed a vodka with orange juice, reading *Time* magazine before preparing supper. Patty had played cards with her brother all her life and mixed the cards like a pro, bridging the cards with an airy shuffle, and dealing with confidence but Bobby knew strategy and almost always won.

"I hate you," Patty inevitably concluded, throwing down her cards and retreating to her bedroom to listen to rock-and-roll on her radio and read romantic novels from the library, the longer the better. Her favorite, she told Harriet, was *Gone with the Wind.*

Bobby preferred to watch TV. Side by side, they watched reruns of the *Twilight Zone.* Sometimes, Harriet pretended that she didn't live next door. That this was her life. Stranger things occurred on the science fiction shows they watched together.

They were sophomores now, used to high school and being together. But Harriet was taken by surprise one afternoon when Bobby turned to her with his eyes closed and kissed her, a warm peck on the lips like a bird tasting seed. She was afraid to move, afraid he might stop, but she knew that Bobby knew what he wanted. For some inexplicable reason, he wanted her. He told her repeatedly that the Valley was full of possibilities. Maybe, at last, he was hers.

✳✳✳

"We're nothing more than animals," Bobby announced at the dinner table.

"Bobby, what are you talking about?" his mother took the bait.

Earlier in the week, Bobby had discovered *Ape and Essence* by Aldous Huxley while showing Harriet his favorite section of the library, the science fiction shelves.

"*Brave New World* is amazing," he told her. "It's like Huxley can see into the future." While locating the novel, he spotted a narrow volume beside it.

By the time he had read the second chapter of *Ape and Essence*, Bobby was re-evaluating his entire view of life.

"Maybe you're an animal, but I'm not," Patty replied. Patty had spent the afternoon re-arranging the letters in "Herman's Hermits" in order to enter a contest she had read about in *Tiger Beat*. She dismissed her brother's foolishness. If she was able to produce the longest list of words, she announced, she would win an autographed picture of her favorite pop star.

Bobby rolled his eyes. This is what the wonders of science had produced?

In *Ape and Essence*, the world, in the hands of intelligent baboons (the author's representation of twentieth-century society) was destroyed by nuclear and chemical warfare.

It made sense to him. "Look at Vietnam, the Korean War. Where has mankind actually progressed?" he asked, sure he had made his point.

The clarity of Huxley's vision was thrilling. Despite the cynicism of the novel, Bobby felt elevated to a higher plane of perception. He was mesmerized by the vignettes of baboons singing as they performed human activities, the surrealistic reflection of humanity as warlike and stupid.

Jack took Bobby's declaration in stride.

"All bright kids go through a period of exploration," he reassured Alice who had listened to Bobby's description of Huxley's novel with horror.

"For this, I dragged the kids to church every Sunday?" she asked.

"Your idea, not mine," he answered.

Bobby ignored his parent's sparring. Life was beginning to get interesting. His family had no idea. As he listened to his growing collection of jazz records and read Huxley's bizarre prose, he dreamed about Harriet.

Increasingly, like the strange baboons, he was metamorphosing into somebody else. Even his body was changing, muscles firming up despite his sedentary lifestyle, wiry hair sprouting in the strangest of places.

"Give me, give me, give me, de-tumescence," the female baboons sang and Bobby, who followed the dictates of his own intelligence, intuitively understood the animal desire that he had discovered not only in the book but also in his own body.

He had kissed Harriet Jackson.

The warmth of that kiss inspired him. Her calm acquiescence reassured him.

Encouraged by the shocked reaction to his first declaration, he made another.

"I'm going to ask Harriet to the prom." Without thinking it through, he gave into the desire to shock his parents, his impulse fueled by the excitement that the memory of her touch aroused.

Patty almost spat out her food in surprise.

"What?"

Alice rolled her eyes at Jack. "Are you sure that's a good idea?"

Bobby already regretted blurting out his intention. After all, intellectuals didn't attend proms. The "rah-rahs" (cheerleaders and football players) did.

As if to confirm his reservations, Patty, for once, stood up for her brother. "Bobby, that's so cool. I didn't think you had it in you."

Later that night, after Bobby had turned off the *Twilight Zone*, he heard his parents in their bedroom. Alice talked as Jack listened and murmured his agreement.

"He could do so much better," his mother said.

"They're kids," his father replied.

Bobby couldn't care less what his parents thought. The longer he listened to their discussion, the angrier he became. Harriet had been through enough. She might not be the brightest girl in his class, but she was the nicest girl he had ever known—mature, responsible and honest. Even pretty, in her own way. She deserved better than his parents' scorn.

His father tried to talk to him the following morning. Bobby refused to reply.

"We think maybe you're rushing into something..." his father said.

Bobby swallowed his orange juice.

Patty watched them both with the same concentration with which she read her romance novels

"It wouldn't be kind to lead the poor girl on," his father said, without much conviction.

Bobby stood up and glared at his father. He should have known better. Even though he knew that Jack was delivering his mother's message, he held both his parents in contempt.

He wasn't a boy any longer.

Huxley was right. Humans were morons.

Picking up his textbooks, Bobby headed out the front door without a word. As he left, he felt Patty watching, her eyes wide in reaction to the family drama.

Harriet was waiting for him at the bus stop. He hurried towards her, still fuming, still rehearsing the answers he had not bothered to give. When he saw her standing in her pleated plaid skirt, she smiled shyly. Immediately he felt his anger ebb. He welcomed the warm wave of desire that rose predictably every time he greeted her.

This was his new science. His brave new world.

Harriet could not believe her luck. Every day after school, she rode home with Bobby on the bus. Holding hands, they walked up the front walkway to Bobby's house. Next door, her mother hid behind windows whose shades remained drawn, but Harriet entered the bright hallway of the Hopkins' house filled with a newly discovered sense of possibility.

This became their routine. Homework, guitar followed by a game of cards, TV, kissing. Bobby never asked Harriet to do anything that made her uncomfortable. She sat next to him on his single bed with its white chenille bedspread. Each kiss a tentative test, like another subject he was mastering. He asked her if he could touch her. He never tried to take off her clothes. He never asked to see her breasts. He tasted like something pure, like the vanilla ice cream they ate for their afternoon snack.

As Bobby filled plastic bowls with ice cream he had taken out of the freezer, Alice nursed her cocktail in silence. If Harriet noticed that Bobby's mother no longer asked about Hiroko or her siblings, it did not occur to her to ask Bobby if his mother was okay. She was, after all, used to her own mother's moods. Besides, she was still basking in the unexpected thrill of Bobby's attention.

When Bobby invited her to the prom, there was no question in her mind that the invitation was the highlight of her life so far.

"Really, Bobby. The prom?" she asked.

Bobby smiled at her enthusiasm.

"I'd love to." She couldn't wait to ask Kat to help her pick out an outfit to wear. Maybe shop someplace else than the commissary. Macy's even.

Kat had started to wear makeup. Lots of makeup. Thick eyeliner and shiny pink lipstick. More and more, Harriet recognized the boys her sister hung out with in the park, high school boys in her own class, the rowdy ones who checked out girls on the quad.

"Kat, be careful," she said as they both got ready for bed the night after Bobby had asked her to the prom. Kat wore one of her dad's T-shirts. Harriet wore her favorite, ruffled rose-patterned nightgown.

Kat dismissed Harriet's warning with a sneer.

"There's nothing wrong with having a little fun. You should try it some time."

Harriet had been keeping a wary eye on her sister. Kat rolled up the waistband of her skirts when she left for school so that they barely covered her thighs. Now Harriet noticed the hickeys on her sister's neck hidden underneath her glossy black hair.

"Those guys shouldn't be hanging out with a junior high school girl," Harriet said, chewing the split ends of her hair.

Her sister, as usual, ignored her.

"Kat, listen to me. You could get in trouble."

"How would you know?"

The role of caretaker had become second nature to Harriet. For longer than she could remember, Kat had been her charge, her responsibility. Even now that she had begun to experience life on her own, she felt obligated to warn her younger sister. But she smarted at Kat's response.

"I know things," she said.

Kat looked over at her and snorted. "Yeah. Like you have so many boyfriends now that you're in high school, right?"

She shouldn't have taken the bait. Her sister had a clue, of that she was sure.

"Where do you think I go after school?" Harriet asked.

"How would I know?" Kat yawned.

She could have said nothing. It was pride that goaded her on.

"You might be surprised to know," Harriet paused and then, unable to keep the secret that sung in every fiber of her being, "that Bobby and I have been hanging out."

"Bobby Glasses from next door?" She had Kat's attention now.

"Kinda like. He even invited me to the prom."

"Kinda like?"

"We kiss."

"You've got to be kidding."

Harriet couldn't help it. She felt a blush spreading across her face, a warm wave of happiness.

"Harriet, you truly amaze me. Who would have thunk it?" Kat gave her sister an enthusiastic punch on the arm. "Good for you."

"Good for me," Harriet repeated, liking the sound of it. She pictured Bobby's intelligent eyes, the cowlick that escaped onto his forehead no matter how much hair gel he used, his photo on the posters asking his classmates to vote for him for Student Council. She told her sister to shut up.

"Don't tell Mom," she took a deep breath. "Will you help me choose a dress for the dance?"

She should never have told Kat about the kiss.

✳✳✳

Two weeks before the prom, Hiroko caught Kat rolling up her skirt. Kat was trying to get off the hook.

"Harriet's the one with a boyfriend," Kat told her mother.

"Harriet don't have no boyfriend. Harriet a good girl."

"Harriet kissed Bobby from next door."

Next door, Harriet and Bobby were finishing their homework. Bobby was attempting to explain how to balance an equation, the process of moving factors from one side of an equation to the other.

"You mean if I move it from here," Harriet stood up from the end of the bed, "to here," Harriet sat down on the chair in front of Bobby's desk, "the room is the same, but the equation is different."

Bobby smiled. "The bed minus one is empty."

"And the girl at the desk doesn't get it."

Bobby stood up and bent over Harriet, kissing her neck. "The factors are the same."

Harriet turned to Bobby, her mouth slightly open, receptive. Before he was able to kiss her, they heard a plaintive howl coming from the street, a furious foreign, almost animal, harangue that brought them both to their feet.

"What the..." Bobby said.

Harriet, with a thud of recognition, felt the blood flow from her head into her extremities. She closed her eyes and stars exploded in the darkness; bombs let loose in the night sky.

Wearing her housecoat and slippers, Hiroko stood on the sidewalk in front of the Hopkins' fastidiously maintained front yard, screaming in Japanese. Yelling, right next to the pruned rose bushes and the expanse of recently mowed grass. When Bobby's mother opened the front door to identify the source of the commotion, Alice's face turned as white as Hiroko's was red.

"Your mom is outside," Bobby whispered. Harriet, afraid to open her eyes, nodded. "Your mom never goes outside," he said, asking for an explanation.

"She knows," Harriet said.

"Knows what?" he asked, clearly confused.

"About us."

Harriet opened her eyes. Bobby was waiting for an explanation. How young he seemed! How totally oblivious.

Harriet grabbed her books and ran out the Hopkins' front door. As soon as her mother caught sight of her daughter, Hiroko pounced, grabbing her arm so firmly that she left a bruised outline of her fury. Hiroko jerked Harriet by her mousy brown hair, exploding at Bobby, who had appeared in the doorway with his mother and sister in front of him like a protective shield: "Bad boy. Fucking, dirty boy." Pointing her finger emphatically, she sputtered: "Nasty boy!" Harriet had never seen her quiet mother so enraged, had never heard the woman swear. "You bad boy, very bad boy." Hiroko continued to rant in undecipherable Japanese. Harriet pleaded, "We didn't do anything," but her mother refused to listen. Pointing and spitting, Hiroko tugged Harriet down the block.

Everyone on the cul-de-sac saw. They heard Hiroko's accusations. Harriet sobbed: "I didn't do anything wrong," but nobody believed her. Her humiliation was public, the buzz on the school bus the next day. Behind the closed shades of the Jacksons' house, Hiroko continued to berate Harriet, sometimes red with fury, sometimes with tears pouring down her face, deaf to her daughter's denials. Harriet's ears rang with her mother's accusations: "Nasty boy. Dirty boy." There was nothing she could say in Bobby's defense. She absorbed the barrage of her mother's words. She was not a good girl. Despite everything, she had let her mother down. The denials that she repeated: "I didn't do anything. Believe me, Mom, I didn't do anything," caught in her throat, swallowed by her mother's fury until even she began to doubt them.

***

Later that night in the quiet of their shared bedroom, Kat apologized profusely for betraying her confidence. "How was I to know that Mom would go ballistic?"

Harriet didn't bother to respond. Her sister would never understand the injustice of her mother's outburst. Kat—beautiful, popular Kat—did exactly as she pleased, unconcerned with the repercussions. Harriet, in contrast, cared.

"Mom hasn't a clue," Kat said. "You can't expect her to understand. If she had her way, we'd have been raised in a convent."

Kat was the one without a clue. Harriet should never have trusted her sister. That was clear now, but the damage had been done.

"Just stay out of my business," Harriet snapped. "You've ruined everything."

"Listen, Glasses is lucky to have found you. Who else would give him the time of day? Just tell him Mom is crazy."

As if it were that easy. As if Bobby would stick around if he thought her mother was crazy. As if she would treat her mother, who she had always protected, with so little respect.

"Give the boy a little," Kat brushed her hair, snickered. One hundred strokes a night and it gleamed like satin. "Something special. I'll show you a few tricks."

"Shut up!" Harriet said, more vehemently than she had intended. "Your tricks got me in trouble in the first place."

Kat raised her eyebrows. "It's not like I was kissing Bobby Hopkins."

Just the thought of her sister's "tricks" brought Harriet to tears. Her sister didn't belong in the same world as Bobby. Kat was tough, defiant. Her long-legged strut declared her independence; the sway of her hips invited attention. Bobby aspired to higher ideals. For a while there so had Harriet.

She wished her sister would stop talking. Kat didn't believe her when she said she had done nothing wrong. Why would she? Kat did exactly as she pleased and didn't fear the consequences.

"Anyhow, I'm sorry," Kat said. "Can't we leave it at that?" She set down the hairbrush and pursed her lips, opening her eyes wider. Even now, Harriet had to admit her sister's reflection was gorgeous.

"Believe me, Sis. There's a lot of fish in the sea."

Harriet didn't want to hear any more of her sister's empty platitudes. The chasm between them was almost as wide as that between the Jacksons and the Hopkins. Kat and Harriet might share a room, but that was all they had in common.

At least, Hiroko had been trying, in her own misguided way, to protect her. Joe understood the sacrifices she had made. Kat couldn't give a damn. She cared only about herself.

"Please yourself," Kat said as if reading her mind. She proceeded to lay out her clothes for the next day before settling into bed with a sigh.

Harriet turned to the wall, hiding her head in her pillow so that Kat could not hear her cry. Waves of anger and disappointment swept over her, each vying for supremacy. She thought of every retort she had not thought to say. She rehearsed convincing arguments proving her innocence, carefully worded justifications for her sense of responsibility that would convince even her sister, who would understand when she evoked Chrissie and her father's absences and the role she had played in holding the family together. In the end, she drifted off, exhausted by the hopelessness of her defense, thinking only: "I am so alone."

✳✳✳

Harriet called in sick to school the next day. Alone in the house, Hiroko and Harriet didn't speak, neither able to arrive at words that could make things right. They walked softly, avoided each other's eyes. Kat reported back that the boys she hung out with were surprised that Bobby had the nerve. She continued to laugh off Harriet's protests that she and Bobby had done nothing wrong, had nothing that they needed to apologize for.

It didn't matter what anyone believed. Harriet had been convicted of a crime she had not committed. For days, she found herself voiceless, unable to feel either anger or repentance. At best, she felt numb. Silenced.

Harriet and Bobby never studied together again. Harriet never returned to the Hopkins' house.

Joe, in a furious Sunday phone call, forbade Harriet to go to the prom "with that boy or any boy." When she tried to explain, he said the words she dreaded: "I have never been more disappointed," he told her. "I thought you had more sense." Harriet, steeled to defend herself, quickly backed down, her surrender settling in her stomach like meat that was beginning to go bad.

On Monday, she got up the nerve to return to school. She was mortified to walk by Bobby's front yard but had no choice. She kept her eyes on the ground, studied her elongated shadow, a silent mockery of the girl who had looked forward to the daily walk to the school bus stop.

At home, Hiroko couldn't look her in the eye. For weeks, Harriet didn't speak to her mother unless spoken to, slowly becoming aware of the despair that began to consume her, an outrage that she had been so misjudged. Over the next month, Harriet and Hiroko continued to fulfill their household duties. They cleaned up after the boys, made dinner side by side in stony silence. Their impasse

101

continued until the day that Kat did not show up for dinner, instead arriving home hours late, drunk, disheveled, and defiant. The next morning, Harriet felt obligated to share her concerns with her mother. Her father would expect her to handle the situation. She had no alternative but to tell Hiroko that Kat had been dropped off by one of the high school boys that Harriet easily recognized as trouble.

If she expected Hiroko to respond with a fury equal to that she had displayed on the sidewalk outside Bobby's house, she was disappointed. Instead, Hiroko asked her to intervene. "Maybe your sister listen to you." Harriet could not help but feel vindicated by her mother's request.

Falling back into the comfortable role of caretaker, faced with her sister's defiant excuses, Harriet began to forget, if not forgive, her mother's enraged face, the blatant unfairness of her accusations. If she could not defend herself, she decided, she could speak to her sister, perhaps with more credibility than before her own misunderstood behavior. Kat might not be able to understand the pain she had caused when she blurted out Harriet's secret, but she was, in the end, family. Here was an opportunity to demonstrate to her parents that they could still rely on her. They were family, she supposed, united as much by the pain they caused each other, as by the rooms they shared, and the history that united them.

✳✳✳

After the night Harriet's mother made a scene for all the neighborhood to see, Bobby stopped riding the bus to school. Alice agreed to drive him before she began her daily house-cleaning routine and he gratefully accepted. The last thing that he needed was to face his classmates' ridicule. He'd had enough of that in middle school. For a while there, the label of "Glasses" had become a familiar taunt. High School had allowed him a new beginning. Arriving at school without Harriet at his side, he discovered that there were plenty of other attractive girls in his class who were a lot less trouble than the girl next door.

Bobby had never liked a scene. His mother's antics had embarrassed him enough for a lifetime. He wasn't looking for drama.

Terri, one of the cheerleaders, a smart one, helped him to hang posters urging his classmates to "Hop on the Wagon: Hopkins for Vice President." If anything, the rumors of his dalliance with Harriet gave him an edge. He was not only smart but also a little bit sexy. Terri was easy to talk to. "A catch," his Dad said. Alice approved and encouraged him to invite Terri to dinner. Patty was impressed by the blonde's easy demeanor, her self-confident smile. Terri demanded little of him. They went on a few dates, during which they discussed their classwork, his chances of winning the race for vice president, and, of much less interest to him, the football team's chances of making the state finals.

Bobby seldom saw Harriet in the hallways of Foothill High School. There were 700 kids in their class and with his course load of AP classes and, after his win, student body responsibilities, their paths seldom crossed. The few times he did see Harriet, she turned away, never acknowledging that she knew him. Her plainness surprised him. He couldn't help but notice her mousy demeanor, the lack of expression on her unadorned face.

Bobby never felt a need to defend his innocence. He never had. His motivations were pure, intellectually justifiable. He hoped that he had been able to help his neighbor through a rough patch, but his mother assured him that he was better off now exploring the many possibilities that high school offered.

In physics lab, Bobby met Zach, one of the founding members of the school's Electronics Club. "Hey man," Zach said. "You gotta join us. The club is rad." Six inches taller than Bobby, Zach was a smooth dresser with shoulder-length auburn hair and a cluster of girls around him at all times. Except on Wednesdays when he convened with twelve brainy boys who shared his love of electronics.

"McCallum," he told Bobby "is awesome." Zach loved the word "awesome," used it every chance he found. "He lets us fiddle with the ham radios." Mr. McCallum, the club's sponsor, peppered every workbench with instruments he had scavenged in his free time: oscilloscopes and TV equipment.

The first time Bobby attended the club, McCallum instructed him on the use of a slide rule. In a corner of the room, there were large bins containing surplus electronics. Bobby was in his glory. Here he discovered a place where he truly belonged, peers who understood him and shared his passions.

Before long, Bobby became a valued member of the club. He loved to show off his creations. Mr. McCallum encouraged his newly discovered love of practical jokes. When Bobby created a siren using circuitry from an abandoned battery and mini-speaker, he decided to give it a test run in the hallways one morning at the end of second period. The entire student body poured into the school's hallways where the siren's scream echoed long after his prank had been uncovered.

If Harriet heard that ear-splitting wail, Bobby never knew. Instead, he basked in his teachers' admiration. He was good at building electronics, making them small and compact, like the little cube-shaped circuit that could be used with an antenna to jam TVs. Even McCallum couldn't figure out how he had made that gadget but asked if he could use it to torture his own children at home.

Life was good. Bobby was busy, and this was only the beginning. Soon he would begin to visit colleges. Mr. McCallum assured him that he would have his choice of the finest technical schools in the country, MIT, Caltech, even Stanford. Nothing could hold Bobby back. With Terri at his side and Mr. McCallum as a mentor, Bobby was confident that he was on the right track. He wished Harriet the best, of course, but that was when he thought of her at all.

Silicon Valley

1990-3

"Am I too late?"

Harriet emerged breathless from the law firm's elevator. Jodi, the ash-blond receptionist was unable to stop the frantic, vaguely Asian, middle-aged lady who insisted she had to see Ms. Hopkins "right now."

Harriet stood in front of Patty's desk, breathing heavily. "Am I too late?" she repeated.

"Harriet, what's wrong? Too late for what?" Patty waved Jodi away with a nod that indicated she had this.

"Did you wire the money?"

"I don't think so. The wires go out at three. Is there a problem?"

Harriet plopped down in the upholstered chair across from the lawyer's desk. She took a deep, ragged breath. "Patty, you're a lawyer. I need you to tell me. Do I have to give my nephew the money?"

"The proceeds from the sale?"

Harriet nodded yes.

"The contract we drew up was between your nephew and the children's parents. You are under no legal obligation. The money is yours to give. Or not. Hold on a second."

Patty picked up her phone. "Mac, I gave you a wire transfer request about thirty minutes ago. Can you hold on to that for now?" After a pause, "Thanks, you're a dear."

"OK, now tell me what's going on?" Patty stepped out from behind her desk and sat in the chair next to Harriet. Harriet sighed, opened her mouth as if to speak and then sat, silently breathing, the exchange of air requiring every bit of her strength.

"Your nephew's a handsome boy," Patty said.

Harriet acknowledged the lawyer's compliment, nodding her agreement.

"A martial arts instructor?"

"A national champion. He owns his own dojo."

"Wow. What's the problem?"

Harriet shot Patty a wary glance, checking to see if she was testing her. "Some of the parents accused him of abusing his students."

"Ouch," Patty said.

Harriet knew that the lawyer had the full account of the lawsuit in the folder on her desk. But she wanted Harriet to provide her own version of the story.

"He's innocent." The words exploded from Harriet's mouth. She had been waiting to be free of them. Then, arguing with herself, she said, "I think he is. He told me that he never touched a student inappropriately."

"It was big of you to offer to help him out." Patty had not been surprised when she read about Harriet's offer. The act of selflessness was consistent with everything she knew about her former neighbor. "I understand the settlement took some time to hammer out. The parents weren't easy to persuade."

Harriet listened attentively, chewing on a loose strand of hair, a habit that Patty recognized from their childhood.

"There are photographs." Patty handed Harriet a manila folder. The details of the case, some highlighted in yellow, others marked with comments in black ink, included multiple complaints of discipline which they claimed crossed over the line.

Harriet paged through the report. Exhibit B included photographs of young boys with bruising on their shoulders and thighs. She studied the photos before speaking.

"Aikido is physically demanding," she said after a long pause, her voice low, almost a whisper. "I practiced myself. Bruises are a sign of effort." She didn't look up. "I had terrible bruises on my forearms and legs when I was learning to break my falls."

"But on the shoulders?" Patty asked.

"I'm sure there is an explanation," Harriet said.

"The parents also said that Eddie brandished weapons, threatened his students if they did not pay attention."

"These students, what do they know?" Harriet said. "Eddie struggles every day to teach the children discipline. The parents never show any gratitude. You can't imagine how much effort is required to hold these kids' attention."

"But, certainly," Patty said, "you can understand the parents' concern. No child should ever be touched in anger."

Harriet put her head in her hands. Curling into herself, she resembled a snail recoiling from the bright light of the sun. Without camouflage, she longed for a hiding place.

"He never hurt them. The kids adore my nephew. I know that to be true. I am there every day."

"Then there shouldn't be a problem."

"But clearly there is." Harriet looked up, angry at the lawyer's condescension.

"But Harriet, there are many ways to resolve this suit. You don't have to surrender all your assets. This doesn't have to be your problem."

"I am the only one in the family with the means to help him." As she offered this explanation, she heard echoes of Kat's accusation, Eddie's pleas, Joe's oft-repeated reminders that she was the one he had counted on.

"You were always the responsible one. I could see that from next door."

"It is what my father expected of me." Harriet recited the line, looking down at her feet and enunciating each word from memory.

"Harriet. This is your choice. The house was in your name. No one else has a claim to the proceeds. That is why the transfer is legally a gift to your nephew. Eddie, and Eddie alone, is the subject of the lawsuit. He is the one who has to pay."

"And if I don't give him the money?"

"Then he will have to get the money elsewhere. Or stand trial. If he's innocent, he will have to prove it."

"He could lose his business."

"Maybe," Patty said. "But if you do give him the money," Patty asked, "What happens to you?"

Harriet didn't hesitate. For the first time that day, she replied with conviction. "I have nothing."

Her face clearly masked a struggle. The restraint that Harriet had learned while watching Hiroko standing wordlessly at the kitchen window dissolved with the realization of the choice that she now had to make. In a rare moment of passion, Hiroko had once dragged her kicking and screaming from Bobby's house. Harriet's unspoken protest: "I didn't do anything. Mom, believe me, I didn't do anything" was seared in her memory, a curtain that had closed on the possibility of a different life.

She didn't want to repeat that error with Eddie.

Hiroko had been wrong to interfere. The decision should have been hers. Harriet had agreed to rescue her nephew from accusations he denied. But instead of saving him, she was about to lose herself for the second time in her life.

"Eddie will have to fight this one on his own," she said.

"You're sure?" Patty asked.

"I am."

Patty stepped out of her office.

"Thank god you're here," Jodi pounced on her. "The phone has been ringing off the hook. The lawyer handling the dojo settlement wants to know why his bank hasn't received the money yet. He insists they need it this afternoon. Offered to pick up the check himself. There's some kind of legal proceeding?"

Patty had heard enough.

"Tell him you don't know where it is. That I was called out of the office, and you will have to get back to him." Patty went down the hall to the accounting office and asked Mac to return the request for the wire transfer. "There's a hiccup here," she said. "Print up a bank check for the proceeds in the name of the seller, Harriet Jackson. We'll sort the rest out later."

On the way back to her office, she leaned over and whispered in Jodi's ear, "By the way, it isn't their money." Putting her arm around Harriet, she said, "Come on. Let's take a drive."

1969

"*Don't go 'round tonight. It's bound to take your life. There's a bad moon on the rise.*" The song playing on Bobby's transistor radio repeated the line like a mantra as he walked the final blocks home. The rhythm, like his heart, beating furiously.

"Look what the cat dragged in," Patty said when he rounded the corner. His sister sat on the front porch, smoking a joint. She wore a peace sign on a lanyard around her neck.

"I want some of whatever you're smoking," he said, sitting down beside her. He turned down the radio as he held the pot smoke in his lungs. God, it was hot.

By this time in the afternoon, the foothills cupped a mustard-colored smog, an eye-smarting mix of car exhaust and industrial smoke that filled the valley where the Pacific fog had once lingered in the early morning. Bobby had arrived in Sunnyvale by bus. His parents had refused to pick him up after he had been expelled from Stanford. He felt his sister's eyes on him, waiting for an explanation. An endless stream of cars streamed by on what had once been a quiet residential street. The population of the Valley had topped one million, and the traffic kept getting worse and worse.

"How are they?" he asked, gesturing inside.

"Out of their fucking minds." Bobby had been expelled from Stanford for hacking into the university's computer. Jack and Alice were beside themselves. So far, Patty complained, she had been the recipient of most of their wrath. It wasn't enough, they said, that they had to tolerate a daughter who attended every war protest but refused to study for her SATs. Now their son, who had graduated at the top of his class after winning two regional science fairs in a row, was returning home in disgrace. After all they had done for their children, they considered the situation unbearable.

"It's bad," Patty told him. "Mom's rants never stop. They get worse when she begins drinking her afternoon cocktails. By five each night, she's in tears, bemoaning the embarrassment that your expulsion caused her." His mother had been avoiding Jack's colleagues and refusing to meet the neighbors' eyes when she ran into them at the grocery store.

Bobby passed the joint, a peace offering of sorts.

"As if the neighbors give a damn," he said. Patty nodded her agreement. The Hopkins were angels compared to the Jackson kids. She brought her brother up to date. Kat had gotten knocked up at fifteen and "had" to get married. Kevin had been in two car accidents since New Year's. Last month he smashed one of his cobbled-together cars into the birch tree outside the Hopkins' living room window. That was what she called trouble.

But Alice wasn't buying any of it.

"I feel sorry for you, moving back into this hell hole."

Bobby had a nice buzz going. Greasy hair hung to his shoulders; his jeans had patches on the knees and his dashiki smelled of patchouli. Instead of a suitcase, he'd slung a ratty backpack over his shoulder.

"What are you going to do now that you've been tossed out on your ass?"

"Zach thinks he can get me a job at Hewlett Packard on the assembly line. Using tweezers and a microscope to place die on the display boards of calculators."

"Dye?"

"No, die. The little pieces of semiconductor material that provide the calculator's functionality."

"Sounds like a blast."

"At least it'll get me out the house until I can figure out what's next. Besides, there are some really smart guys working there now. Zach and I might try to set up our own business."

"That'll be the day."

"You'd be surprised, there's money in the air." Bobby exhaled expansively. "The military and NASA used to get all the money for the development of new electronic devices but that's changing now. They're starting to call this area Silicon Valley."

Patty raised her eyebrows skeptically. "Good luck with that."

"So, Sis, what's new with you?"

"Trying to stop this stinking war and elude the raging elders," Patty said. "At least until I can blow the coop."

"Be sure you don't hack any computer systems."

"Wouldn't dream of it." Patty pinched out the joint and shook her head to clear her vision. "Are you ready for the firing squad?"

"Let's do this," Bobby picked up his backpack, and they headed inside.

***

Next door, Harriet's nephew Eddie burst in the door like a 34-pound dancing dervish. Behind him, Kat balanced a diaper bag and a miniature scooter. She struggled to keep her over-sized pocketbook from slipping off her bronzed shoulder. Gold bracelets tinkled. "Look what Daddy bought me," Eddie said to his aunt.

Harriet admired the scooter, moving it to the side of the entryway. "We can take it to the park this afternoon."

"He had another accident last night," Kat opened the conversation with a complaint about her wayward son. Harriet adored him.

"I told Mommy I needed to go," the three-year-old whined, "but she didn't hear me." Harriet wondered if Mike and Kat had been at it again. The passion of their marriage was matched only by the intensity of their arguments. During the day, when Harriet babysat, Eddie was nearly toilet trained but at home, he lost all control. Harriet suspected that his parents, absorbed in the drama of young love and overwhelmed by the responsibilities that came with a youthful marriage, had eyes only for each other.

Kat was more beautiful than ever. You would never guess that she had a three-year-old son. Marriage and motherhood had transformed the teenage rebel who had run with a wild crowd. There was little left of the junior high school girl who had hung out with the Chicano sons of migrant laborers and the high school football stars who drove her to the dam to watch the "submarine races" on a Friday night. Those submarine races left Kat pregnant and yet still defiant.

Her sister, clearly, had embraced her new life.

Kat's husband, Mike, ran a successful gas station on the busy corner of Mariani Avenue and Foothill Boulevard. The same one that Harriet had once watched explode and which, after demolition and insurance settlements, had been available for reconstruction at a bargain price. The opportunity had been a gift from Joe. Mike, a senior who had intended to enlist in the army when he impregnated her sister, had agreed, to all of their surprise, to marry Kat instead.

Babysitting was Joe's idea. He saw it as yet another rescue. Harriet's father was used to being a hero, saving victims from disasters. Hiroko had been the first of many. Harriet had saved a drawer-full of articles documenting their father's heroism. When Harriet was still a girl, Hank D. Richards, 23, had crashed his A-7E Corsair on a mountain about 10 miles north of Crater Lake while on a routine training flight. Her father had responded to the crash. Joe was always there when someone needed him. When Mike agreed to marry Kat, Joe took out a second mortgage on the house to buy the newlyweds the property for the gas station.

Soon after their shotgun wedding, Mike supervised the station's reconstruction. Six months later, he scheduled a grand re-opening of the service station. By the time, Eddie was born, Mike and Kat were the proud owners of a promising Silicon Valley business.

As usual, Joe's rescue required Harriet's assistance.

Harriet, about to start her senior year in high school, offered to babysit the new baby so that Kat could help her new husband out. Joe and Kat agreed that she was the best person to step up, keep the crisis in the family. Besides, ever since the scene in Bobby's front yard, Harriet had been looking for a way to prove to her father that she was the responsible daughter he had always counted on. His look of approval told her, at last, that she had been forgiven.

Once she had made the offer, there was no looking back. Despite the advice of her high school guidance counselor, Harriet had not planned to apply to college. When asked, she had told her classmates that she was considering attending Foothill Junior College, but, in truth, she had no interest in studying there. Instead, she had been considering applying for a job in the record store downtown, the one where she and Bobby had once searched for cheat sheets on how to play the guitar. The chance to surround herself with the songs of her favorite artists appealed to her. She couldn't get enough of Joan Baez's exquisite interpretation of classic folk songs. Most mornings she woke up with Judy Collins' rendition of *Both Sides* Now fading from a recurring dream.

Harriet no longer aspired to sing; she accepted her lack of talent. But she relied on music to get her through the long, lonely days of school. When her father agreed to her offer to drop out and take over the care of her newborn nephew, she was relieved to have an excuse to avoid the grating enthusiasm of her classmates who couldn't stop talking about their college plans. She was happy to step up during the family crisis.

Eddie was an easy baby. Now a rambunctious toddler, he filled her days. She felt useful, better prepared than her younger sister to care for him.

Kat dressed for work in a mini-skirt and sateen purple blouse. Her over-sized gold earrings brushed against well-toned shoulders.

"Mike says an attractive woman is good for business," she told Harriet. "It never hurts to remind a man what he's got."

No wonder the couple's arguments often resulted from Mike's jealousy. He never took his eyes off Kat. Kevin said that Mike had given Kat a job at the station so that he could keep her close to his side. His possessiveness had become a family joke.

Now, Mike honked his horn in the driveway. "I gotta run, Harr. Have fun," Kat said. "I might be a little late tonight. There's a sale at Macy's." Blowing an air kiss to her son, she forgot to close the door behind her.

Harriet moved the diaper bag out of the way and waved as the car pulled away from the curb before closing the door.

"What do you want for breakfast, Tiger?" she asked Eddie.

Kevin, already late for school, tousled his nephew's hair, grabbed a piece of toast and headed out to his car, the latest he had rescued from the junkyard.

"Don't hold dinner for me," he told his sister.

"What's new?" Harriet replied.

In the kitchen, Hiroko poured orange juice for Eddie. Joey was practicing Japanese vocabulary with his mother. The only child in his family who had expressed an interest in learning his mother's native language, he had been thrilled when the junior high school added Japanese to their list of language offerings.

"Do you want some *gyuunyuu*," he asked Eddie, pointing to the milk bottle.

"What?" Eddie asked.

Harriet poured raisin bran for the young boy. "*Gyuunyuu*," she echoed and looked at her mother for approval.

Hiroko laughed.

Joey tucked his vocabulary list into his backpack. "Better watch out, Ma. Your secrets are no longer safe with us."

Joey, the youngest, had always had a special bond with his mother. He understood Hiroko when none of the other children did. As a young boy, he had learned to sing Japanese lullabies. Now as an adolescent, he had decided to be the one to translate for Hiroko. A few years ago, learning Japanese might have been difficult, but Japanese electronics companies were popping up all over town and with them, programs to integrate the children of employees into the school's culture.

Joey had been the first to sign up for the new Japanese language class and recently he had joined the Japanese/American club. Mr. Ito, the high school's popular principal, was the club's faculty adviser.

"Sayonara," he said now, kissing his mom good-bye.

"Sayonara," Harriet said, as her brother passed her on the way out.

"Sayara," Eddie tried to imitate the others.

"Eddie, are you ready to use the toilet now?"

"Go poop," he said, following Harriet to the bathroom. Hiroko cleared the breakfast dishes with a rare smile as she and Harriet settled into their daily routine.

Today, she would teach Eddie *Frere Jacque*s.

***

"This is a job for robots," Bobby complained. His eyes were red and watery with the strain of looking through a microscope while placing die in perfect figure eights destined to light calculator display boards in an array of squared-off digits. The assembly line at Hewlett Packard was a mindless grind.

"Now that's an idea," his friend Zach replied. "Let's make robots."

"Sure, right after we finish our prototype."

Zach and Bobby were the only college students on the Hewlett Packard assembly line. The other employees, mostly women, had worked at the electronics company for years. They easily met their production targets while talking about what they were going to do on Saturday night, their husband's gambling problem, or their baby's colic.

Zach and Bobby used the time at their microscopes to plan. Since Bobby had returned home, they had bonded over their shared project, the creation of a personal computer which they had almost finished building in Bobby's garage.

Bobby figured he had another month or two before they would finish the prototype. In the meantime, he found that the repetitive work of the assembly line allowed him to write code in his head. When the bell signaled the end of their shift, the two friends pushed their way past their dawdling co-workers, oblivious to the giggles of the women who found the two computer nerds a source of constant amusement. Bobby and Zach, deep in concentration, didn't notice the titters that followed them out the door of the factory. After work each day, they headed directly to their workshop.

"I think we're almost there," Bobby said one spring evening, reviewing his coding from the night before.

Zach watched flickering letters dance across the TV screen which Bobby had hooked up to his central processing unit. More impressive, Bobby showed him a short program which added a column of numbers as he typed them on his keyboard.

"Whoa," Zach said, "good-bye calculators."

"Let's not get ahead of ourselves. But yeah, goodbye calculators."

Both boys hooted. They had seen enough calculator boards for a lifetime.

Bobby's dad walked into the garage, lighting a cigarette. He stood behind Zach, watching the demo.

"I think we're ready to dazzle the Cock-eyed Computer Club," Bobby said. The techies in the Club were the best and brightest computer hobbyists in the Valley. Many of them, like Bobby and Zach, were graduates of Foothill High School's Electronics Club. Bobby couldn't wait to impress his fellow club members with what he had concocted. "Unlike most of their crap, the Seed," which was what Bobby had nicknamed his computer, "has a video screen." This machine was bound to blow their minds.

"Pretty impressive," Jack said ignoring Alice who was calling him in for dinner. Bobby's Dad had gotten into the habit of heading right to the garage when he arrived home from work. He still wore his suit and tie.

"You know, guys," he said. "I think you might have something here. Maybe it's time to think beyond the Cock-eyed Club." Bobby and Zach watched as Jack took off his thick glasses and cleaned the dirty lenses with the white handkerchief that Alice put in his pocket every morning. "Zach, do you think you're up to preparing a presentation for a couple of my engineering colleagues?"

Jack had recently been put in charge of the computing capabilities at his company. He told the boys that a room-size computer now handled his company's payroll and supply inventory system. The computer had become integral to the company's business. But the machine was expensive, required constant supervision, and the programming was beyond the understanding of most employees. Bobby saw the opportunity. Soon after Bobby had arrived home, he had asked his father: "What if a smaller computer could be manufactured for individual use? Imagine a computer small enough to keep on your desk at home, straight-forward enough that Mom could write letters. Think about it. People could balance their checkbooks, prepare schoolwork, or even maintain personal financial records."

He was sure he was on to something.

"Hell, yes," Zach said, scratching his chin through his unkempt beard.

Bobby was already back at work. "I've got an idea for a new routine," he said. That was how it began. He would be up all night coding. Who knows what application he would be antsy to show them the next morning?

"Our boy genius," Zach said to Bobby's father. The salesman of the two, he was already working out his pitch. If they could procure some funding for the Seed, they could quit their day jobs and develop the project full time.

The techies at the Cock-Eyed Computer Club could keep on playing their war games, the Seed was ready to sprout. The creation had grown like the orchards that once stood where their garage workshop now hummed with activity.

Alice called Jack again. "Dinner is getting cold. How many times do I have to tell you to take off your good shirt before you get grease on it?" She stood in the doorway with a cocktail in her hand. Jack winked at Zach before pulling up his tie as if to hang himself. Zach laughed but Bobby, mumbling to himself as he composed elegant computer code, was oblivious, already lost in the endless possibilities of the machine he had created.

1973-1974

At six, Eddie began studying judo and aikido. He was a natural. Every day after school, Harriet drove him to the dojo, a sunny storefront on the El Camino Real in a strip of neon-lit stores, service stations, car lots, and taco stands. On a nearby corner, a stranded apricot tree huddled, strangled by the surrounding subdivisions and never-ending traffic.

The entire Jackson family supported Eddie in his new undertaking. Hiroko's face lit up when her grandson announced that he wanted to learn the Japanese martial art. Joey told his young nephew that aikido could be translated as "unifying with life energy." Eddie quickly progressed from yellow belt to brown. As Harriet watched Eddie working out in the dojo, she could see where the discipline was also an art.

"Look, Auntie Harry," he said. In his starched *dogi*, he showed her how he had been taught to use his opponent's force to resist rather than repel the attacker. Harriet adored the seriousness with which her nephew approached the challenge. She watched him compete; his confidence grew by the day.

Eddie's instructor, Max, a large man with a surprising high giggle, worked with each child individually but Eddie was obviously a favorite. Like Eddie, Max called Harriet "Auntie Harry." Often, as Eddie practiced, Max sat down beside her. Harriet was younger than the mothers in the bleachers and felt self-conscious when the instructor singled her out.

"That boy is amazing," he told her. She watched Eddie, admiring his rapt attention, his precise movements.

"He's good, right?" she inquired.

"His talent is remarkable. He takes to the discipline like a natural," the instructor replied.

No surprise there. Joe, after all, was Eddie's grandfather.

Harriet was more comfortable when her father, handsome in his uniform, sat beside her. When Joe was in town, he insisted on joining her when she drove Eddie to the dojo. He admired the discipline required by martial arts and shook Max's hand vigorously. "Atta boy," he cheered on his grandson, never needing to raise his voice to be heard. The war in Vietnam was finally winding down and Joe was home more often these days. The United States' role in the region, he told her, had been reduced to providing assistance to the South Vietnamese army while negotiators in Paris hammered out a peace agreement and withdrawal strategy. Her father was considering leaving active duty to join the Reserves. As a reserve captain, he would be closer to his family. Soon, her father would be coming home for good, a decorated veteran. When Joe talked about the war, he never mentioned the high cost of the conflict, the hundreds of thousands of fatalities. Despite having watched nightly news coverage of protests against the war, Harriet never questioned her father. She was happy to have him home.

Eddie glowed at his grandfather's compliments, stood taller when Joe was in the audience.

"Discipline" was a word that Joe used a lot. He took great pride in telling his grandson about his role as a Commander in the Navy, entrusted with building men. "My own boys will tell you," he said, gesturing over at Kevin or Joey, "I never missed an opportunity to set them straight. Sometimes my actions might have seemed severe," he looked over at Joey who, he made it quite clear, was somewhat of a softie. Despite the fact that his younger son often easily ended up in tears when disciplined, "They always knew it was for their own good."

When Eddie advanced from one belt to the next, the whole family attended. They filled the front two rows of the dojo, a rowdy crowd of supporters. Eddie beamed, especially when his grandfather singled him out for attention. "You and I are cut from the same cloth, boy," he would say. Harriet knew that feeling. Eddie had been granted Joe's benediction, a two-edged sword, a blessing that bestowed the responsibility of living up to Joe's high expectations.

Kat sometimes complained when her son came home with bruises. Joe was the first to defend Max, the instructor. "Skill does not come without discipline. Aikido is, after all, a martial art."

Eddie defended Max. "He sometimes corrects me with his bamboo pole, but I can't even touch the weapons until I am a black belt and have demonstrated to him that I am a serious student."

Max put an arm around his star student. "Eddie gets it," he said. "A few bruises are a small price to pay for mastering the art."

"I guess," Kat said, "just take good care of my boy."

In January 1973, the Paris Peace Accord was signed, the US withdrew from Saigon and Joe retired.

By that time, Max had asked Eddie to be his assistant. Under Max's supervision, the seven-year-old began to teach younger children. His confidence was impressive, his concentration unflagging. Harriet saw in her nephew maturity that reminded her of her own childhood. He too had accepted responsibility at a young age, but, unlike her, he was frequently recognized for the talent that he exhibited. Often Max drove him home and Joe invited him in for dinner.

Under Hiroko's watchful eye, Harriet found it hard to participate in the conversation at the dinner table. The burly instructor made her nervous. When he spoke to her, she never knew what to say. Fortunately, Eddie had no end of questions for his instructor. Joey took advantage of the visits to show off his increasing Japanese vocabulary.

"Eddie is my superstar," Max told her mother, reaching for another serving of Harriet's homemade lasagna. Eddie's muscular build was complemented by a twinkle in his eye. With Joe home, Harriet had dialed up her cooking, pulling out her father's favorite recipes. Max, who had a bottomless appetite, ate the pasta with gusto.

Kat and Mike often begged off from the family dinners, citing work obligations. Harriet suspected they took the opportunity to spend some time on their own.

One morning when Kat stopped by to drop off the family laundry, she asked about Max. "He's so good for Eddie," she said. Looking at her sister with a knowing smirk. "When are you guys going to get together?" It had never occurred to Harriet that Max might be attracted to her as anything but Eddie's loyal guardian.

Harriet blushed. Kat laughed. "Eddie says Max is sweet on you." Seeing Harriet's confusion, she raised her eyebrows. "He seems like a good guy."

Harriet, hands deep in soapy water, was caught off guard. Max was a frequent visitor to the Jackson household because of his attachment to Eddie, his star pupil. But, she had to admit, he did seem to enjoy her lasagna. Even Hiroko welcomed the aikido instructor to the dinner table, often complementing him on his knowledge of the Japanese martial arts. Had Harriet, intent on welcoming her nephew's instructor into their home, missed something that all the rest of her family could see?

Kat laughed at Harriet's discomfort causing her to blush.

"It's about time, Sis, that you get yourself a man. Think about it."

***

Joey ushered Harriet and his mom to their seats in the high school auditorium. Four of the Jackson children had attended the high school, but this was the first time that Hiroko sat in the modern auditorium with its plush, movie theater-style seats and professional lighting system. She had dressed for the event in her finest blue dress, purchased from the commissary for a Christmas party soon after Joe's return from Vietnam. A party where she sat quietly in a corner while her husband held forth, entertaining the wives of the men in his squadron with tales of their valor.

Now she wore a simple pearl necklace. Harriet noticed that her mother had purchased new nylons for the occasion.

Joey greeted his classmates from the Japanese American Club and introduced his mother to Mr. Ito who spoke briefly in Japanese. Hiroko giggled self-consciously and replied in her usual broken English. "Honor to meet son's teacher. Very kind. Thank you. Thank you." Harriet stood to the side, unrecognized by her former vice principal.

Mr. Ito spoke to the assembled students and their guests about the Japanese Internment Camp where his family lived during most of World War II. Joey had heard the story before but had struggled when trying to discuss the treatment of Japanese Americans during and after the war with his mother. Joe had refused to accompany the family to the lecture.

"I've always protected your mother. Why do you need to open that wound up now?" he had answered when

Harriet had asked her father whether he wanted to come along with them to the high school.

But watching her mother's face was answer enough. Mr. Ito, despite the gravity of his presentation, frequently broke into a benevolent smile as he calmly related his family's experiences during the Second World War. When Mr. Ito described the treatment that his own mother had received, the names she was called, Hiroko reached for her son's hand. Harriet could see that her mother understood every word.

During World War II, over one hundred thousand Japanese Americans had been interned "for their own protection" following an executive order by President Franklin D. Roosevelt.

Just like Joe had protected Hiroko, Harriet couldn't help thinking.

Mr. Ito told the rapt audience that the Japanese were labeled "a dangerous element," "totally unassimilable," whose loyalties could not be determined. On the West Coast, all Japanese with dual citizenship had been stripped of their belongings and shipped to internment camps.

Mr. Ito expressed no bitterness, only a desire to educate. For so long, the treatment of Japanese Americans during the war had not been discussed, he told the students. Only through education could such abuses be avoided in the future.

After the talk, Hiroko thanked the principal profusely. Joey could barely keep up with her animated Japanese as she told Mr. Ito about the scorn she had felt from the other wives on the Navy base, the suspicion, the hurtful things that the American wives had said to her.

"When I came to America, war was over, but not for me," Hiroko told them in the car on the way home. Increasingly, Harriet's mother had become comfortable talking about her background, especially when she was in the company of her youngest son. With Joey, she was no longer the silent mother of Harriet's, Kat's and Kevin's childhood. Joey told his siblings that their mother was an inspiration. Her struggle to adapt to a foreign country had taken place behind closed doors. Listening to him, Harriet recalled her mother singing lullabies to her baby brother in a language that no one else in the family could understand.

When they arrived home, Joe didn't look up from his football game. Hiroko made a cup of tea and went to her room to take off her blue dress. Harriet thanked Joey for inviting her to the lecture.

Joey answered, "I'm glad you could come. It good for Mom to talk about how hard it was at first."

Harriet raised her eyebrows. "But she was never in a camp. Dad rescued her."

Joey's silence reminded her of her mother's.

"I suppose that's what she's been writing to her mother all these years." Harriet was dying to know if her brother had read her mother's letters, or better yet the responses she received.

"Mom was fifteen, the same age I am, when she left Japan. She has never seen her family since. Those letters have been a lifeline." Joey chose his words carefully. His mother's secrets were safe with him. "Imagine, how lonely she must have felt."

Harriet, who had no trouble imagining loneliness, sighed. "I suppose. But try not to aggravate Dad, okay? It's hard enough for him to adjust to civilian life. I'd like him to stick around for a while this time."

"Gotcha," Joey said. Harriet heard his answer, but she could not read his face and knew that his feelings were more complicated than he let on.

The Jackson family had, as a result of a ceasefire in Vietnam, finally come together. Next door, the Hopkins family's unity was disrupted by battles of their own.

"God, I wish they would shut up," Bobby said to his father.

The closer Bobby got to completing his project, the more his family drove him up a wall. The presentation to the Cocked-Eyed Computer Club was only two days away. He had discovered a glitch in the program's display, and he couldn't concentrate. The din of constant arguments taking place in the house was impossible to tune out. Angry words filtered through the wall into his workshop in the garage.

Patty and Alice had been going at it all day long. Even with his headphones on and Mahler's 5th Symphony pumped up to maximum volume, Bobby couldn't shut out the growing acrimony between his sister and mother. It began when Alice decided to donate Patty's unused flute to the church fund-raising drive. Alice had arrived home and announced to the entire family that when she handed the instrument case to Mrs. Hitchcock, the intimidating chairman of the woman's club, a baggie of marijuana had dropped onto the table in front of her.

"You are an embarrassment," Alice exploded at her daughter before slamming the front door of the house. "The last thing I need is for those women to know how utterly I failed in raising you." His mother's glare swept the room like a cop's spotlight.

All Bobby wanted was a little peace and quiet. Five minutes without hysteria. Was that too much to ask?

Alice saw the whole affair as personal, something Patty had done solely with the intention of causing her embarrassment.

Both women were bonkers as far as he was concerned.

His sister was unrepentant. "Is it my fault that she's a lousy mother?" she asked Bobby as he tried to walk by undetected, heading for the bathroom.

Bobby wanted nothing to do with his sister's complaints. He had more important things on his mind.

"I refuse to put up with her nonsense. I'm just lucky she's not in jail!" Alice declared.

Despite knowing better, Bobby made one futile attempt to intervene. He was willing to try anything to end the hysteria that made it impossible to think.

"Mom, everybody smokes. Calm down."

"Calm down? You're telling me to calm down." Alice was in a tizzy now, pouring more vodka into her glass with every word.

"What's the big deal, Mom," Patty said. "I smoke. You drink."

"I am your mother," Alice screamed.

He'd had enough. His mother's incessant drinking only made things worse. His sister was hopeless, raw emotion which couldn't be reasoned with.

When Bobby returned to his workbench, Zach snickered. He found the situation amusing. "My house is so boring," he said. Bobby would happily settle for a dose of boredom.

While Alice berated her daughter, "I have a good mind to march you down to the police station myself right now," Bobby tried to concentrate on his coding. Zach had been running test programs with Jack all afternoon, preparing the presentation for potential investors. If they aced this presentation, Bobby could move out before the check cleared the bank. He couldn't wait to rent a quiet apartment of his own.

Bobby retreated to the garage, wiping his hands of the whole mess. Zach looked up from his computer.

"I'll be so glad when we can get out of here," Bobby said to his father.

"You are a lucky boy," Jack said and returned to his printout. Bobby would never understand his father who, despite his rebellious quips, was committed to staying with Alice. His father thrived on family drama. And he enabled his wife's drinking, keeping up with her glass for glass.

In the kitchen, Alice was warming up. "You are nothing but a leach," she spat at her daughter. "Look at you. What man would have you with those fat thighs? What were you thinking, choosing a major in comparative literature? You don't have a sensible bone in your body."

Patty responded with equal furor. "A leach! How dare you call me a leach while my golden brother tinkers with computers in your garage after being expelled from college?"

"Get out!" Alice screamed, so loud that Bobby figured even the Jacksons could hear next door. "Get out of this house right now!"

"With pleasure. Have a good life, Mom," Patty slammed the front door behind her. For a moment, Bobby listened to his sister pause outside the open garage. He hoped she wouldn't stop and try to convince them to take her side. He refused to be dragged into this mess. A moment later he could hear her boots stomping down the block. Bobby didn't blame her. In twenty years, their father had never come to her rescue. Her mother always won. She couldn't expect that to change now.

Thank God, the house was quiet at last. Maybe now he could actually get some work done.

Mahler's 5th got better and better. Written when the composer was in his twenties, the opus tackled the riddles of the universe through technique and musical theory. Bobby wanted no less of his coding. Quiet precision. Even perfection. He wasn't about to let the din of family around him interfere with the waves of inspiration that began to flow with the Adagietto, a glorious escape from the bravado of the previous movements. The strings and solo harp brought him back down to earth. Focused him. He was on a roll now and wouldn't stop working until the morning sun woke him from his reverie.

***

Harriet was on her way to pick up Eddie at the dojo when she saw Patty walking on the side of the busy road, a denim bag thrown over her shoulder.

Walking on Foothill Avenue was never a good idea. The endless stream of cars zipped around pedestrians without regard for their safety. After a moment's hesitation, Harriet pulled over.

"Do you need a ride?" The two women hadn't spoken in years. Harriet hardly recognized her neighbor. Patty had worked hard to transform herself, her long hair hung in a braid to her waist, her t-shirt was tie-dyed purple. Her tight jeans had improvised patches.

"Do you mind? I need to get to the bus station by three."

"Not at all. I have to pick up my nephew in twenty minutes. Are you leaving on a trip?"

Harriet was curious. Kevin had told her that Bobby was back home. Last she'd heard, he'd left for college. Maybe Patty could explain the recent activity in the Hopkins' garage.

Patty hesitated. Harriet felt self-conscious, an old habit. The Hopkins didn't speak to the Jacksons. They came from different worlds. She didn't mean to put Patty on the spot. What business was it of hers where Patty was headed? Still, Patty had accepted her offer of a ride.

"I'm blowing this place for good," Patty said. "I'm as good as gone."

"Hop in." Harriet pulled away from the curb. "You're in college, right?" she asked.

"Was. NYU. In New York City."

"Wow. I've never been out of the Bay Area."

"Never? Your dad's a pilot. I would think that you could go anywhere."

All these years and the two girls, women now, had never discussed their families. Harriet was surprised to find the subject painful. Once the Hopkins' house had been her refuge, now it seemed as foreign as another country where people spoke a language she didn't understand.

"Yes, but after we bought the house," Harriet looked at Patty, acknowledging the one thing they had in common, "my father never took us with him when he traveled." In explanation, she added, "He spent most of the last ten years in Vietnam."

"Ouch."

"He's a captain in the Navy, you know," Harriet thought this, at least, would impress her neighbor, but Patty's reaction caught her unprepared.

"That's shitty. We should never have invaded Vietnam. What we're doing to those people is a crime."

At the mention of the war, the conversation died. Harriet snaked her way through the thick traffic.

"You're leaving the Bay Area?" Harriet asked.

"I'm going back to NYC. My mom kicked me out; I couldn't be happier. I hate this valley with its cookie-cutter grid of houses and highways. The mountains here are nothing more than a smog trap."

Harriet couldn't hold back a smile. Patty had never been short on passion. The girl who sang with the Beatles. Looking at her surroundings through Patty's eyes, Harriet knew that her neighbor was right. Where once there had been open space, now there were only strip malls and fast-food restaurants on every corner.

"What is New York like?" she asked.

"Amazing. You'd love Greenwich Village," Patty told her. "You can find anybody there—artists and writers, people of every color and background. In the Bay Area, one hardly ever sees a black face. In New York, you can be an actress, an artist, a jazz musician, even a millionaire. Everyone rides the same subway."

Harriet listened, entranced. She tried to imagine living in a city which would allow her to re-invent herself. Who would she choose to become? Patty positively vibrated with the possibilities. How could two neighbors grow up side by side and see the world through such different lenses?

The Greyhound bus station was several miles away.

Patty worked herself up into a righteous indignation. "Here in the Valley, the Chicanos, the families who worked in the fruit orchards and canneries for generations, are hidden away in pockets of poverty on the wrong side of 101. Even they are being pushed further and further away now that property values are going through the roof. Everyone you meet here is the same: self-centered high achievers looking for the next promotion."

But Harriet wanted to hear more about New York. "It must be amazing to live in the City. You are so lucky." Harriet tried to imagine where she would choose to go if she could go anywhere. In New York City, would she choose to spend her time with a man like Max? Or would she decide to live alone? Would she have the nerve to seek out the Greenwich Village clubs where the music she loved originated? Would she miss her family, the comfort of their need? Would Joe resent her absence? Would Hiroko write her letters?

"Yeah, I suppose." Harriet's enthusiastic response obviously surprised Patty, who seemed to have expected sympathy, not envy. Watching Patty's confusion, Harriet realized that she knew very little about her neighbor. And her neighbor knew nothing about her.

"What are you up to these days?" Patty asked after another uncomfortable silence.

"Not much. I help Kat out with her kid. And my mom needs a hand around the house." Harriet hesitated. "I hear Bobby's home." Harriet's heart fluttered as she asked about Bobby, but Patty only yawned in response.

"The golden boy was kicked out of college. Now he's brewing some kind of computer business in our garage."

Harriet couldn't imagine Bobby failing at anything. She was certain there was more to the story than Patty was letting on. If anybody she knew was destined to succeed, it was Bobby.

"Sounds like our house when Kevin was small. He was always trading car parts."

"Yeah," Patty said, although her expression made it clear that it was not at all the same. The Jacksons and the Hopkins had nothing in common. There was no point in pretending otherwise.

When Harriet dropped Patty off at the station, the rumble of idling busses muffled her neighbor's final words, but Patty's description of New York lingered. As Harriet continued along El Camino Real on the way to Max's dojo, she tried to imagine the city, a place "where you could be anything you wanted." But the momentary thrill of the fantasy was gone. Eddie was waiting for her. Dinner needed to be cooked and Max's smile seemed to be evolving into a leer that she hadn't yet decided how she was going to handle.

But still, she was oddly pleased to realize that things in the Hopkins household were far from perfect. Bobby kicked out of college and Patty running away on a Greyhound bus. Harriet chuckled to herself.

✳✳✳

Max asked Harriet to accompany him to the carnival set up in the parking lot of St. Simon's Church. She asked if she could bring Eddie along. Kat had been on her case, insisting that her son seldom had a chance to "have fun." She complained that Eddie's responsibilities at the dojo were filling the time that a young boy should be outside playing with other children.

"You're his mother," Harriet protested. "If you were around more, maybe he would have a chance to play with the kids in his own neighborhood." When Kat looked annoyed, Harriet quickly apologized. "You know I love your kid. Give me some credit. Eddie never looks as happy as he does at the dojo."

The night at the carnival would placate her sister. Max picked the two of them up in his bright yellow Karmann Ghia. Eddie climbed into the cramped back seat. The back seat barely fit her diminutive nephew. Harriet resisted the temptation to climb in beside him. Her place was obviously beside the imposing aikido instructor. She let Max open the right-side passenger door for her and perched uncomfortably in the bucket seat. The seat had been adjusted so that she was practically laying down. With effort, she sat upright, looking nervously out the window.

Eddie chattered away happily in the back seat. "I've never been to a carnival. Will there be rides?"

"Ferris wheels and twirling cups," Max answered. "Cotton candy too."

141

At the entrance to the fair, Max bought them a long roll of red tickets. Families and crowds of excited children surrounded them.

They rode on the Ferris wheel together, Eddie in the middle of the rocking car, hand grasping the metal bar, knuckles white as they rose over the neighborhood. "Look at those lights. People look like ants!" Eddie squealed. "We are unbelievably high!"

Max chuckled, putting one arm around the excited boy and resting the other on the shoulder of Harriet's white cardigan sweater.

Eddie wanted to try everything. He tasted the cotton candy skeptically. "Can you believe, Auntie Harry, this is actually sugar! It's like a spider web," he said, waving the cardboard cone with awe.

Long after Harriet began begging off from another dizzying ride, Eddie insisted on trying everyone, bravely sitting alone in the twirling coffee cup and pretending to drive a red, miniature race car with solemn concentration.

"What prize would you like?" Max asked Eddie as he prepared to toss a ping pong ball into a platform crammed tight with glass vases. Eddie gravely considered his choices. With a successful throw, Max said he could pick the stuffed animal of his choice.

Harriet watched Eddie choose as if his life depended on it; he had never been given so many options.

"The German shepherd," he said at last, indicating a noble looking stuffed dog at the top of the shelf.

"He's yours," Max said, artfully aiming the ball. They watched the hollow ball arc gracefully and slide right off the edge of the vase.

"It's rigged, you know," Max said, before buying a dozen more balls.

"What's rigged?" Eddie asked.

"They grease the edges of the vases so that you can't win."

Eddie's face scrunched up in concentration, trying to figure the trick out. "That wouldn't be fair," he said, "I'm thinking they are trying to make it a challenge." Max laughed and put his arm around the boy.

Harriet watched Max, his easy affection, his obvious pride in Eddie's keen observation.

"Max, thank you so much for inviting us here tonight," she said.

"My pleasure," Max answered, tossing one last ball which balanced on the edge of a vase for what seemed like an eternity, before falling into the glass with a satisfying click.

"We won!!!!" Eddie cried, his usual maturity melting in the victory of the moment. He jumped up and down yelling "We won, we won," oblivious to the amusement of the crowd that surrounded him. Harriet and Max stepped aside so that the boy could point out the German shepherd to the blasé carnie who removed the large stuffed animal from the top shelf with a hooked stick. As he handed Eddie his prize, a wayward cloud opened up over their heads and it began to rain.

The three of them ran to Max's car, Eddie hugging his new dog, Max holding Harriet's hand, each of them laughing at the perfect timing, this perfect ending to a perfect evening.

On the drive home, Eddie said: "The most unlikely thing occurred to me. As we were running, a raindrop hit my face. It felt like a tear, but really it was only a raindrop."

Harriet smiled at the young boy's observation. The innocence revealed. Maybe her sister was right, Eddie needed more opportunities to be a child. Yes, he thrived on the attention he received at the dojo. As a young girl, she had also thrived on the responsibility that Joe had entrusted to her. But she would never want to deny this precious boy the joy of that raindrop trickling down his cheek.

"You look happy," Max said after they had dropped Eddie off at Kat's.

"I am," she replied, realizing that the smiling man was watching her and that it didn't bother her. As a matter of fact, she felt amazing.

1976

"Don't cook tonight. Call Chicken Delight."

"Very cute," Amy punched Bobby in the arm as she walked into his apartment. "I told you I would cook tonight, and I'm a woman of my word."

Bobby let it go at that. He would have been content to order in a bucket of fried chicken for dinner. His girlfriend, Amy, wasn't much of a cook. Her specialty, rice and frozen vegetables, lacked both flavor and substance. But he wasn't about to complain. When he wasn't knee deep in one of his projects, he was grateful for his petite girlfriend's company. Besides, Amy was as big a *Star Trek* fan as he was and never objected to watching TV while they ate. Watching *Star Trek* during dinner, now that was the life. The sex wasn't too bad either.

Amy puttered in their tiny kitchen, managing to produce a busy-sounding clatter despite the fact that the meal required only one saucepan. Bobby flopped onto the rust-colored couch. They had rented the Cupertino apartment with a bare minimum of furnishings: a two-seater couch, an unmatched and flimsy armchair, a Murphy bed in the closet and a small veneer-covered dresser. Sometimes when they had smoked a little too much grass, Bobby and Amy tried to read the scratches on the coffee table as if they were hieroglyphics.

"I think it says, "Dobie Gillis lived here," Amy would giggle, taking off her glasses to examine a particularly deep scratch. "What, me worry?" Bobby would answer and they would end up rolling on the worn rug in hysterics. Bobby was happy in the modest apartment. The best part of living on his own was not having to answer to his mother.

"How is Alice?" Amy asked over flavorless rice and cardboard-tasting string beans."

"Not my problem," Bobby answered, never taking his eyes off the TV screen. It had been a mistake, introducing his girlfriend to his mother. Both women had made too much of it. All he had wanted to do was visit his dad and see how he was holding up now that Alice and Jack were alone in the house. Amy made a point of putting her best self forward, offering to clear the table and complimenting Alice on her cooking. The best he could do now was to change the subject and hope that Amy didn't notice.

"I played that Star Trek text game all afternoon," he told her.

"Tough job there," Amy said. "You should have to stand behind a teller's counter all day."

"Are you implying that being in command of the USS Enterprise is an easy task? Today I was on a mission to destroy an invading fleet of Klingon warships."

"Oh, well in that case..."

"It was awesome, I tell, you."

"But, the question remains, is it really work?" Amy remained skeptical about the practicality of Bobby's job. More than once she had expressed surprise that Bobby and Zach had actually received funding from a venture capitalist.

In her own quiet way, Amy had ambitions.

"You would be surprised." While playing the Star Trek game, Bobby had successfully tested a new programming language for the upcoming Seed release. Zach had appreciated the efficiency of his beta trial. Together they played two rounds. Bobby won them both.

"Did I tell you," Bobby asked, "that Zach and Lara have pooled their resources so that they can write a script and produce a Star Trek film? Lara is going to make the sets. So far, she has spent two months researching materials, building sets and props, collecting costume patterns, producing make-up prosthetics for Klingons and Organians."

Lara was Zach's girlfriend, a dark-haired beauty who he had been dating since high school.

"If they want, I could print enlarged slides for screen projections," Amy offered. She lacked Lara's flair for the dramatic but was a willing spectator, ready to do her share.

"Right now, I wish Zach would concentrate on getting the Seed to market."

Amy cleared the dishes and curled up at Bobby's side. He held her hand. They watched *The Trouble with Tribbles*, season two, episode five, with devoted attention. They could recite the show's dialog without even looking at the TV. Bobby strutted the length of the room as he mimed the bureaucratic Federation commissioner's speech. Amy pretended to be the peddler selling the furry, purry hungry little tribbles as pets.

Bobby couldn't resist the tribbles.

Sometimes when they made love, they did it in character.

Amy was petite. Even that first day when he met her at the bank, she had looked up at him through the teller's window. When he said "Live long and prosper" as he pocketed his cash, she had almost jumped out at him in excitement.

"Are you a Trekkie?" she had screamed. Her voice was high, almost squeaky. They had been an item ever since.

"Are you up for ice cream?" he asked when the last of the credits rolled across the screen. He was starving.

The show had energized him. After they finished their Bascom Robbins rum raisin ice cream, Bobby pulled out the Murphy bed and turned to Amy, his arms wide. They made love, right in the middle of the living room. Amy pretended to be a furry, purry tribble and Bobby conquered her eagerly with soupy kisses to her neck. When they were done, he waited for her to doze off. The soothing rhythm of her gentle snoring filled the room. He extricated himself from the tangle of their sweaty limbs, slipped out of bed, and returned to his computer to go over the day's coding one more time before joining her underneath the comforter that they shared.

***

Rita, the dojo's bookkeeper, was in a bad mood again. The short, dark-haired woman glowered at the front desk once a month when she came to the gym to collect the student's tuition. When the parents dropped off the monthly check for their children's classes, Rita didn't thank them. She simply pocketed the check and wrote out the receipt. Max stood beside her, smiling apologetically as the students filed in.

"Rita," Max said, "it wouldn't hurt you to smile at the parents every once a while."

"Why would I?" Rita asked, stowing the checks in her briefcase. "This is business, not some cocktail party."

"Don't pay her any mind," Max said, lighting when he saw Harriet arrive in the lobby. "Rita woke up on the wrong side of life."

Rita looked Harriet over, evidently not happy with what she saw.

Harriet and Max were an item, even Rita must sense that by now. With her father's encouragement (Joe called Max *Mr. Saturday Night*), Harriet had been dating the instructor for almost a year. Max was a frequent guest in the Jackson household, watching football with her father on Sunday nights, and cheering on Kevin at the San Jose

Speedway where her brother had become a minor celebrity known for his speed and skill at driving sprint cars around the oval dirt track.

"Best restaurant in Sunnyvale," Max would chuckle as he finished off another plate of Harriet's meatloaf. Now he handed her sweater and left it to Rita to close up the dojo for the day. They dropped Eddie off at his parents' house.

Harriet cherished the idea of sitting by this powerful man's side in a dark theater, his large hand resting on her thigh. Max had taken her to see *Rocky* half a dozen times.

"You'll always be my Adrian," he told her later as they walked up the stairs to his studio apartment. Harriet wasn't thrilled at the comparison to the plain Jane love interest of his favorite movie, but she figured that he intended the attribution as a compliment.

Max kept things simple. He let her know exactly where she stood. She liked that.

On their very first date, Max had told her that he was separated from his wife. End of story. No name. No regrets. No questions asked. He never mentioned his life before they met. His marriage never came up around the Jackson dinner table.

Max's apartment felt more like a hotel room than a home, but Max had resisted Harriet's attempts to give it a woman's touch. The framed photo of the Santa Cruz mountains that she hung above the dresser disappeared before her next visit. The place mats she put on the folding card table he used as a kitchen table ended up unused in a drawer. Even the blue blanket she bought to cheer up his single bed was cast aside, ending up crumpled on the dusty floor.

"Honey, this is my man cave. Let it be." Despite her weekly visit, the apartment was clearly his and obviously meant to remain that way.

Bed was another story. For once in her life, Harriet was the center of attention. No complaints there. Kat might have begged for details, but Harriet wasn't about to talk about it. Instead, she told her sister that Max was generous with both his money and time. She told herself the same thing. Harriet, who had never had any money of her own except a small, weekly allowance from her father, now wore a slim gold chain around her neck. Max took her to the mall. He insisted she model tight fitting skirts and mohair sweaters that clung to her breasts. When she tried on a pair of black high-heeled pumps, he whistled and called her "hot stuff" right there in front of the salesclerk.

Despite, Harriet's discomfort at Max's showmanship, Eddie commented that he had never seen his aunt so happy.

"Adrian!" Max called out now as he came, thrusting a victorious fist into the air. Harriet never asked him when his separation would become a divorce, but she was conscientious with her birth control. The last thing that Joe needed was another daughter who got knocked up before she was married. Her father encouraged her to date Max, but he had also told her not to lose her head. Ever since Bobby, Harriet had promised herself that she would never embarrass her family again.

"Yo, Adrian, ready for another round?" Max stubbed out his cigarette. Harriet, lost in the memory of Bobby's cautious kisses, didn't hear him until he started tickling her. She turned towards him, wishing that he would treat her more gently but aroused, as always, by the size of him, the strength of his muscular arms, the confidence with which he drew her to him. Her nephew might have bruises as a result of his training, but hers were acquired in moments of passion and came in the shape of the burly man's fingers.

Max always drove her home before midnight. No problem there. They both preferred to wake up in their own beds.

✱✱✱

Max and Harriet watched as thirty sprint cars spouted alcohol, their huge overhead wings struggling to keep the vehicles on the ground. With the right rear tires twice the size of the left rear tires, the cars pitched gracefully into turns but wobbled precariously on straightaways.

Kevin was the star of the California Rebel Cup Race.

It was bad enough that Harriet had spent half her childhood terrified that her father's plane would crash into the sea or careen onto a poorly lit runway. Now that her father was home, her brother had inherited his thirst for danger. Max might think watching the C-cars smash into the tire barricades was a hoot, but Harriet had been clenching her fists all afternoon. Max made fun of the drops of blood under her fingernails. In response, she clasped her hands tightly in prayer.

During the qualifying race, the car in front of Kevin's collided with the wall on the second turn. Kevin barely avoided leaving the track and ramming the tire barrier.

The cars kicked up clouds of dirt. By three o'clock her skin was coated with dust. She watched the eager kids who waved checkered flags as the cars made their first turn around the track. Max stood up and cheered when the yellow flag shot into the air. Harriet heaved a sigh of relief when Kevin won the final sprint to the finish.

Kevin waved his trophy overhead, flashing it in their direction to share his victory. The $1500 he'd won was only a fragment of the money he had spent on the car and spare parts, but he was clearly thrilled. The kids in the stands clustered around him asking to try on his helmet and admiring his souped-up car.

Max lit a cigar as they walked out the gate. "What a rush," he said.

"All my childhood, I cut out articles about plane accidents," Harriet told him on the drive home. "Somehow I imagined it would keep Dad safe. Now I have to worry about Kevin in that crazy car."

Max continued to puff on his cigar, his arm casually resting on the open window. The bright sunlight danced in the smoke.

"Boys will be boys," Max said at last, coming to Kevin's defense. "After all, Joe made it home in one piece, didn't he?"

"Thank God." Looking over at Max, Harriet realized that she was once again waiting on a man. Her father, now Max, who never mentioned his ex-wife, who seemed content to spend his Saturday nights with Harriet without requiring, or desiring, any further commitment. Harriet tried to picture Max with another woman, but his sparse apartment provided few clues. Despite their intimacy, the man beside her remained an enigma. As Max backed the car out, insinuating his way into the line of exiting traffic, refusing to yield to less aggressive drivers, Harriet thought about the intensity of hostility that seemed to exist between Max and his bookkeeper. Rita, who jaw clenched with unfathomable fury as she tallied the checks. She wondered if there was something more there than met the eye but then Max smiled over at her and said. "Honey, sometimes you just need to enjoy yourself. Stop worrying."

Harriet had been trying to get up the nerve to ask Max if she was too old to join one of his aikido classes. Eddie would undoubtedly try to talk her out of it. The dojo, after all, was his world, but she had been thinking a lot about the need to take care of herself. She was tired of being in the stands, holding her breath waiting for something awful to occur. She liked the idea that she could use her own strength to determine a match's outcome.

She couldn't figure out how to start the conversation. How could she explain her need to Max? How would she make Eddie understand?

"I've got to check my messages at the dojo. Rita is paying the monthly bills and asked me to stop by to sign the checks. You don't mind if I drop you home? I'll be there by dinner time." Before she had a chance to answer, Max had already made the turn onto Mariani Avenue.

"No problem," she said, unnecessarily, feeling unsettled at the mention of Rita. Another day, she would ask him if she could join a class.

Max drove off before Harriet had the front door open. She was startled to find Joey was sitting on the living room couch with an arm around her mother.

"What's the matter, Mom?" Harriet asked.

Hiroko looked up. The blank expression on her face evoked a memory of the silent mother of Harriet's childhood.

"Mom's brother died," Joey said before their mother could respond. Right after lunch, he explained, the phone rang, long distance from Japan. In twenty years, Hiroko had never received a phone call from Japan.

Joey, hearing his mother's frantic Japanese, had hurried to his mother's side.

"Mom wants to go to his funeral," Joey said now.

"In Japan? Does Dad know?"

"No, I haven't been able to reach him."

Max had invited Joe to the race today, but Joe had business to attend to at the base. Lately, her father had been spending more and more time away from home.

"Did you know that Mom's brother, Haru, never spoke to Mom after she got pregnant?" Joey asked Harriet.

"He wrote her off, told her she was an embarrassment to the family and no longer his sister." This was news to Harriet.

Harriet pictured all those letters, a correspondence maintained in secret between Hiroko and her mother all those years.

Harriet sat down on the other side of her mother. So animated in recent days, her mother was wordless once again.

"Mom, I am so sorry." Harriet had no idea how to comfort the mother who had maintained a stoical indifference to her past. She would call Max and tell him that she couldn't go out tonight. When Dad got home, she'd convince him to let Hiroko go home for the funeral, to be at her mother's side. Joey agreed, it was the right thing to do. As her mother began to pack a bag, they strategized. The best way to approach their father would be to convince him that it was his idea, an act of generosity.

It would be strange though, this house without Hiroko. Everyone else in the family came and went, but her mom had always been there.

With Hiroko off in Japan, Joe spent more and more time at the base. The house was frequently empty. Kevin, who was working for Mike and Kat at the gas station, had moved into an apartment with friends from the track. Joey frequently stayed late at school where Mr. Ito was helping him with his college applications despite Joe's adamant insistence that he should enlist after graduation and take advantage of the Language Program at the Presidio in Monterrey. Eddie demanded less of her time. The ten-year-old preferred to help Max out at the dojo after school where he often stayed until Max closed up after the 7 pm class. Mike and Kat were happy to have their son dropped off on Max's way home; it saved them the trip to Harriet's. Frequently Joey and Harriet ate dinner alone.

Joey called his mother in Japan once a week. At first, he told Harriet, the conversations were about her brother's funeral.

"Mom was nervous about attending the wake," Joey told Harriet. "She didn't know if she would be welcome."

"Why did her brother treat her so badly?" Harriet asked.

"Haru never forgave her for marrying an American. America, after all, was the enemy."

The story her father told was one of rescue. Of an innocent teenage girl he had taken under his wing when everything around her was crumbling. When her parents, once wealthy, were struggling for food and their house was in shambles, he had been the one to assure Hiroko's survival.

Joey told a different story. "Before he died, her father warned her not to leave. But by then she was pregnant and did not feel like she had a choice. She was so ashamed."

"She told you this?" Harriet was amazed.

"Not in so many words, but she missed her family. She treasured her mother's letters. It meant everything to her that her mother was willing to stand up to her brother and refused to cut her off entirely.

"The war left people on both sides of the conflict bitter and very angry," Joey said. "Her father hated the Americans and once she was in the States, Mom felt judged, resented by the Americans she met. I think for most of our lives, Mom believed she was the enemy. Her father told her as much."

No wonder her mother had been livid when she discovered Harriet at fifteen kissing a boy. For Hiroko, that was a disastrous act, an irreversible mistake. A high school crush set her life on a path that she had never been able to escape. Sexuality, in her world, led to a young girl's ruin.

"It must be so weird for her, to be there after all these years."

Joey was silent, weighing his words. "I think Mom is happier now that she has been at any time in our lives."

"To be with her mother again?"

"Yes. But also, to see her brother. Prior to cremation, her family held a traditional wake. Mom was able to see Haru dressed in a kimono on the altar. When her mother, according to Japanese ritual, laid a pack of cigarettes in the coffin as a gift to take to the other side, Mom gave him candy. At least for her, this was some form of reconciliation."

Joey had been writing his senior paper on Buddhism. Now he told her, "His body would have been placed with his head towards the north or west. In Buddhism, this orientation reflects the realm of *Amida.*"

Harriet could not imagine her mother in Japan, among Buddhists.

"Mom was allowed to sit with her family and offered incense to the deceased at the wake. At the funeral, she placed flowers around her brother's head. She considered it a great honor."

"Her family?"

"He was her elder brother, you know. He was a soldier fighting in Chungking when Dad took Mom away."

"Mom never spoke about a brother."

"Remember, except for her mom, her family saw her as sleeping with the enemy."

"I can't imagine." Years of sadness suddenly took on a new reality. Her mother's silence, head hung in shame. Her father's strict adherence to routine. The many years he left her alone to care for the family.

"I never knew."

Joey nodded.

"When she comes home, I feel like I owe her an apology. All those years, I've never understood."

"If she comes home..."

Harriet, startled, looked up at her brother. Joe had insisted that his wife be back by the end of the month. He had bought her a return ticket at the same time that he had agreed to her unexpected trip.

"If?"

"Don't you ever think that maybe, for Mom, Japan is home? Maybe, she's been waiting for a chance to go back?"

"That's ridiculous. Sunnyvale is home. Mom would never leave her family." For all those years, Harriet had tried to protect her mother. Sacrificing for home and family. Now her brother was suggesting that her mother might leave them behind, abandon her. Strangely, Harriet was not angry. Instead, the emotion that overtook her was jealousy. Her mother had a life to return to, a world so different from the world that they had shared.

Joey raised his eyebrows, watching his sister's face and unable to read her reaction. "Maybe, if Dad had gone with her..."

That ended the conversation. They both knew that Joe would never have accompanied his wife to the funeral. That might have required an apology and if there was one thing that Joe Jackson never did, it was apologize.

***

"Gregg says the Seed is going to explode." Zach had convinced Bobby that the time had come to move their company out of the two rooms they had rented in the Orchard Industrial Park, but he had yet to succeed in prying his partner away from his keyboard.

Gregg, a chip industry veteran, had been working on a business plan with Zach. "He's projecting $500 million in sales over the next ten years."

"What have you been smoking?" Bobby looked up from his computer, sure his partner was joking.

"I'm not shitting you." Zach was wearing the designer suit and tie he had bought for entertaining potential investors. He was freshly shaved and had spent $50 on a haircut. Bobby, in his usual jeans and red-and-black-striped t-shirt, had kicked off his huarache sandals and walked barefoot over to the mini refrigerator. He depended on an endless supply of Diet Coke to keep him going. "We're going to be millionaires," Zach repeated. "Time to get this show on the road.

Bobby couldn't care less about real estate. All he required was a computer and a screen, but he understood the need to ramp up production if they were going to sell the computer kit he had designed. He preferred that someone else took care of the details. Gregg, who had offered to get the ball rolling with an investment of $250,000, provided the business expertise and the direction that they needed if they were going to incorporate into a legitimate business.

"This is where it starts, my friend," Zach said now. The computer kit that Bobby had designed was scheduled to go on sale for $750. "We've projected revenue to double every six months."

Bobby had already moved beyond the kit. He was hard at work on the color graphics of the Seed II which he planned to introduce at the California Computer Fair. He had been working on the design of a removable floppy drive for storage of data and a program that would use spreadsheets to store numerical data.

"I don't have the time to go shopping for office space. Can't you and Gregg handle it?"

"Done, my friend." Zach produced a signed lease with an exaggerated flourish. "We're moving on up," he sang, Jeffersons-style. The eight-room office suite was available immediately. "And one other thing..." Gregg had suggested they hire at least two additional people to assemble the kits for sale. "I've hired Lara. She can keep the books," Zach added. "We need to keep an eye on the bottom line if we're going to get funding for your Seed II."

Lara, who, as far as Bobby knew, had never held a full-time job, seemed an unlikely choice for a bookkeeper. Amy would certainly have been a better choice, but rather than argue, Bobby nodded in agreement; Zach knew how to make a sale.

They hired two more of their friends from the Cock-Eyed Computer Club before moving into the new offices as well as a manager recommended by Gregg.

The day they packed the final box, Jack visited the office, looking bereft. "I'm gonna miss working with you kids," he said. Alice had reclaimed her garage. "I already miss the days when we worked together until midnight." He bent to pick up one of the cartons. "I'm thrilled at your success, but I have to admit, Alice is happy to have her house back."

It had been several months since Alice had urged Bobby to return to college. Jack told his son that he had assured her that Bobby was on the right track. Begrudgingly she had admitted that the projected revenue for his new company was impressive.

"And that Amy. She's a keeper," she said this to Bobby every time she got the chance. "Feel free to bring her by for dinner anytime."

"Don't worry about it, Mom. I think I can afford to buy her dinner now." In fact, Bobby had rented a new, larger apartment around the corner from the new office so that he wouldn't have to waste time commuting. In addition to a large master bedroom, the apartment had a second bedroom where he could set up a home office. He knew that Amy was hoping that he would ask her to marry him. The commodious apartment was clearly a step in that direction. For now, though, the move would have to be enough. When he had a little more time, he would have to decide whether he was ready to commit to sharing his life with the diminutive Star Trek fan. Right now, he could barely keep up with the changes taking place at the Seed. His life was rapidly spinning out of his control.

1980

Zach opened the bottle of Dom Perignon.

"Hey, man," Bobby protested, bending over to shelter his workbench from the spray. When Zach burst into his workspace, Bobby had been reviewing the latest prototypes for the Seed III, checking the color resolution, evaluating how much speed had been compromised.

Zach had received a confirmation from their broker. The Seed IPO had raised $100 million dollars.

Nattily dressed in a turtleneck and khaki pants, Zach shook hands with each of the 18 employees in the room. He was the benevolent CEO. Each of them was now a multi-millionaire. Bobby, in his usual ratty jeans and t-shirt, took a moment to realize what was going on. He had been in the middle of a calculation and was reluctant to stop midstream.

"We did it!" Zach shook his partner's shoulders, "Wake up, man. This is huge."

Caterers entered the room dressed in black and white and carrying more champagne and trays of finger food.

Employees continued to gather as the news traveled throughout the building.

"Reporters will be here any minute," Zach announced. *MachineWorld*, the computer magazine based in Palo Alto, wanted to do a group shot for the cover. Seed, the reporter had told Zach over the phone, was emblematic of the explosive emergence of the microcomputer industry in the valley.

"Explosive," Zach said now, opening his fingers like fireworks lighting up the night sky.

Bobby got it. He was dancing to the music, cranking up the sound system.

Zach twirled around in dizzying circles. Queen sang "Another One Bites the Dust." "I love you, man," he said, bear-hugging Bobby and then leading the other employees in a conga line around the lab.

"Captains of industry," he said.

"Knights of the realm," they replied.

Bobby drained his glass of champagne, taking off his fingerprint-smudged eyeglasses and rubbing them clean so that he could watch the celebration more clearly.

Last year, Zach had almost walked out of the business in a dispute over expansion slots. Zach wanted two; Bobby wanted six. "Go get yourself another computer," Bobby had said in the heat of the moment.

But that was behind them now. The phones were ringing off the hook.

Real estate agents eager to sell them houses appropriate to their new status.

High-end car salesmen ready to take them for a ride.

Architects hard at work designing an appropriate campus for the Seed Headquarters.

"I'm going to buy myself a plane," Bobby announced jubilantly. He was flying now. He'd take Amy to visit Patty in New York. Hell, he'd take her to Paris and propose to her in the shadow of the Eiffel Tower.

The sky was the limit.

Bobby headed home at 2 a.m., short of sloppy drunk. Fortunately, the usually congested streets of Silicon Valley were clear of traffic early in the morning. Without the steady stream of headlights, stars burned brighter overhead. He would travel among them, examine the heavens, free to fly wherever he pleased. First, though, he needed to figure out why the Seed III kept overheating whenever he attempted to upload the latest version of their software.

✳✳✳

Amy insisted that Bobby hire a financial advisor. "We have to be smart about how we invest the IPO money," she said, flipping through a jewelry catalog and folding down the corners of pages that displayed wedding rings that she admired. The IPO had earned Bobby $116 million dollars. Catalogs overflowed their bedside table.

Christmas was coming. Amy had never been subtle. Bobby pulled the blanket up over his head. The phone rang.

"You take it," Amy said.

Bobby should have told her not to answer the phone. Since the IPO, he seldom answered the phone at all, leaving it to Amy to keep the world at bay. Lately, there had been overtures from long-lost friends who "had been thinking about him." Now that his name was a household word, he was determined to distance himself from forgotten friends and his family's never-ending drama.

Amy handed the receiver to Bobby, no longer bothering to curry favor with his family. Like Bobby, Amy had learned to screen his mother's phone calls, judge her level of sobriety. She never had time for Patty's enthusiastic late-night rants.

"He's dead," Patty sobbed as soon as he said hello.

John Lennon had been shot by a fan outside his apartment building in New York City. The rock star was pronounced dead on arrival at Roosevelt Hospital.

Bobby groaned. Even over the phone, Patty sucked the air out of a room. He didn't need his sister's drama. Patty, who had remained a big fan, took the murder personally.

"Poor Yoko," Patty said. "What happens to their double fantasy now?"

Like John Lennon, his sister had made New York her home. When he and Amy had visited on their way to Paris to celebrate the IPO, John Lennon, in his NYC t-shirt, had smiled from a poster on Patty's wall, right above her law school textbooks, across from the bed which she shared, she had proudly announced, with her lover, Robin.

The implication had been clear. Bobby might be rich, but Patty was in love. John had Yoko Ono, his soul mate for whom he was willing to sacrifice fame and fortune. Patty had Robin, who worked for a foreign policy think tank. Despite Bobby's recent success, Patty dominated the conversation later that afternoon as they drank vodka in the Russian Tea Room on 57th Street. Amy insisted on ordering caviar, more intent on swirling the little fish eggs in sour cream than following the conversation. She had spent the afternoon shopping on Fifth Avenue. A line of bags from Saks lay at her feet.

He hadn't been able to decide which woman ticked him off more.

Amy was certainly no Yoko. At first, he had been proud to have his best friend on his arm for those first press photos, but Amy's companionship was becoming suspect. Some days he was convinced that she was in love with his new-found fame and fortune more than the penniless engineer she had met in the bank. They hadn't watched *Star Trek* together for months.

Now he listened to Patty bemoan her loss and felt a stab of sympathy. "Last night, I was listening to Lennon's *Double Fantasy*," his sister sniffed back tears. "Such a brave album, opening up John and Yoko's inner life like a wound." Amy turned over and placed a pillow over her head to shut out the noise. "It's like John was speaking directly to me. "

Bobby had to admit, seeing Patty in love and filled with enthusiasm, had been a highlight of the trip to Paris.

In France, Amy had insisted on a whirlwind of sight-seeing and serious shopping. Since their return from Paris, conversations with Amy had centered on acquisitions which she deemed necessary for their new status in life. Designer dresses, luxury apartments, purchases that would appropriately reflect his success. And of course, endless discussions about marriage and the possibility of having a baby.

Success—even the word was beginning to piss Bobby off.

Before hanging up, Patty inhaled raggedly and encouraged him to "Come visit often. I miss you." He assured her that he would, as soon as he got his pilot's license. He was, after all, family. Then again, he had a company to run and a girlfriend who, at this very moment, was flipping through real estate ads. Bobby took away the newspaper and put his arms around Amy. "Poor Patty," he said—and, swept up in a wave of sympathy for his lovelorn sister, "Should I get a condom?"

Amy wiggled from his grasp and faced him. "Is that really necessary?" she wheedled, her tone flirtatious but her expression dead serious. "We have all the money that parenting could possibly require."

With a sigh of exasperation, Bobby turned over and clicked off the light.

The persistent financial adviser that Amy had contacted, a fast-talking MBA named Stan, began to call them, every Monday at 9 a.m. to update them on "wise" investment opportunities. Strategic investments where wealthy investors could "park " their windfall in a safe, tax-free haven.

Before agreeing to look at the advisor's proposals, Bobby placed an order for his plane. A turbo-charged single-engine, six-seat Beechcraft Bonanza A36TC. As a boy, Bobby had shut himself in his bedroom to escape his family's drama, now he suspected he would need the whole sky to hide in.

Most of the advisor's recommendations lacked inspiration. Amy insisted that Bobby peruse the proposals before they went to bed each night. Commodities like oil and precious metals, stock in faceless conglomerates and schemes offered by private equity firms. One night he saw the pitch for the theater. Located in downtown Sunnyvale, the building was rundown but strategically located. Minimal investment, maximal return, the request for proposal touted the acquisition's value. Bobby examined the photo, an idea taking shape as he reviewed the terms. He could easily hire a contractor to do the necessary renovations. Open the theater as something more upscale which might appeal to the Valley's changing demographics. An art theater maybe. A venue sure to inspire.

Bobby decided then and there to buy the theater. He would personally plan a Science Fiction marathon to take place when the theater reopened.

The more he thought about it, the more excited he got.

"We'll host the opening night," he told Amy over drinks the next night after work. They sat at the bar of one of the many restaurants that had recently opened in the shadow of the busy Seed campus. "A red-carpet gala." He could see that the idea appealed to her; their wealthy new friends walking the carpet like paparazzi, flashbulbs popping. "We'll showcase *Star Trek*," After all, the mythic story had brought them together. Maybe, its reprisal might re-ignite the magic of their early relationship.

"After the opening," he said, on a roll now, "I'll fly you to Montana." By then he would have flown 50 hours with an instructor. He was ready to pilot his plane on his own.

Amy had an uncle in Montana who made custom jewelry. She mentioned him often, unveiled hints that it was time for Bobby to commit. None of the wedding rings she had marked in her stack of catalogs compared in originality or beauty to her uncle's stellar work. The small diamond engagement ring Bobby had once pointed out to her at the mall paled in the light of their new circumstances. Her uncle had offered to work with them on a personalized design.

Bobby swallowed. He imagined taxiing down the runway, gaining speed in preparation for takeoff. Amy at his side, their whole life in front of them. What was he afraid of? When he said, "The trip could be the start of something good," Amy jumped into his arms with a girlish squeal. "We're engaged," she announced to the patrons of the bar, unable to contain her excitement.

"No *Star Trek* crap," she whispered to him when the applause died down. While he accepted the congratulations from strangers, she began sketching interlocking ring designs on her napkin.

"I bet Yoko didn't give a hoot about a ring," he whispered, settling in beside her. And then, louder, so the patrons of the bar could hear. "What's important is that we do this together. Like John and Yoko. Share a vision for a better world."

Right on cue, the jukebox began to play "Imagine."

Under her breath, Amy added, "John and Yoko had a son, so obviously there's more to love than idealism."

He'd forgotten all about Sean. Would he ever be able to please her?

No matter. They ordered drinks all around. By the end of the evening, Bobby was hugging strangers, and sharing his vision of a downtown theater that would bring the arts to Sunnyvale, his enthusiasm confirmed by Amy's happy glow and the patron's boozy benevolence.

"Trust me, baby," she said when they arrived home long after midnight, arm in arm. "Ours will be a journey that makes even *Star Trek* fade in comparison." She could not have chosen more perfect words to seal the deal.

"Merry Christmas," he said, carrying her to bed, loving the smallness of her, the ease with which she guided him inside her. This time, he didn't bother to ask about a condom.

"Let's make love like married people," she said, and, for better or worse, he did.

***

"The key," Max told the class "is responding to your attacker's movements in a way that enables you to control their actions."

Eddie stood in front of the dojo, poised to demonstrate, his black belt secured around his waist. He carefully avoided looking at his aunt who sat among the students, cross-legged on the floor.

Besides Harriet, most of the students were children, giggling in the bright white jackets of their uniforms. Harriet, too, wore a *dogi;* she was one of only a few adults in the class. Two young women had introduced themselves as interested in self-defense and three teenage boys looked too eager for a fight. Max had asked her if she wanted to join the beginner's class. He would have been happy to tutor her himself, but Harriet insisted on being treated like everyone else. She looked forward to being a student again, at last. Standing among the others in her white pants and jacket, she relished her anonymity.

When she had paid for the class, Rita looked over her registration slip. "Feeling a need to defend yourself?" The surly woman chuckled as she wrote out the receipt, more words than Harriet had heard from her in all the years Eddie had attended the dojo. She examined Harriet's check, turning it over as if suspecting it was counterfeit, and then dismissed her. "Good luck, you'll need it." Once again, Harriet wondered why the bookkeeper was entrusted with the Dojo's income.

"In Aikido," Max continued, "we study both the physical and mental aspects of training. We start by learning how to safely fall or roll. When you have mastered the fall, we move on to strikes and grabs, throws and pins."

Wordlessly, Eddie gave an example of each of the techniques they would learn. His opponent, a fellow student from the academy, allowed himself to be tackled and pinned to the floor. Eddie's face remained expressionless, almost robotic, as he executed each technique in slow motion. The demonstration reminded Harriet of ballet, the rhythm of bare feet on the mat, the carefully aligned posture of the combatants. Her nephew's mastery of the art was flawless.

After the demonstration, each student was assigned a partner. Harriet was relieved to be paired up with the mother of a young boy who sat on a bench at the side of the room.

"Almost every technique you will learn involves a fall," Max said. "This is where we begin. A successful fall is elegant and well-executed."

Harriet's head pounded from the intense concentration required, but by the end of the class she had successfully executed several of the falls. She faithfully imitated Eddie, moving her hands in a circle, pushing with her legs into a forward roll, placing her weight on her shoulders so that her head did not contact the floor.

"Falls depend on the attack."

Harriet's partner went through the motions but lacked Harriet's commitment.

"My son adores Eddie," the woman said. "And I liked the idea of defending myself, but this is a little more than I anticipated." Harriet was careful not to push the woman too far. She was obviously delicate and not about to fall.

"I think it's back to the gym for me," her partner said, at the end of the class, her words like an apology to Harriet who she clearly viewed as invested in the dojo.

Harriet understood the woman's hesitation, but she found the lesson empowering. The intensity in the eyes of the teenage boys at the mention of an attack, oddly thrilling. The teenagers were only a little older than Eddie, yet in them, she sensed an undertone of violence, a titillation that the careful choreography of the movements could not disguise.

After class, the boys clustered at the wall where weapons were displayed. While Max chatted with the parents of the younger students, Eddie explained the use of the Aikido weapons to the older boys, teaching them the terminology, having them repeat *Jo* when he lifted the staff, *Tanto* when he held up the knife and the *Bokken* when he took the sword off of the wall.

At twelve, Eddie was as tall as any of the students and his confident routine granted him total control of the room. The Japanese terms he used during his demonstration were fluent. He spoke comfortably of the cultural heritage of aikido.

Only Eddie was allowed to touch the weapons. Eddie explained to the students that the weapons in aikido were never intended for combat. Holding the *Bokken* in his hand, he reminded the students that its purpose was for teaching the important principles of control, responsibility, *irimi isoku* (entering in an instant), and *awase* (blending and harmonizing). Eddie had studied for many years before Max had instructed him in the use of the weapons. Those sessions had been private, serious, and intimate. Even Harriet had been banned from observing. The one-on-one sessions had been the ultimate demonstration of the trust Max had placed in Eddie.

In the car on the way home, Harriet asked Max about the role aggression played in the study of Aikido. Max reminded her that aikido was a discipline. Only the most dedicated devotees progressed far enough to handle weapons. There was no denying, however, that they were part of the lure that kept the undisciplined students coming back for more.

"Eddie is the exception. His focus was amazing from day one. I am proud to have him as my apprentice."

In class, Eddie had called Max "Sensei."

Watching the interaction between the two, Harriet sensed an intimacy far more profound than she had with the instructor. Max explained to her that the relationship he had with Eddie was integral to aikido. A Sensei often selects a *jikideshi* or personal pupil to mentor. It is not unusual for this student to be groomed to become the next head of the school.

"But Eddie's only 12," Harriet said. Max's intensity alarmed her. "Besides, you better not go anyplace until I earn my brown belt."

"No worries, Auntie Harry," Max teased. He hadn't called her that for in a while. Perhaps joining the class had not been such a great idea. Max refused to take her seriously.

If her nephew could become a *jikideshi*, Auntie Harry could at least learn to harness her own strength. Max could laugh at her as much as he wanted, but he wasn't about to stop her.

That night, bruises bloomed on Harriet's skin. During the week that followed the black faded to blue and then red followed by green and finally a sickly yellow. She admired each bruise like a badge of accomplishment, something she had done, not for others, but for herself.

When she showed the discolorations to Max, he laughed at her determination and asked what she was preparing for dinner. When it came to food, he always called her "Babe."

***

Joe said he would be eating dinner at the base. He told Harriet he was meeting with buddies from the "good old days," but Joey didn't believe him. He figured his father probably had a girlfriend on the side. "It isn't like Dad to remain idle. Something is occupying his time and keeping him on the ground."

Harriet, arriving home after her aikido class, listened for her father's footsteps and let out a sigh of relief. She was beginning to enjoy a quiet house. Taking a yogurt out of the refrigerator, she stretched out on the recliner normally reserved for her father.

"Think about it," Joey said, joining her with a box of pizza he had picked up on the way home from school. "Dad doesn't ask about Mom anymore. He knows I call her on Sundays, but he doesn't ask when she's coming home. And he certainly doesn't make any effort to call her himself."

"It's his pride. He doesn't like to beg. I'm sure he's as anxious as we are for her to come home."

Joe wasn't the only family member with secrets. Joey had been accepted to Swarthmore College where he had applied because of their exchange relationship with the University of Tokyo. He intended to continue his study of Japanese there but hadn't gotten up the nerve yet to ask his father if he would be willing to contribute to his tuition. Fortunately, Mr. Ito was helping him apply for financial aid.

"Ask him," Harriet said. Joe had taken out a second mortgage on the house for Mike and Kat to buy them the gas station. He had even helped Kevin out when he ran short on funds for his newest race car. Certainly, her father would be proud of her brother's accomplishments.

Besides, the value of the house kept going up and up. Her father certainly could afford to pay his share.

"I'm not counting on it," Joey said.

Harriet and Joey turned on the TV to watch *Bosom Buddies*, the shenanigans of two men dressed as women. At first, they didn't notice when Joe arrived home, smelling of beer, and royally pissed.

Then they did, with alarm.

Joe stood in the doorway, a menacing shadow.

"She's not coming home."

"Who's not coming home?"

"Your mother." Joe opened the refrigerator. "I see you don't bother cooking anymore, Harriet."

"Dad, what are talking about?"

"I called your mother and told her to come home." Joe opened a beer and helped himself to a piece of Joey's pizza. "Your mother says she's not coming back."

"Dad, I'm sure she didn't mean it."

"What the hell do you know?" her father's words were as painful as a slap. "After all I've done for the bitch, she's decided she needs to stay with her mother." Joe shot an angry look at Joey as if he too were complicit. "Well, I told her..." Harriet was afraid her father was going to punch a wall. He was coiled so tight that she could see the blood pulsing blue on his forehead.

"It's over." His voice the bark of a commander, don't-argue-with-me or else. "We're getting divorced. What use is she to me now?"

"C'mon, Dad. Her brother just died."

"Her brother called me the bloody devil. She couldn't wait to run home to her precious family. I should have thrown her out a long time ago. Fuck!" He threw his beer can into the sink. "I'm such an idiot."

Harriet was speechless. Joey kept giving her looks that said *I told you so.* Harriet, rehearsing defensive aikido moves in her head, watched her father pace like a caged cat. What a joke; she would never be able to resist him with her own strength. He could break her in two. Looking at them with undisguised disgust, Joe picked up his keys. "That's that. I just thought you kids should know. I can't stand to be in this house right now."

He gunned his engine as he pulled out of the driveway. They could hear his muffler fade away into the distance.

"That was fun," Joey said.

"Do you think he means it?" Harriet asked.

"I know he does." Joey looked at her, gauging her reaction. "Mom must be so relieved."

"What are you talking about?"

Joey shifted in his chair stalling. Then he turned to her and looked directly into her eyes. "When Mom went home, she started spending time with a man she knew in high school. That's why she is staying in Japan. I think that Mom is in love."

Harriet put her face in her hands. Everything she thought she knew was a lie.

"Believe me, Dad is no saint. They'll both be better off." Joey sat down beside her and took her hand. "Harry, this is a good thing. You're almost 30 years old. You have a boyfriend. Mom and Dad have treated you like a slave for too long. Kat and Mike have been more than happy to pick up where they left off, letting you practically raise their son. This could be your chance to begin living a life of your own."

Her brother was young. What did he know? "Joey, that is not who I am. I love taking care of all of you. And Max and I aren't serious."

Her brother's look, more pity than sympathy, broke her heart.

"That bastard will end up on his feet."

"Or ship out any day now," she said, trying to smile.

"Yeah, that's about right," her brother answered, turning up the TV volume.

✳✳✳

But Joe didn't go back to flying right away.

The next morning, he invited Harriet to lunch at the base. "There are some things we need to talk about, honey," he said in the early morning phone call.

All morning, Harriet had listed the possibilities. He had accepted a pilot's position for a commercial airline; he was selling the house. After dropping Eddie off at school, she made sure to put the house in order and planned an elaborate dinner to demonstrate that she was the one her father could depend on, that he would always have a home to return to.

In darker moments, she wondered if he would be alone when she met him. Or if, as was often the case, he would be surrounded by officers from his days in command. If there would be a woman among them.

But Joe was by himself, enveloped in cigarette smoke and looking raggedly hung over when she arrived. "Hey, Honey." He stood up and pulled her chair out for her. To her surprise, her father looked embarrassed. "Sorry about last night. Your mom caught me off-guard."

Harriet waited. This time she knew better than to come to her mother's defense.

"It's just you and me now, Pumpkin," he said.

She looked at the menu.

"I met with my lawyer this morning. I've decided I'm not going to contest the divorce."

Wait. Had Hiroko initiated last night's discussion? Harriet felt herself softening. "Daddy, I'm so sorry."

Joe's face flashed "Don't go there," and Harriet concentrated on drinking her iced tea.

"You know you are the one I have always depended on." At the familiar phrase, Harriet struggled to swallow. Unspoken retorts stuck in her throat like un-chewed meat. She coughed but said nothing. Every response that occurred to her she knew she would regret.

"I'll give your mother a small settlement. Nothing more than I have to by law."

Harriet nodded, studying her hamburger like a map.

"There are some other legalities I have to attend to. I'm leaving the house to you in my will. The other kids have gotten their share when they needed it and I know I can trust you to keep the family together if anything were to happen to me."

"Daddy! It's bad enough that Mom's is gone..."

"I know, sweetheart, it's just a technicality. But I want you to know that I'll always take care of you. I know how much you have sacrificed for the family."

There was a time when his words would have warmed her, but now Harriet trembled. Maybe it was the air conditioning. She recalled her brother telling her about the Japanese attitude of *Taisho*. Now, her mother's lesson in stoicism was there to hold her up. She smiled gently at her misguided father and said softly "Thank you."

Joe ate his hamburger as if he had some place else to be. Harriet no longer cared where. She did, however, decide there was one more question she needed to ask.

"Dad, one other thing."

"Yes, Love."

"You know that Joey has been accepted to college, a good one. Do you think you could take out a mortgage on the house to help pay his tuition next year?"

Joe responded immediately.

"Not on your life. If Joey would enlist like I told him, he could request assignment to the Army Language School at the Presidio. It's a fine program and it wouldn't cost me a dime." Her father struggled to maintain his calm, but anger reddened his face.

"Dad, please. You know there is equity in the house. House prices in Sunnyvale just keep going up and up."

"Honey, don't be a softie." Joe signaled for the check dismissively.

"Harriet, you are too good for your own sake." He reached for her hand. "I worry that people can too easily take advantage of you." Harriet did not move her hand away, but she thought of her aikido holds, wondering which might bring him to his knees."

"Like Max. One day we really should talk about Max."

And that did it. Before he could see the tears in her eyes, she pushed away her plate, food uneaten, and stood up.

She had already turned her back to her father when she thanked him one more time for lunch.

The bastard, she thought as she walked out of the room, the selfish bastard.

✳✳✳

Amy vomited as soon as they arrived at the airport. She doubled over in the shadow of a sign which proclaimed "Welcome, Pilots Center." Bobby paced outside the small white service building with its friendly blue trim. He listened to her retching inside. The sound made the coffee he had drunk in the pilots' lounge turn to acid in his stomach. Just what he needed on such a momentous day.

He had planned the trip for months. A leisurely drive up the coast, a romantic night in the picturesque inn and spa. He had booked massages for the night before their flight to Montana, planning to take off from the Scott Valley Airport.

Instead, Amy canceled the massages and perched on the king size bed with its view of Mt. Shasta, announced that she was pregnant. Sick as a dog. She emerged from the bathroom of their tastefully appointed room, ignored his suggestion that she might feel better after a soak in the outside hot tub or sauna, and said: "Do we really have to do this?" She pursed a napkin over her mouth, prepared to spew at any moment. Clumps of vomit clung to her hair.

The champagne remained on ice. Of course, she couldn't drink now.

This was supposed to be his maiden voyage. With 50 hours of instruction under his belt, Bobby had been cleared to fly on his own at last. His plane was waiting. Fueled, serviced and parked in one of the tie-down spaces on the apron adjacent to the scenic one-thousand-foot runway of the airport.

Amy had been dead set on getting pregnant. He was doing this for her. When she made her announcement, he responded that he had no intention of canceling the flight.

The sympathetic innkeeper gave them a box of crackers for their journey. Bobby handed Amy one now, trying to ignore the green tinge of her skin, the miserable downturn of her dry, white lips as she emerged from the airport service building.

"I'm sure you'll feel better by the time we are in the air." His heart pounded at the prospect of taking his seat in the cockpit. She wasn't going to take this moment away from him. To placate her, he said. "Your uncle will be thrilled to hear the news."

She chewed at the cracker, her face scrunched up, miserable. "Well, I hope somebody is," she said. He pointed to the vomit in her hair, and she used her napkin to dab at the stinky curd.

She had been fine the night of his theater's opening, dressed to the nines, and holding court in the lobby of the recently renovated building. Explaining to the assembled press that *Star Trek* had always played an important role in their relationship, that her "fiancé" was a man of rare vision—as if that meant something to her.

"We're flying our plane to Montana," she said. "Bobby is becoming quite the pilot." Their financial adviser, Stan, had been there too, recruiting clients from among Bobby's Seed colleagues. Just as the opening credits of *Star Trek* began to roll, Stan had cornered Bobby. "We really need to discuss real estate," but Bobby had shaken him off, annoyed to miss even a minute of the movie he loved.

Amy and Stan had spent much of the evening together while Bobby gravitated to an enthusiastic cluster of science fiction nerds, those wealthy enough to have been invited (many recipients of funds from the Seed IPO themselves). He bragged about the upcoming movies he had booked, his goal of growing their community of like-minded fans. For the first time since laboring with Zach in his parent's garage, he had ridden the wave of possibilities, optimistic and ambitious. Psyched about the trip he had planned and thrilled at the prospect of his upcoming flight. It had required every ounce of self-control he could muster not to brag about his good fortune.

He should have enjoyed himself while he had the opportunity.

Now he insisted they walk to the plane. He wanted to cherish every moment of his first flight. Amy moaned when he insisted she climb up the plane's stairs. Determined to distract her, he babbled on about the plane's outstanding craftsmanship, the power of the piston engine. "First-class technology, comfort and world-class quality," he said, quoting the brochure to the back of Amy's matted head. The Bonanza took his breath away, even now, and he trusted in its allure, but Amy slumped down angrily into the seat beside him and stared gloomily out the window.

He handed her a vomit bag, relieved to see that a stack of the small white bags had been stowed in a pocket in front of her seat.

All around them, nothing but open sky.

"The views on takeoff are spectacular," he enthused, proceeding methodically through his checklist. "We'll go right around Mt. Shasta and over Kangaroo Lake."

He started the engine. The plane seemed to shake itself awake and then purred in readiness. Amy held the vomit bag to her mouth, refusing to look at him. He was determined that she would not spoil this moment. He watched the propeller begin to spin. Here, at last, he was the master of his own domain. He had done the work, put in his time, was fully prepared. Despite Amy's gloom, he gave in to the exhilaration of control as he began to taxi down the scenic runway, watching the console dials move as the Bonanza gained speed.

"Yahoo!," he yelped, pointing the plane's nose into the clear blue sky, aiming for the heavens. Higher. He would show Amy the liberation of leaving the earth behind. He needed her to understand. He jerked the plane's silver nose up even higher, ignoring the alarm in Amy's eyes. He would climb higher, change her mind. He refused to give in to skepticism, tuned out her gasps of panic until the moment he too felt the plane stall. Shit. The engine died with a dull gasp.

The plane had almost cleared the car park of a skating rink. Later Bobby would wonder if Amy had accidentally leaned on the controls when she doubled up, preparing to vomit. He was certain he had not climbed too abruptly, but for whatever reason, the powerless plane tumbled back to earth, careened through two fences, metal crushing metal. Amy screamed as they came tumbling down, the plane rolling, its incomparable workmanship busted to pieces around them.

1990-4

With Harriet beside her in the passenger seat, Patty drove out of the valley, steering her blue Camry up into the foothills of the Santa Cruz Mountains on a two-lane street discretely dotted with the houses of the wealthy beneficiaries of Silicon Valley. By mid-afternoon, the daily fog bank had retreated towards the Pacific Ocean revealing Spanish Style mansions with impressive views. The properties' landscaping was impeccable. The houses' windows crystal clear.

Higher up, the narrow road meandered through redwood forests and golden hillsides where majestic oak trees towered over the ups and downs of untamed terrain. Grassy ridge tops overlooked ravines filled with the orange-red bark of madrones. The higher they went, the fewer houses they saw. Rolling down her window, Harriet inhaled breezes that hinted of the Pacific Ocean on the other side of the mountain range. Puffy clouds cast complex shadows on open fields of dry grass.

Harriet watched the valley disappear below her. She had no idea where Patty was taking her. The movement of the car soothed her; she didn't want to interrupt the calming silence. The events of the day, the closing, Eddie's desertion, and her realization that she was on her own overwhelmed any curiosity as to where they were heading.

Finally, Patty pulled into an unpaved parking lot with a sign indicating that they were in the Adobe Creek watershed of Hidden Valley Park.

"I have something I want to show you," Patty said. The two women walked up an unmarked trail until they arrived at a hilltop with 360-degree views.

"From here," Patty said, "you can see all the way from San Jose to San Francisco."

Harriet looked out in amazement. "My father must have seen views like this every time he flew." She said. "It makes the houses look pretty insignificant." Harriet took a deep breath of the pungent air. "The houses where we used to live, I mean."

"I come here often," Patty said, "to remind myself that I have choices. It's a big world out there."

Harriet turned to the lawyer.

"Do you think I am an awful person, leaving my nephew hanging like that?"

"Honey, your nephew is a strong confident man. Talented, I'm told. He'll land on his feet. I'd bet anything on it."

"And it's legal to hold on to the money?"

"The money is yours. The house's title was in your name, no one else's. Your family had no right to ask you to give it away."

"My sister never forgave my dad for giving me the house. She was adamant that the house belonged to all of us."

"But your father knew you had earned it. Harriet, you know that." Patty watched Harriet's face, waiting for acknowledgment. At first, Harriet seemed ready to protest but then a quiet smile settled on her troubled face.

Patty stood up. "Before the sun sets, there is another special place I want to share with you."

Skyline Boulevard traversed the ridge of the mountains that separated the bay area from the Pacific Ocean. Patty stopped the car at a bucolic overlook with views of lush forests of pine and redwood trees fading into the Pacific Ocean.

"I come here whenever I have decisions to make."

Harriet was mesmerized by the sea. "I would never have dreamed the ocean was so close," she said.

Fog flirted with the coastline.

"The beach is the perfect place to clear your head."

Neither Patty nor Harriet mentioned her nephew again. Harriet watched the sunset to the West, sinking below a horizon that she had never seen before, that had been hidden behind a mountain range she had never had a chance to explore.

"Isn't the San Andreas Fault around here somewhere?" Harriet asked.

"Why?"

"I remember Bobby telling me that there is a park up here where a fence straddles the fault."

"Knowing my brother, he probably stood with one foot on either side, just so that he could say that he had."

"It's just science," Harriet said, imitating the young boy. Patty laughed, relishing the memory they shared. Her brother had always believed that there was a scientific explanation for everything.

"This is crazy," Harriet said to Patty. "I don't even know where I'm going to sleep tonight. All my things are at Kat's, and I can't imagine how I'm going to face her now.

"There's no rush," Patty said. "I know where you can stay until you get your bearings.

It was dark by the time they drove down the mountain. Only the ebbing moon and the lights of houses discretely tucked into the hillside marked their passage. Long before they descended into the glowing lights of the busy valley, Patty turned into a long driveway that led to an expansive, three-story house built into the hillside. Marble stairs lined with dwarf plum trees led up to a two-story entryway which glowed in the darkness like a beacon.

"My brother's house," Patty said, parking the car next to the three-car garage. "He won't even notice you're here."

1982

Bobby's head ached.   His head always ached. Air closed in on him like an invisible wall, pulsing pain through his veins. The throbbing never went away. He couldn't remember his own name.

A baboon stomped around his hospital room, eyes bright in its furry, or was it furious, brown head. It declared that God was dead, and doctors were his sad successors.

If only Coltrane would leave out the high notes that threatened to split his tender skull. The horn's screech painted the inside of his eye sockets redder than the display on the giant computer screen that the doctors insisted on mounting on his wall.

He couldn't uncode their coding. He didn't understand what the baboon was trying to tell him.

"I was standing in the subway car with one hand wrapped around a dirty metal pole to keep my balance and the other shielding my briefcase from the press of the crowd," the ape said. "A man sitting in front of me opened his newspaper to the business section and your ugly face stared back at me from the other side of the page."

Bobby tried to focus, but Coltrane and Mahler competed for his attention. His head was twice its normal size, wrapped like a mummy in white bandages. The voice implied that the National Safety Board suspected that his inexperience as a pilot had led to the crash that landed him in this room.

Even in his compromised state, muddled by pain medication, Bobby knew that his sister's presence at his side signaled that something was very wrong.

Patty. Why was she here? Where was he? Why couldn't she be quiet?

He preferred silence. It hurt less. He cherished the days when the only people who entered his hospital room were nurses. He liked the swish of white uniforms, the business-like quality with which medical personnel checked his monitors. Smooth days, unlike those when the woman named Amy, a small twitchy thing, sat at his bedside checking her watch.

Another woman who said she was his mother had a pungent, familiar smell. A man with glasses often accompanied her. Only the man did not make the pain worse. He didn't expect anything from him. When Jack sat by Bobby's bedside, the orchestra played more softly. Coltrane blew whispers that sounded like lullabies.

He was coming along. That's what they all told him. There was an airplane crash. He was going to be alright.

That's what Patty was saying when he opened his eyes.

"You're going to be alright.

"Mom told me you were in the hospital. Stanford, the best. She said you don't remember the night of the accident."

"I cleaned up the guest room for her," the white-haired woman next to her added. In a rare moment of clarity, Bobby thought: The guest room, that's Patty's old bedroom. He was sure, it was not in need of cleaning.

Since the accident, Bobby's life had dissolved into a painful blur. He woke up each morning unable to remember what had taken place the day before. He couldn't remember his girlfriend's name or whether she had been in the single-engine plane when it had crashed.

There was something familiar, though, about having his family here at his side, his sister chattering on about who knows what, his parents watching her stiffly from the end of the bed. Something comforting that went way back. He tried to listen to Patty but eventually, he succumbed to a wave of exhaustion. The last thing he heard before drifting off was Patty chirping away about robins. A*h, spring must be coming at last.*

✳✳✳

The private nurse who had been hired to watch over Bobby, wheeled him through the maze-like ward to a sunny room, filled with cards and flowers. No more Critical Care: she was moving him to a private room, an important step, the doctors said, on the way to recovery. The young, but no-nonsense and efficient, nurse shifted him from the wheelchair to his bed, tucking him in securely. She plugged in his computer and placed the monitor on his bedside table. Once he was settled, the nurse sat in an armchair doing crossword puzzles, asking his advice on the toughest clues when she was unable to figure them out.

When his parents entered the room, Bobby didn't look up from the game he was playing on his computer.

"Look, Bobby," the nurse said brightly. "Your family has come to visit."

"Hi." The music from Bobby's computer game continued to tinkle merrily as he poked the computer's keys intently.

"I don't believe I know you?" the nurse extended her hand to Patty who was checking out the view from her brother's window. "I'm Trudy. Bobby's private duty nurse."

"I'm Patty, Bobby's sister."

At the sound of her voice, Bobby looked up. "Hey, Sis. What brings you to California?" His delighted smile made it clear that he had no memory of his sister's previous visits.

"Just thought I'd check out my brother now that's he's fallen from the sky," Patty said, handing him a box of Ghirardelli chocolates. He accepted them eagerly; this was the medication that he required.

Bobby's head was wrapped in bandages and an IV drip was taped to his arm, but beneath the bandages, Bobby was beginning to put the pieces back together again. When asked by his physician, he could list the essentials: He was Bobby Hopkins, the computer whiz. He had crashed his plane. His knew that Amy had been by his side and that she had yet to forgive him for the miscarriage she suffered after the accident.

Jack took Bobby's daily ups and downs in stride. "What game are you playing?" he asked, sitting down on his son's bed to get a better look.

The game, Bobby told him, was an upcoming Seed release. Playing helped him to restore his memory. He credited the program's repetition with healing powers that rebuilt synapses. The problem-solving that was required to progress from level to level was re-igniting his damaged brain.

As Jack watched Bobby progress from level to level, Alice and Patty chatted with the nurse, an attractive woman who appeared quite fond of Bobby.

"He's really made remarkable progress," Trudy reported. "Yesterday we walked to the solarium. He's beginning to talk about going home. Returning to work."

"Bobby," Patty said, "it's great to see you doing so well. You had us scared there for a while."

Bobby nodded briefly, still clicking away at the computer keys.

"Hanging in there," he replied. When Trudy asked, however, he didn't remember that his family had visited him every day during his lengthy hospitalization. Still, his daily progress was impressive.

Trudy reassured them that he was going to be okay. Alice eyed the nurse's hand, which rested on Bobby's thigh with a familiarity she didn't quite trust. There was no wedding ring on her finger.

"How's Amy?" she asked her son.

Bobby ignored the question, hooting with glee as he completed the final level of his game. "That's a record!" he shouted, and Trudy clapped in appreciation for all the progress he had made.

"Poor Amy," Alice said, tucking in the sheets of his bed and putting his bedside table in order.

"Let it go, Mom," Patty said. When, at last, it was time for his family to leave, Bobby breathed a sigh of relief. He turned to Trudy as the door shut behind them.

"Trudy," he said, "I have something I want to discuss with you."

✳✳✳

Joe invited all the kids over for dinner "like old times." "Make lasagna," he told Harriet. "We'll put the leaf back in the dining room table."

Harriet had finally gotten her brown belt. Since she had asked Max about Rita, he had been putting her through hell. The *Ki* tests, questions regarding meditation and a demonstration of breathing techniques had been the easy part. The *Jo Kata Two*, all twenty-two movements, had required every ounce of her strength and hours of practice. She suspected that the proposed dinner was her father's attempt to remind her that her proper place was at home.

Reluctantly Max had admitted that Rita was still his legal wife, if only because she owned half the business.

Unlike Eddie's promotions when he was a boy, no one from the Jackson family had been there to watch her take the rigorous test. No siblings witnessed her mastery of specific grasps, nor watched her defeat a standing attacker from a seated position. She had struggled for weeks with *Maegeri Kokyunage*, a front snapping kick and timing throw, spending every waking hour at the dojo. Eddie never gave her a break. Max insisted on perfection.

"I invited Kevin over and his new gal," Joe said when she arrived home. "Kat and Mike'll be over after they close up the gas station." Harriet had been hoping to take a long bath to soothe her aching muscles. Instead, she headed out to the supermarket to buy groceries.

When she returned, Eddie and Max were sitting in the living room with Joe discussing the 49ers. The Super Bowl champs had started spring training but there were rumors of a strike.

Harriet chopped onions and peppers for tomato sauce. She waited for Max to congratulate her on passing the test.

Mike arrived with a gallon of cheap wine. "Where do you keep the glasses these days?" Kat asked, digging in the drawer for a corkscrew. "I thought we'd never get here."

As a result of the gas shortage, all the local service stations were being required to implement odd-even gas rationing. "It's a madhouse," Mike said. "Price controls were bad enough, now we are expected to police gas lines."

Joe, overhearing their conversation, entered the kitchen and gave Kat a kiss. "You look beautiful, Darling," he said. As he watched his younger daughter pour the wine, he said: "This is such bullshit. The oil companies are creating shortages so they can jack up prices. Honest businessmen like Mike are the only ones that suffer."

Mike couldn't agree more. "The whole mess is a hoax. But tell that to the yuppies lining up at the station. You'd think I was personally responsible." During that morning's commute, the lines of cars at the station were more than a block long.

Kevin arrived last. He held the front door open for Mercedes, his latest, who handed Harriet a covered container. "Mercedes makes a killer flan," Kevin said. Harriet thanked the attractive Hispanic woman and placed the dessert on the counter. Mercedes flashed a model's smile at Joe, who was already pouring her a glass of wine. "I'm so happy to finally meet you." Glancing over at Harriet, busy layering noodles, cheese, and tomato sauce, he said to Mercedes, "It's hot in here. Come take a load off. It looks like it will be a while before we eat."

When the lasagna was finally in the oven, Harriet asked Eddie if he would set the table. Eddie and Max were whispering intently in the corner and didn't acknowledge her request, but Mercedes jumped in. "Let me give you a hand." Kevin kissed his girlfriend's fingers as she passed, never taking his eyes off the TV set.

"How long have you and Kevin been seeing each other?" Harriet asked.

"Six months. We met in Arizona at the Indy Car world series. Kevin placed 15th. By the time we finished partying, I had moved to California."

Harriet had heard this story before. Kevin demanded nothing more of his minor celebrity than a pretty girl to share it with. Mercedes, who seemed very sweet, was one in a series.

"Your brother is a real sweetheart," she said. "A cutie." Lowering her voice, "and a really sexy guy."

Max walked into the kitchen, looking for a refill. "How's dinner coming along, babe? I'm starved."

"Mercedes this is my aikido instructor, Max." Harriet could have said *boyfriend*. She waited to see if Max would tell Mercedes about Harriet's accomplishments during the day.

"Aikido? Is that like tai kwon do?" Mercedes asked.

And Max was off. Harriet had heard his lecture about aikido more times than she could count. Besides the lasagna was beginning to brown.

***

Over dinner, the family discussed the usual topics: car races, the 49ers, the price of gas. Joe hinted he might be flying again soon.

"McDonnell Douglas is recruiting test pilots for their Joint Task Force at Edwards Air Force Base."

"Test pilots?" Kevin asked, his interest peaked.

Max said, "Hey, Harry, do you have any garlic bread."

Joe was happy to explain. "The Air Force Logistics Command, Tactical Air Command, Army and the USMC have all assumed logistical roles in the military flight test program for new aircraft designs. The Air Force provides the facilities and chase aircraft, but McDonnell Douglas hires the engineering personnel and test pilots."

"Sorry, Max. No bread tonight." Joe's announcement didn't surprise Harriet. She figured there was a reason for this get-together. Her father had been home every night this week. Whatever had been keeping him grounded had come to an end. Her father had probably already signed an employment contract weeks ago. She'd be willing to bet he would be leaving any day now.

Max excused himself before dessert, apologizing to Mercedes. "That flan looks spectacular," he smiled a marketer's smile, "but I've had a long day. I've got to hit the road." Eddie stood up to walk his Sensei to the door. At the last minute, Max returned to give Harriet a kiss on the cheek.

"You did good today, Sweetheart," he said, zipping up his jacket.

"Thanks," Harriet said. "Sorry about the bread."

"No problem," he said as if he thought that she had been waiting for him to forgive her.

***

After dinner, Mike and Kat invited Kevin and Mercedes to head out for a drink and some dancing while the night was still young. Even after a long day of work, Kat loved to put on her silver stilettos and cut up the dance floor.

"The Miami Beach Club?" Kat suggested.

"Do you know how to salsa, Mercedes?" Mike asked.

"Do I salsa?" Mercedes brown eyes sparkled with excitement. "Am I Puerto Rican?"

Kevin laughed. "My girl can shake her booty."

"The Miami Beach Club it is, then," Mike said. "You're going to see, Mercedes. This place has amazing dancers," Mike winked at her, "but a warning, once Kat and I hit the floor, no one can keep up with us."

"That's a race we can win," Kevin said.

Even Mercedes did not offer to help Harriet clear the dishes from the table.

***

By the time Harriet had finished cleaning up the kitchen, Joe and Eddie had settled on the couch to watch the basketball playoffs.

"What was up with Max tonight?" she asked her nephew. Taking a deep breath, she added, "Dad, did I tell you I passed my brown belt test today?"

"Yeah, he seemed out of sorts," her father said to Eddie.

Eddie looked at his aunt warily. Harriet wondered if Max had said something about her promotional test. Whether her passing had been an act of charity. She suspected she had been too cautious, had not executed the movements with the expected air of authority. Perhaps Max was having second thoughts about awarding her the belt.

"Nothing. He and Rita are at it again," Eddie said.

Joe nodded. "Can't live with her; can't live without her. I know that drill," her father said.

Harriet busied herself, clearing the dirty wine glasses that had been left behind on the coffee table.

Even she had noticed that Rita had been acting even more pissed off than normal. She hadn't expected the bookkeeper to congratulate her; Rita never did show much interest in the discipline itself. But she had been taken aback by at the look of disgust on Rita's face when Max tied the brown belt around Harriet's waist.

"Don't worry about Rita," Max had said years ago. "She woke up on the wrong side of life."

Now it all made sense.

Turning on the dishwasher, Harriet was glad for its noisy cover.

Of course, Rita had all the power. After all, she collected the checks.

What really hurt was Eddie's and Joe's indifference. Neither of them had even bothered to include her in their discussion. The least they could have done was congratulate her on passing her test.

Eddie sidled up behind her. "You knew, right?" he whispered in her ear.

"Of course, I did."

So much for defending herself. She had failed miserably.

She was through with aikido.

"Eddie, do you think I could learn to salsa?"

"Of course you could, Aunt Harry. You are in great shape." At last, she received the compliment she had been waiting for all evening. She would ask Mercedes to teach her. She had loved Latin music ever since discovering Santana. She had made tentative, if unsuccessful attempts, to teach herself the steps that the passionate songs demanded. Especially now, with her father leaving town, she needed to get out of this stifling house.

***

Harriet wasn't the only one on Picaflor Court chafing at a parent's interference. Despite his parents' support during his recovery, after his discharge from the hospital, Bobby avoided Alice like the plague.

Alice had been horrified when he told her that Amy had moved out of their apartment during his hospitalization. In typical fashion, she hadn't made any attempt to mute her disapproval.

"This is exactly the time that you kids need each other the most," she said.

Fine for her to say. His mother had benefited from Jack's unwavering support. Bobby's father might have the patience of a saint, but Bobby had his hands full putting his life back together. The expectations awaiting him on discharge were overwhelming. The last thing he needed right now was twenty-four hours a day of Amy's silence. Her unspoken reproach.

Bobby could barely remember life before the crash. Amy lived there, could speak of nothing else. The cocktail parties, the celebrity. The unplanned pregnancy that she had seen as a beginning and which he, even before the plane crash, rued as an ending.

"Don't say it," he had said to her each time she visited him in the hospital.

But she had been unable to say anything else. "We can try again."

"Amy, don't you see. I'm in no shape to be a father now."

"You're getting better every day."

Amy's disappointment trumped her sympathy. If Bobby hadn't insisted on his toys, especially the Beechcraft Bonanza, she would be only weeks away from delivery. She railed at him; she cried. Soon Trudy began to guard his bedside, concerned for his safety, convinced that Amy was desperate enough to harm him.

Amy, furious, demanded that he fire the nurse. Instead, he told Amy to leave him alone. She had done exactly as he had asked. Her visits, fewer and fewer, deteriorated into negotiations. By the time he was cleared for discharge, the couple had decided to break up.

Bobby knew that his mother didn't approve of Trudy, but he had come to depend on the private duty nurse who had cared for him at the hospital. When he told his mother that he had hired Trudy as a live-in aide, Alice snapped: "A gold-digger if you ask me."

But the nurse asked nothing of him.

He had been relieved and grateful when Trudy agreed to move temporarily into his apartment. He didn't need to justify his actions to his mother, but he wasn't about to argue with Alice's suspicions. He supposed that Alice was hoping he would get back with Amy. She held him responsible for the failure of the relationship.

But as he and Trudy played their nightly game of Spades, he knew he had made the right decision. Trudy understood that recovery was all he could handle right now. She didn't try to win. She had witnessed firsthand his estrangement from Amy, watched as they faced each other with nothing to say.

"Amy and I have so little in common," he confided in her as he dealt another hand. "Amy loved being the focus of the Valley's attention. I still feel like an elephant in a crystal shop.

Trudy answered softly, "The baby you lost is always there, between you."

Trudy was a healer, what he needed to help with his convalescence. She assisted him without complaint, helping him to reconstruct his daily routines. She was content to occupy herself with his therapeutic requirements. She had even learned a few of his favorite computer games and proved to be a worthy competitor. Shortly before his decision to return to work, she agreed that *Star Trek* wasn't so bad, and the simplicity of vanilla ice cream had its own allure.

When they both agreed he was ready to return to work, she packed her bags, knowing that the time had come for her to leave.

****

The Jacksons must be entertaining. Bobby looked for a place to park on Picaflor Court. The cars overflowing the Jacksons' circular drive, included a beat-up race car, a snazzy Kharmann Ghia, and an assortment of dated, seen-better-days jalopies that Kevin had probably pieced back together with duct tape and spit.

His parents' house appeared serene in contrast.

His sister complained that their parents' house on Picaflor Court smelled of cigarette smoke. But the pungent odor of the Jacksons' eucalyptus tree greeted Bobby when he finally located a parking spot on the opposite side of the cul-de-sac. He had agreed to join them for one final dinner before Patty returned to New York.

"Every night like a broken record, Mom offers me a glass of wine and gossips about the Jacksons," Patty said when she opened the door.

"As if twenty-five years of old cars in their driveway wasn't enough, now the Jacksons play Spanish music all day long," Alice, who was standing beside her daughter, said.

His parents' house was immaculate, no surprise there. Even retired, Jack's pants were pressed, and Alice still complained when the ash from his cigarette left a charcoal smudge. Bobby's old room had been transformed into an office.

"Dad spends all his time on the computer," Alice complained, enjoying the audience that her children provided. She had redecorated the "guest room," painted Patty's old bedroom a neutral beige and decorated it with photos from their recent trip to Australia.

"Mom is thrilled that you finally accepted her invitation for dinner," Patty whispered, looking at him for an explanation.

"Well, I'm here now," he said.

Jack and Patty sat stiffly in the living room chairs. The room was still used only on special occasions. Only Alice sat on the living room couch, the one that had been off limits to Bobby and Patty when they were children. Alice leaned forward hungrily to catch every word of their conversation. Bobby wondered if his mother's hearing was beginning to go. To fill the uncomfortable silence, Patty prattled on and on about her job as a corporate lawyer. It was sad to see how much his sister still needed her parents to acknowledge that she had turned out all right.

Alice was the one who asked about Robin.

"She's in Beijing on business, import and export," Patty said. "A six-month assignment."

"I gather you're gay now," Alice said. Bobby couldn't believe how calmly his mother confronted Patty. "My generation, we never had a choice, a woman got married, and she had kids."

Patty's and Bobby's eyes met. Their mother was full of surprises, especially after a few glasses of vodka.

Jack sipped his Manhattan, a guest at the cocktail party.

"Who knows what I would have chosen? I certainly wasn't meant to be a mother."

The comment hung in the air between them, an unexpected ·apology. That, he supposed, was as good an explanation as anything else. Family—he had no idea what to make of it. Here was a sentiment he could clearly recall from before his accident. That even a profound re-set could not supplant.

They all had baggage.

Nothing like an evening with his family to prepare him for his imminent return to his former job. Bobby was more than ready to let go of the list of grievances that had been his childhood. Maybe a fresh start was what he needed to get up the nerve to re-dedicate himself to his work.

Jack announced that he and Alice were thinking of downsizing.

"Why?" Patty asked.

Bobby figured his parents stood to make a ton of money if they sold their house. That was the story in the Valley now, everyone was getting rich.

"More than thinking," Alice added. A local doctor had made them an offer. "He's going to gut the house, modernize everything. At least that's what he says."

"Add a second floor with a master suite and Jacuzzi," Jack told them.

It didn't matter that Alice knew the house was scheduled for a complete renovation, she was already complaining that she needed to clean every room once they had packed. Bobby was certain that not a speck of dirt would remain when his parents closed the door behind them.

✳✳✳

The evening headed downhill from there. Alice passed out on the couch after her third glass of vodka and a rant about the Vietnamese who were taking over the neighborhood. She began to cry when she described the neighborhood shopping center that was a mecca for Asians in the area. Ash fell from the cigarette still smoking in her hand when her eyes closed. Jack hadn't said a word when he removed it from her fingers. He cautioned Bobby not to wake his mom. "Let her sleep," he said. Bobby had forgotten how tender his father could be with his mother. After his hospitalization, he recognized the grace of unspoken compassion.

Jack was dozing off in front of his computer when Bobby went in to tell him good-bye. Patty was busy packing in the muted guest room that had once been filled with incense, black lights and Joni Mitchell dreaming of being a free man in Paris during the era while Alice had simmered outside her door with unfathomable anger.

It was strange to be home. Everything the same but different.

"Thank God I am only visiting," Patty said. "You take care of yourself."

"Don't be a stranger," Bobby answered. "I can't believe it, but I think I'm actually going to miss you."

"Likely story," his sister said, her voice already more confident as she snapped the suitcase shut.

"Come here," Bobby said. "There's something I want to show you." Patty followed Bobby into the unlit garage where Alice's fastidious cleaning had erased all traces of the workspace where he had once built the original Seed. Turning on the overhead light, he pointed to a corner below the utility sink. Patty knelt down on the cold cement floor. The date 6-10-59 remained visible on the cloroxed concrete, right under the impression of a handprint left by a little boy. They each took turns placing their hands on the small imprint that Bobby had made the day the floor was poured.

"It all began here," he said.

"And now you will remain here forever," Patty said. "So, go spend your millions. Have a good time. Remember to keep your feet on the ground."

"You too, Sis. You too."

They stood in the dark garage awhile before Bobby headed home, wherever that might be.

1985

"Do you write recommendation letters for college applications?" The prospective student's mother had ash blond streaks in her hair and a diamond the size of a small vegetable on her finger. Her son, a wired boy of four, stood at Harriet's desk, already feigning jabs and punches.

Harriet couldn't help but feel that she was seeing the dojo through Rita's eyes. A parade of hyperactive kids and their protective parents. Sitting at the reception desk, she felt like a doorman, babysitter, salesman, teacher and keeper of the peace, all at the same time.

While the mother carefully read over the standard disclaimer, Harriet asked the young boy if he was excited.

"I'm going to be a Ninja," he told her, eyes as wide as Christmas morning.

Eddie, six feet tall, muscular and handsome in his starched white *dogi* and black belt, shook the newcomer's hand. "Would you like to see the studio?" Eddie asked. He didn't need to raise his voice. He was clearly in charge, the dojo's Sensei.

Harriet had never intended to enter the dojo again. When Eddie had asked her to help him out, her immediate instinct had been to say *No way in Hell.* The last thing in the world she wanted to do was enter Max's studio, face his surly wife with her knowing sneer, submit in any way to Max's domination. Even worse, pretend she wasn't aware of the pity in their eyes.

Ever since he was a baby, Eddie had known how to pull her heartstrings.

He chose his opportunity well, over breakfast and in front of his grandfather. "Aunt Harry, if we can't keep the studio going, everything I've worked for will be lost." His voice trembled, his teenage macho threatened by boyish tears. Joe, back in a pilot's uniform and on his way out of town to join the test pilot program at Edwards Air Force Base, snapped to attention. Opportunities to be a hero were far and few between these days. One by one, his family had left home, and he had been increasingly restless since retiring from the Navy.

"What do you mean, son?" Joe asked.

"Max and Rita are taking a leave of absence," Eddie said. "They're talking about closing the dojo down while they work on their marriage." Neither Joe nor Eddie looked at Harriet. "It's not fair. Since the article in the *Mercury News*, our enrollment is way up. I have more students than Max ever had. But if they close the dojo now, I'm screwed."

Joe set down his cup of coffee, clearly mulling the situation over. The article from the *San Jose Mercury News*, with a quarter page photo of Eddie, was attached to the refrigerator door with a magnet. "National Champion at 17," it reminded him. Joe was shipping out in 48 hours.

"I can teach, but I'm not old enough to take over the lease," Eddie sniffled.

"Besides," Harriet reminded him, "you have school."

"But the classes I teach are in the afternoon and evening."

Joe put an arm around his grandson. They were head to head now, Harriet noticed. Cut from the same cloth.

"I have an idea." Harriet could almost see her father putting the puzzle pieces together.

Max, after all, had liked Joe. Joe had never judged his grandson's teacher for the affair he had with Harriet. Maybe Joe could make this right. Heck, even come up with a job for Harriet in the process. After all, once he'd shipped out, his daughter would be left alone in an empty house.

Harriet watched her father. He might as well have switched on a light bulb over his balding head. Joe was going to kill two birds with the same stone.

The plan fell into place before Harriet had a chance to weigh in. By the end of the day, the dojo's lease had been transferred over to Joe. Max agreed to let Eddie run his business for three months, to be evaluated at the end of the term. Harriet would be hired as the temporary receptionist and bookkeeper. Lawyers were contacted. Papers were signed. Max and Rita booked their flight to the Caribbean.

"Extracurricular activities carry a lot of weight," the attractive mother skimmed the registration disclaimers. "I don't want my son to get hurt."

"Eddie is a national champion," Harriet reassured her. "All the kids love him."

Enrollment at the school was at an all-time high. The dojo was a hive of activity. Harriet, for the first time in her life, had a full-time job and a regular paycheck. As well as enough money to take salsa lessons from her new friend Mercedes.

Joe headed to Southern California with a clear conscience. Harriet was relieved to see him go. Her father embraced her with renewed passion. The spring in his step as he packed his bags said it all: he was heading back to the open sky knowing that he had done the right thing for the loved ones under his charge.

This time, Harriet hoped, he might be right.

Eddie wanted to add a class on weaponry to the dojo's curriculum.

"Do you really think that's a good idea?" Harriet asked.

"The kids are fascinated by weapons. They need to learn respect. It's important that they learn to handle the traditional weapons as they were meant to be used."

Eddie sat at Harriet's desk at the end of a busy day, enjoying the silence of the now empty gymnasium. These days, the dojo was busier than ever. Eddie taught four classes a day; each had a significant waiting list. With Max gone, Eddie was making the business his own. He would graduate from Foothill High in two months and was already looking for ways that he could embellish the dojo's reputation.

"Listen to this," he said and read from a martial arts newsletter that he had received in the mail:

"*If a student does not master their function, he will never do full justice to the weaponry. Even though the heart may be strong, if the form is not appropriate, the stroke will fall where it should not fall. If one deviates from the principle of technique, one will not attain what one desires.*"

The quote, from *Tengu Geijutsu* Ron, inspired him.

"I don't know," Harriet answered. Sometimes Eddie morphed into the grandfather he adored. What the Navy had instilled in Joe, aikido had come to represent for Eddie. Discipline. Excellence. But also, an absolute truth that could not be questioned.

"Do you really think your students are ready?"

Harriet watched the young students as they left his classes. They were children. They wanted to be entertained, but their attention spans were short. They were not serious. "Would it really be wise? Max once told me that only the most dedicated aikido devotees were allowed access to weapons."

Eddie responded with confidence. "I would never permit a student to handle a weapon if they were not properly trained."

Max had personally trained Eddie. Maybe that influenced her reaction to his proposal now. Any mention of Max made her recoil. The embarrassment of her naïveté. Her family's complicity. Although Max had never raised a hand to her, in the end, the bruises he had inflicted were far more painful than those she had received from the practice of aikido.

The weapons on the wall bothered her.

"I think you should be careful," she told Eddie.

"I always am," he answered. "But it wouldn't be right to withhold essential components of the discipline."

"There's right and there's right," Harriet answered, willing to leave it at that.

"Basho said: 'Seek not what the old masters did; seek what they sought'," Eddie said.

Harriet had totaled the month's receipts that morning. The business was flourishing. She was reluctant to challenge her nephew whose passion had finally opened a door to her independence. She wished she had as much faith in the indulged boys and girls that were his students. She listened to their parents in the attached lounge. They spoke of entitlements and opportunities. In their discussions, their children, she noticed, were always in the right. One mother, with perfectly styled jet-black hair, attributed a broken bed frame to the hired help, not her hyperactive son. Another, who wore a different pair of designer yoga pants each week, complained incessantly about gardeners and housecleaners who refused to follow her instructions. Hired help, the mother said, seldom performed their jobs satisfactorily. As she spoke, she ignored the tussling of her twin boys at her feet.

Earlier that afternoon, Harriet had walked into the dojo and watched Eddie demonstrate the elegant moves of the ancient art. He struggled to hold the students' attention. In a moment of exasperation, Eddie brandished his bamboo cane, a technique he used to hold his students' attention. For one flash of a second, Harriet thought her nephew was about to strike one of the fidgety students giggling at his feet. She gasped; her nephew turned to her, clearly perturbed by the interruption.

"Sorry, Eddie," she said, retreating to her office. *I'm jumping to conclusions. I know this boy like my own heart. He is not capable of violence.*

Eddie, despite appearances, was only seventeen. He had assumed so much responsibility at such a young age with grace and commitment. Harriet knew that early maturity came at a cost, but it could also be easily misread. How close she had come to judging Eddie for an act that had not occurred. To reliving her mother's assumption of guilt which she had never been able to forgive. Would Eddie have been able to understand that she wanted nothing more than to shield him from the heartache she had experienced? Wasn't it more important to gift him with the trust he had so clearly earned?

Watching Eddie polish the weaponry with loving care, she got it. The countless repetitions. The striving for excellence. The mindful applications of essential principles.

"*Jim-dori, tachi-dori,* and *tantō-dori* are not violent moves," he insisted. "The disarming techniques that I demonstrate teach courage. They develop reflexes necessary to enter inside the arc of a moving object."

He deserved her support.

It was late. With a sigh, Harriet closed the books and turned off the lights. Eddie punched in the dojo's security code and, confident that his precious dojo was safe for the night, followed her to the car.

McDonnell Douglas test pilot and retired Navy Captain Joseph Jackson was killed while landing an F-20 jet at Edwards Air Force Base. Captain Jackson had positioned the F-20 Tigershark into a climbing roll with flaps and landing gear extended when the aircraft stalled and crashed. The prototype overturned, trapping the pilot underneath the inverted airframe. According to the director of the Company's Combined Test Force, "The crash crew worked feverishly for about 30 minutes to free the strapped-in pilot from the cockpit. The crew eventually brought in a crane to lift the front of the jet fighter high enough to pull him out." Despite spilling its fuel, the aircraft did not burn. Jackson was airlifted by Life Flight helicopter to the Air Force Medical Service Hospital where he died at 10:25 a.m.

Capt. Jackson is survived by four children. A daughter predeceased him. He served as a Navy pilot in the Pacific theater in World War II. After the war, he continued to serve in both the Korean and Vietnamese wars. His decorations included the Distinguished Flying Cross, three awards of the Air Medal and the Navy Commendation Medal. After retiring from the Navy, Captain Jackson resumed his work with airplanes at McDonnell Douglas where he tested aircraft under development for the Joint Task Force. — The San Jose Mercury, June 1, 1985

***

Joey's flight from Japan arrived two hours before Joe's funeral was scheduled to start. Harriet paced the international lounge at San Francisco Airport, dressed in black. When her brother finally appeared at the end of the skyway, surrounded by Japanese tourists, she looked in vain for her mother by his side. For the first time since two police officers had appeared at her doorway, she fought off tears.

The rest of the family waited in the kitchen on Picaflor Court. Mike held Kat's hand while Mercedes took over Harriet's duties, refreshing coffee cups. Eddie paced back and forth. Grief would not allow him to sit still. When a delivery boy rang the doorbell with an armful of flowers from the neighbors, Mercedes set the vase on the kitchen counter. The sickening sweet aroma of lilies hung over the family like a looming storm cloud.

Harriet pulled up to the curb in front of the house behind a shiny black stretch limo provided by the Navy. The car idled outside the Jackson home, the driver in full uniform. "Look familiar?" she asked, as Joey eyed the house. "We don't have much time."

Joey deposited his overnight bag in the front hallway, an old habit. *It used to be his backpack,* Harriet thought. Kevin gave his brother a vigorous hug. "Hey, Bro, it's about time."

All the questions that they could not ask hung in the air, scented by funeral flowers.

Harriet, who had never attended a high school prom, had never ridden in a limo. The family perched on the car's plush upholstery, uncomfortable in their formal clothes. Two wide seats faced each other, making it hard to avoid one another's eyes. Mike asked the driver how many miles the car got to a gallon. Joey whispered to Kevin: "What happened?"

"His drag chute didn't open. The commanding officer thinks Dad tried to stop using only his brakes." Kevin spoke quickly. Joey nodded but the toll his 24-hour flight had taken was evident. "They're trying to figure out why the aircraft's canopy landed several feet away from Dad's aircraft. He might have been trying to eject before the craft rolled over. Of course, it's s all speculation at this point."

A seasoned racetrack driver, Kevin was more comfortable describing the details of his father's accident than wearing his rented black suit. Mercedes smiled apologetically at Joey. Despite the fact that she had not been introduced to the youngest Jackson sibling, she assumed the role of caretaker for the shell-shocked family.

Airmen lined the road into the cemetery, all in full uniform—hats low on their brow, white gloves, chins held high. Standing tall as Joe had his entire life, they paid homage to the fallen hero.

Kevin and Joey joined four other airmen lined on either side of their father's coffin. As they walked, they imitated the stiff-legged, stuttering march. At Kat's side, Eddie raised his hand in salute. Mike, at first surprised, joined him.

In the cloudless sky overhead, airmen performed the Missing Man Formation, the flight leader at the point of the V, his wingman to his left.

Taps. The Folding of the Flag. Eddie, with the stoic dignity of his practice, stepped forward to receive the flag, all that would soon remain to remind him of his beloved grandfather.

Throughout it all, Harriet remained quiet. Joey, this stranger at her side, did not cry. Like his mother at the funeral of her own father, he maintained *taisho* and Harriet followed his lead. Only Kat whimpered, soft but heartfelt sobs as she clung to her husband's arm.

After the ceremony, Kevin shook the airmen's hands, still digging for information about his father's accident.

The reception was held at the officer's club. As the family sat in folding chairs at the front of the club, Kevin rattled off what he had been able to learn from the uniformed men. Officials said the aircraft had computerized landing and takeoff systems, and a computerized anti-skidding system. "They're looking at the landing gear and aircraft's wheels to see what went wrong."

The doctors at the hospital had assured Harriet that her father died almost immediately after the crash severed his spinal cord.

The commanding officer told Kevin that Joe had booked nearly 4,000 flight hours, but fewer than 43 in the F/A-18 Hornet, a new airframe which was being flown to test its design. Investigators were focusing on the planing link of the undercarriage as a probable cause. The link may have caused the starboard wheel to be slightly out of line causing the airframe to swerve so sharply that Joe had been unable to maintain control.

Joey sat in the straight-backed chair, his eyelids nearly closed. Harriet noticed that he was the only one in the family whose Japanese heritage was apparent. Kat, in her black sheath, smoking her cigarette as she crossed and re-crossed her legs, could easily have been anything. Kevin was American through and through.

She had no idea how she was supposed to act, what was expected of her as each of them bided their time, waiting until the Commanding Officer indicated that the limo had arrived to take them home.

For thirty years, Harriet had clipped articles about planes falling from the sky. Dreaded this crash. Waited for the news. Now that it had arrived, she felt nothing. Her stoic expression was not a mask. The polite smile of gratitude that she directed at the officer who gently guided her by the elbow to the waiting car was effortless.

In the limo, the air conditioner was cranked up high to counter the bright California sun. At first, she thought the trembling she felt was the car itself shaking, the motor in a wrong gear, a passing truck heavy on the road. Then she realized that her own body was betraying her. The shaking that overtook her was violent, waves of grief that refused to be denied, shivers of guilty relief and a roiling regret that seemed to come from deep inside.

Joey, the baby who had now become a man, put his jacket over her shoulders.

Kevin raised his eyebrows. No one said anything as the car slowly made its way through the endless afternoon traffic.

✳✳✳

Joe had never informed Harriet's siblings that he was leaving the house to her. Harriet read the shock on Kat's face when his lawyer recited the terms of the will. Kat and Mike had undoubtedly already planned how they would spend the expected windfall. Kevin simply said "Shit" and then apologized. She could count on Kevin to roll with the punches.

The ownership of the house was not the only surprise in the will. When the base lawyer reviewed the allocation of Joe's resources with the family, he told them that her father had set aside an account for Eddie; funds designated for one use only—for his grandson to set up a dojo of his own.

Harriet, seeing the dismay on her sister's face reminded her. "Dad did the same for you."

Her father's collection of cars, of course, went to Kevin. "Even the Porsche?" Kevin asked, immediately pacified.

The rest of Joe's assets were to be split three ways, between Harriet, Kevin, and Kat.

Nothing for Joey.

Hiroko's name did not appear in the will.

✳✳✳

"How is she?" Harriet had asked Joey on their drive home from the airport.

"Mom is fine," Joey said briskly. He was tall now. Imposing. He wore a well-cut suit. "She lives in Tokyo with Sunichi, her husband, a professor of medicine at the hospital."

Sunichi, Harriet assumed, was the man that her mother had returned to.

After the funeral, Harriet handed her brother a box of letters that she had discovered in her parents' closet when she was cleaning out her father's belongings. Letters written in feathery characters that told a story that Harriet could never decipher. There had been a time when Harriet had studied the thin pieces of stationery paper looking for answers, but now she asked Joey to return them to her mom when he went back to his adopted country.

"I assume they are from him."

Joey flipped through the box. "Not really. Most of them are from her mother." Harriet watched as he skimmed a letter here, a letter there. "Mom was always so lonely. So terribly homesick. Her mother was afraid for her, told her that she must respect her generous husband."

At the mention of her Dad, Harriet felt a need to apologize "Joey, that wasn't right. Dad leaving you out of his will."

"Mom was the one who insisted I come back for his funeral. I didn't come looking for anything."

"Do you think she ever loved him?"

"Love is a strange thing," Joey said, choosing his words carefully. "You've got to understand. War brides were regarded as traitors in Japan; they married former enemies. Mom didn't feel entitled to love. The question I have never been able to figure out is—Did Dad love her?"

Neither sibling attempted to answer his question. Joey continued to flip through the letters until he found one from their mother's new husband, written when the surviving Jacksons were still young children at their mother's feet.

"My precious Hiroko," it began. Translating the letter, Joey spoke English as if his native language felt unnatural on his tongue.

"He said even then that he would wait for her. I think Mom never learned English because there were things she couldn't tell us, but Harriet, you know she stayed in California for us, despite the discrimination she experienced, despite him. When Chrissie died..." Joey was the only one of her siblings who ever spoke about Chrissie. The sound of her name on his lips caused Harriet's tears to spill at last.

Returning Sunichi's letter to the box, Joey's face once again became unreadable. "I want nothing from my father. I have a family of my own now." Only then did her brother pull out photographs of his wife and two children and showed them to his sister. His youngest daughter wore rubber boots imprinted with yellow ducklings. She held her brother's hand; the young boy wore glasses and a school uniform. Joey's wife stood behind the children, smiling warmly at the photographer.

"I'm leaving in the morning," Joey said after she had returned the photo.

✳✳✳

"Give Mom my love," Harriet said when the airport van arrived to take him to the airport. When her brother left, she returned to her empty house and pulled down the shades, shutting out the incessant sunshine. Laying down on her single bed with a wet cloth across her forehead, she waited in the dark bedroom for her headache to abate.

✳✳✳

Bobby walked up to the front door of his parents' new condo wearing a red, white, and yellow umbrella hat. The two-bedroom condo, one of five adjoining units recently constructed in the Cupertino foothills, was only miles from the Seed headquarters. Real estate signs plastered the hillside, advertising new multi-use developments: "Coming soon." The foothills, once home to grazing cattle and a Jesuit monastery, were being carved out into a suburban grid. The rain was coming sideways. Bobby parked his new BMW on the dead-end street, before dancing a jig up the front walkway.

"Good evening, beloved parents," he said, bowing at the waist when his mother opened the door.

"Take off that silly hat," his mother snapped. "I wouldn't want the neighbors to see you." She took his dripping raincoat and hung it in the red-tiled entryway so that it would not soil the brand-new carpeting of the small but tidy living room. "You certainly seem in fine fiddle tonight." Alice's mouth pursed skeptically, an expression he knew so well. "I gather things are going better at the Seed?"

"You might say that, Mom. I've quit. I am happy to inform you that the Seed and I have parted ways."

Alice sighed. "Again?" This wasn't the first time since his accident that Bobby had resigned from the company he had founded.

"For good, this time. Zack's the businessman. I keep reading in the papers that he is the one with vision. I am just an engineer."

"And a damn good one at that," his father managed to insert.

Bobby didn't have to be anything. He'd already made enough money for several lifetimes.

Bobby made no effort to justify his decision to his mother. He left it to his dad to reassure Alice that his son knew what he was doing. These days, Bobby preferred the declarative flourish. When he told friends and colleagues about his new status, he liked to imitate Howard Beale in the movie *Network*, pretending to hang out his office window while yelling "I'm as mad as hell, and I'm not going to take this anymore!"

It felt good, venting his righteous anger.

The truth, of course, was less dramatic. He continued to draw a salary. He owned a significant part of the company. He simply had arranged to step down from day-to-day operations.

Additionally, he'd sold a ton of his stock.

"What's Amy have to say about this epiphany of yours?" Alice asked.

"Not a damn thing. I haven't spoken to her in ages."

Alice's frown clearly reflected disapproval. "What are you going to do now? Shack up with that nurse? Do you even have a plan?"

"Don't worry yourself about me. I have no intention of moving home and building a computer in your garage." Bobby grinned, pleased with his comeback.

"That's good. Your father and I don't have a garage anymore."

"Touché. Actually, I've been thinking about finishing up my BA at Stanford, maybe teaching. Who knows?"

"Bobby Hopkins an undergrad. I'd like to see that," Alice said.

"I can apply under a pseudonym. What do you think of Dylan Coltrane? Or maybe something ethnic that might give me an edge? Pancho Villa might fit the ticket."

"You are so weird." As usual, his mother said whatever crossed her mind.

"No weirder than my hippie sister becoming a lesbian lawyer in New York."

He enjoyed sparring with his parents. He hadn't had a chance to do enough of that in high school. He had been driven to succeed, to excel at anything he tried. Now he was enjoying the chance to screw it all up for a change. To fuck up if he wanted to. His mother would never understand.

Over takeout Chinese food, in the diminutive but well-appointed kitchen, his mother announced, to his surprise, that Patty had decided to move back to the Bay Area. Had, in fact, accepted a job at a Sunnyvale law firm which specialized in high-end real estate and IPOs.

"Is Mrs. Patty moving too?" Bobby asked.

"I liked Robin you know," his mother said, challenging him to respond. "She can hold her liquor."

Bobby hadn't realized that Patty had introduced her lover to their parents. She had obviously confided in Alice.

"Robin accepted a job in Beijing." his mother informed him.

Jack said nothing. As usual, Bobby could not read his father's reaction. He envied his father's ability to go along for the ride.

Two sheets to the wind, Alice was warming up: "Why can't any of my children stay in a relationship. Jack, what did we do wrong?"

Jack stubbed out his cigarette. "The sooner I get your mother to bed, the more likely it is that she will pass out before she says something she might regret," he whispered as if Bobby had agreed to be a co-conspirator.

As perhaps he had. Perhaps they all had.

"Nothing has changed here, I see, despite the new digs." Bobby put his boots up on the coffee table, knowing it wasn't allowed.

For too long he had let his life revolve around doing the correct things, getting A's, pleasing authority figures, chasing money and success. Now, as he watched his father walk Alice up the stairs to their bedroom, he saw his choices in a different light. His mother seemed frail as she leaned into his aging father, her back no longer straight. Slurring her words, she continued to bemoan the fates of her wayward children. "I want them to be happy." Jack nodded his agreement, supporting his wife's weight with obvious effort. Bobby could hear his father struggling to catch his breath.

"They're good kids, Alice," Bobby heard Jack say as they turned the corner.

That, he had learned, was the tricky part. Money was a lot easier to understand than the unfathomable riddle of whom we love and why

.

✳✳✳

In the morning, Bobby called his sister. He offered to let her stay with him until she got settled back into the Bay Area. "My apartment has more rooms than I know what to do with," he told her.

"An apt description for your life, I would guess," she said.

"You have no idea."

"Who am I to talk?" she chuckled sympathetically.

Bobby understood. His sister was hurting.

"Been there, Sis. I mean it. Mi casa es su casa."

"Thanks. I might take you up on that offer. Can you believe Mom and Dad sold their house and moved into that tiny condo?"

"They seem happy, in their own way. One thing is certain. The house sure is clean."

"And everything is new. Mom must think she has died and gone to heaven.

By the end of the call, Bobby and Patty were giggling like kids having trouble falling asleep at the end of a long day.

1989

Zach and Lara's *Star Trek Fan Film* had become a classic. Trekkies couldn't get enough of the legendary Zach Packer transformed by a rubber mask into Mr. Spock. The image of Lara, alien green and flailing around in a revealing lime green tunic, didn't deter any die-hard fans.

Bobby still had his copy of the Super 8 film.

Amy never made the background slides.

The film was scheduled to be shown on the final night of the 1989 Star Trek Convention to be held in July in Los Angeles.

Bobby had never missed a Star Trek convention yet. After the TV show was canceled, he continued to watch syndicated episodes, viewing each of the Star Trek movies multiple times. The *Search for Spock,* directed by Leonard Nimoy, blew him away. Nothing matched the show's deft use of science and space to explore contemporary issues like civil rights and the Vietnam War. Even now, when Bobby was trying to keep his head down, finish his studies and figure out his next move, he had made a note of the May date when tickets would go on sale through Ticketmaster. He programmed his Vodafone VT1 to speed-dial the number the minute that tickets were available.

"I got 'em," he hooted when the confirmation came through. "Mr. Spock, here I come." His classmates were conscientiously completing their final exam, but they were already used to the disruption caused by their famous classmate. Bobby's pseudonym was as flimsy as his early attempts to conceal his identity. What other college seniors could brag that the millionaire Bobby Hopkins sat beside them in calculus?

"I've seen every episode 20 times," the woman sitting behind him whispered. A slightly chunky brunette in a tank top, she gave him a thumbs-up. Like Bobby, she was older than the rest of the students.

After they had handed in their exams, his fellow Star Trek fan tapped him on the shoulder.

"Hi, I'm Sharon. You wouldn't happen to have purchased any extra tickets to the Convention?" she asked. "Ever since I got back from the Peace Corps, I have been jonesing for a Star Trek hit. You know, a clean fight between good and evil."

"I'll see what I can do."

Sharon's lack of pretense reminded him of his former neighbor, Harriet. Her sincerity. He had learned over the years that Star Trek saga attracted good people, people with hearts in the right place.

He gave her the ticket as a graduation present. "I hope I'll see you there," he said, waving away her enthusiastic barrage of *thank you*s. He didn't plan to attend the graduation. The publicity that his presence would generate would blow his cover for good. How would he explain to the press that he had spent the last two year's preparing for a new career—that of high school math teacher?

Besides, he wanted to work on his outfit for the convention. This year he was thinking of something more dramatic than the long-sleeved yellow tee-shirt with black trim and Star Trek logo. When he pulled out his box of Star Trek paraphernalia, he discovered that his old costumes no longer fit. The thirty pounds he had put on while completing his college degree made it necessary to start from scratch.

And that, he decided, was not necessarily a bad thing.

✳✳✳

Zach and Lara arrived at the convention for the presentation of their Fan Film in a black stretch limo. As was his custom, Zach was dressed as Mr. Spock, prosthetic ears and all. Lara wore a sparkling lime-green gown, her spiky dark black hair infused with glitter. The most glamorous alien Bobby had ever seen. The couple arrived in a shower of shooting stars as the flashbulbs of hundreds of cameras pursued them.

"My man, how are you?" Zach put his arm around his former business partner. "You are looking well." Bobby knew Zach, ever the salesman, was full of shit. Still, it was good to see his old friend outside the corporate arena.

"Lara is stoned out of her mind," Zach whispered. "She dropped a tab of acid on her way over here."

Zach, himself, was buzzed. "Look at these dudes!" he said, gesturing at the fans who were overjoyed at being the object of his attention. Their costumes were elaborate, the faces familiar. Dozens of Captain Kirks, even more Spocks. A few thousand fans gathered in the convention center, all in costume.

Zach jumped into the middle of it all, signing autographs, his eyes dazzled by speed or cocaine with an intoxicating mix of fame. Bobby watched from the sidelines, Lara, disoriented at his side.

"He's a force of nature," she said. "I don't even try to keep up anymore."

"Who can?" Bobby asked.

Lara studied his face. He wondered what she saw there. The teenager she once knew or the overweight student he had become?

"How are you doing, Bobby?" she asked.

"I'm hanging in there," he answered, holding her hand, overwhelmed by the impulse to protect her from the costumed throngs.

"Hey there, Lt. Sulu," Zach appeared out of nowhere. "Hands off my alien bride." Lara dropped Bobby's hand. "Bobby, you look like you need a drink. I happen to have a flask right here. Fortify yourself, young man."

Bobby shook his head, but Zach was already pouring a capful of tequila.

"I hear you've been slinking around the UC Campus," Zach said. "What kind of life is that for a billionaire?"

Bobby's choice to dress as Lt. Sulu was apparently the right one. He felt he was in the torpedo room, preparing for an alien attack.

Zach led him to the front row of the screening room. In Zach's shadow, Bobby, too, was lit by the flashes of cameras, barraged by eager Trekkies asking for his autograph.

He swallowed a second shot of tequila. He hadn't gotten high since his accident, but if any occasion required fortification, this was it.

He could swear that Lara had stars in her eyes. He had forgotten how beautiful she was. They watched the familiar film, mesmerized. The simplicity of the vision. The hope for the future frozen in time. Awe filled him as he watched the moral tale unfold. He admired the characters portrayed; he felt complete in the company of his friends. The screening room was populated by a family that could never be broken.

"I love you, man," he said to Zach on the way out of the theater, oblivious to the fans following his every move.

Lara watched the two men hug, tears rolling down her lovely face.

"Hey," Zach snapped his fingers, his eyes lit up. "I have a fabulous idea."

Bobby, in his old friend's thrall, listened.

"A dude I know, wealthy as all hell, is selling his house. A veritable mansion on a beautiful piece of property up in the mountains. He's looking to get out of town without a hassle. Moving to Zurich, don't ask me why. I'm going to hook you up. It's what you need, a vantage point on the hillside. Enjoy your good fortune for a change."

Bobby watched Lara watching him.

"Do it, Bobby. Ride the wave, Bobby."

Zach was already on the phone, selling the deal, promising Bobby's cash payment on the spot. Bobby didn't bother to stop him. Bobby was lost in the image of the two officers sharing the helm of the USS Enterprise side-by-side. The inevitability of their friendship.

He was flying once again.

When he had returned to college, Trudy had resigned from her position as his personal nurse, comparing Bobby to a bird who had broken his wing. Now that he had been rehabilitated, she told him, it was time for him to take off.

Not about to buy another plane, he had been having a hell of a time figuring out how he was supposed to do that.

Zach hung up the phone. "We've got ourselves a deal." He shook Bobby's hand.

Sharon, Bobby's college classmate, tapped on his shoulder. He didn't recognize her at first.

"It's me, Sharon," she said. "Lt. Sulu, I haven't thanked you for the tickets. This show is awesome!"

"And who, may I ask, is this lovely maiden," Zach asked.

Sharon, in her Star Trek tee-shirt, blushed.

"A classmate of mine," Bobby answered. "A fellow math major. Sharon, meet Zach, my former partner."

"Like I don't know who you are," Sharon said. In contrast to Zach's manic dialog, Sharon's voice was calm, moored. "The pleasure is all mine. Of course, I only know Bobby as a fellow math geek."

"A math geek he may be, but the man just bought himself one big-ass house," Zach laughed, bracing himself against Lara who was visibly fading by the moment. "If you would excuse us, I have a limo waiting outside." With a flourish and a courtly bow, Zach and Lara disappeared into yet another adoring crowd.

Bobby and Sharon watched him go.

When the clicking of cameras faded, Sharon turned to Bobby. "You bought a house?"

"Apparently," he said.

Sharon suggested they watch the simulated game show that was about to begin in the adjoining conference room—a Star Trek Trivia game based on Family Feud—Klingons vs. the righteous wrath of the Federation. By the time the show was over, Bobby had begun to sober up, but the euphoria of the afternoon had not faded.

Not since Trudy had resigned had he felt so comfortable at a woman's side. In the company of his fellow Trekkies, he could finally be himself.

Zach was right, he needed a home. Maybe today he had found one.

"A math nerd with a big ass house, huh?" Sharon laughed.

"Next year we'll find you a better costume," he said.

✱✱✱

Everywhere Harriet looked, there was construction.

The Klein's house next door was in a perpetual state of renovation since the Hopkins had moved out. Where Bobby had built the first Seed, a three-car garage sheltered a Mercedes SUV and two high-end sports cars. Where there had once been floor to ceiling windows illuminating Alice's pristine living room, there was now a fortress-like brick facade. The modest Eichler had gradually been transformed into a two-story, brick-faced mansion with columns on either side of an over-sized front door. The arched picture windows of the additional second story hovered over the neighboring one-story homes. The fortress-like walls cast dreary afternoon shadows on the Jacksons' eucalyptus tree.

The house's front bell, which rang out like a church's noon call to prayer, was in constant use by the drivers of a never-ending parade of vans. Electricians, plumbers, tile layers and carpet installers vied for the limited parking spaces on the cul-de-sac. Despite the minuscule size of the Klein's backyard, once a week a fleet of gardeners arrived with mowers and trimmers and blowers to maintain the little plot of sod that had been rolled out like a red carpet one hot August morning. Despite a worsening drought, two times a day the new homeowner's programmed sprinklers hissed on, and the neighborhood birds danced and bathed in the man-made mist.

The apricot tree in the backyard was the first to go. In its place, carefully pruned shrubs huddled miserably in redwood mulch.

Kevin once said that the Klein's house was like a huge container ship with Harriet frantically paddling in a little rowboat along its side.

And it wasn't only Picaflor Court.

Pavement and buildings had slowly covered over most of the absorbent soil of the Valley. Serious flooding was becoming more common on the low-lying streets when it rained. The heavy demand for water threatened almost constant drought. Governor Deukmejian had recently proclaimed that mandatory water restrictions (more extensive than the familiar *flush for two, not one*) were inevitable. The town's water table was so depleted that the ground was sinking around City Hall and in the neighborhoods near the Bay which had, unwisely, been built on fill.

The air itself was sated. Discolored by car exhaust, poisoned by the glut of automobiles. The morning fog that once crept across the Santa Cruz mountains had been permanently replaced by a yellow-tinged smog that remained trapped in the valley created by the San Francisco Bay.

At last count, one-and-half-million people inhabited this valley.

Inspired by the frenetic construction around him, Harriet's nephew Eddie had also set out on a building project of his own. When he turned eighteen, he had come into his inheritance and, with Harriet's help, had purchased a storefront for his dojo.

The space Eddie had purchased was on a busy corner of the old downtown where an odd mélange of businesses competed to survive with the enclosed malls being built in the suburbs. Down the block, a shuttered retail space was sandwiched between a Bank of America branch, an auto-body shop and a school of music. Across the road, there was a windowless semiconductor company called Synerchip and a bustling southern Indian restaurant.

For the past six months, Eddie had dedicated himself to his school's decor. Mike and Kevin were drafted to sand floors and paint the walls a crisp white with glossy black trim. Eddie insisted on interlocking mat squares on the floor of Dojo #1; his brothers re-laid the interlocking red and blue checkerboard pattern three times before he was satisfied that the pattern was perfect. Harriet hung adhesive mirrors on one wall so that the students could monitor their posture. The floors of Dojo #2, the smaller gym, had to have five coats of polyurethane before Eddie gave his approval to the quality of the gloss. Eddie designed the lobby himself, hired a carpenter to build the counter to his specifications with built-ins for displaying fliers and sign-up sheets and blond wooden chairs with black leather upholstery where parents could comfortably wait when picking up students.

From Japan, Joey contributed hand-painted Japanese ideograms on white silk to hang on the walls.

Harriet had never shopped so much: coat racks, storage armoires, bamboo benches. She barely had a moment to herself.

There was no denying that Eddie knew exactly what he wanted. He paid particular attention to the purchase of the weapons' rack, ordering an elegant black rack from Japan on which to display the dojo's collection of handmade wooden weapons. He carefully weighed the advantage of snakewood over cocobolo, insisted on holding each weapon in his hand. Each *tanto, bokken, jo,* and *shinai* was the finest he could find. Displayed on the wall without a visible screw or hanging device, the elegant weapons conveyed a message of quiet power and control.

By the time the new dojo had been completed, Harriet's office was enclosed by translucent sliding screens. The sensei's carpeted suite had a high-end glass table where Eddie could counsel students in a private setting. The pro shop was stocked with gym bags and t-shirts embossed with the dojo's logo.

When everything was right, when Eddie no longer paced the floors looking for imperfections, the business was officially opened. Eddie, the business owner, cut the ribbon in front of a photographer for the *Mercury News*. Harriet, shades of Rita, was introduced as the business manager.

The timing couldn't have been better. In 1988, Steven Seagal made his acting debut in *Above the Law*. A 7th-dan black belt in aikido, the actor became all the rage and students flocked to the new school to remake themselves in the actor's image.

Harriet, who had recently completed a bookkeeping course at Foothill Junior College, couldn't take in the checks fast enough. Sitting in her secluded office, she greeted the affluent parents of Eddie's students with a composed smile. The parents had titles like CEO, CIO, CFO, COO, Sr. Manager, and Marketing VP which they handed out like corn chips for her to chew on as she entertained waiting siblings and made sure that the departing students didn't forget their expensive, if unnecessary, ski jackets. It was her responsibility to make the bank deposit at the end of each day.

There was never enough time. At the end of the day, Harriet retreated to her home on Picaflor Court. Mercedes, Kevin's long-time girlfriend, had moved in soon after Joe died. Kevin had suggested the arrangement. A regular on the national NASCAR circuit, he was away on the road most of the time. Harriet had been glad for the company.

After a long day's work, she was content to put her feet up. Mercedes, a sales associate at Macy's, joined her. Neither of them had the energy to dance anymore though their friendship had blossomed when Mercedes taught Harriet salsa steps during the lonely days after Joe had died. "Start with your feet together. Hold on the first beat. On the second step forward with your left foot. On the third, rock back with your right. On the fourth, step back with your left." Her patient instruction had served as a soothing litany which Harriet recited to herself on those nights when she found it difficult to sleep.

The intimacy and rhythm of Mercedes' instruction had gotten Harriet through the hard times. Now Eddie's business demanded everything she had left. Despite the constant hammering next door, Picaflor Court remained her only refuge, an oasis of peace in the midst of the Valley's prosperous din.

✳✳✳

Kat and Mike, in a rare gesture of hospitality, had invited Harriet and Mercedes to their new house to watch Game Three of the World Series. Mercedes drove Harriet's Chevette, while Harriet read Kat's penciled directions. "Two lights, then turn left onto the Central Expressway." They were heading towards the bay. As dusk descended, they drove toward the shadowy outlines of the mountains on the other side of their long, flat valley through crowded concrete and neon strips of stores, service stations, and car lots. Turning, at last, into her sister's subdivision, Harriet passed rows of townhouses built side by side with tract homes with flat roofs that huddled together, back to back and side to side. Unlike the neighborhood surrounding Picaflor Court, here there were no open spaces, parks or sidewalks. Although the homes were relatively new, they already slouched, their gravel roofs showing wear. Flimsy fences surrounded sparse dirt yards. Painting exteriors were already beginning to fade. Finally, Harriet spotted her sister's house in the middle of a quiet block on Arques Avenue.

In an all-Bay Area series, the San Francisco Giants were playing the Oakland Athletics at Candlestick Park. Mike, a long-time Giants fan, had closed the gas station early so that he wouldn't miss a minute of pre-game coverage. Harriet suspected that he had money riding on the San Francisco team.

By the time Harriet and Mercedes arrived, Mike had already settled into the couch, a beer in one hand and a plate of nachos in his lap.

"Hey girls."

"Hi, Mike. Where's Eddie?" Harriet had chuckled that morning when the normally serious Eddie showed up for work with a Giants' jacket over his *dogi*.

"Some sort of parent-teacher conference at the dojo hung him up. He says he'll get here as soon as he can," Kat had a twin on each hip. Her second stab at motherhood became her. When her sister had announced the unexpected pregnancy, Harriet had been glad that her job prevented her from being drafted into babysitting again. To her credit, Kat didn't even ask.

"Strange, Eddie didn't mention a conference to me when I closed up the office."

Mercedes reached out for one of the twins, tickled his chin, and cooed adoringly.

"Kevin better watch out." Mike chuckled, never taking his eyes off the TV set. I can hear someone's biological clock ticking."

"62,000 people in the stands," the broadcaster said. "The entire Bay Area is watching this game."

Harriet helped herself to a cheesy nacho.

"When does the game start?"

"Any minute..." Just as Mike began to answer, the house shook, shifted to the left, shook again. The TV went blank.

Every Californian knows that when an earthquake hits, the safest place to stand is a door frame. Mike shot up from the couch and hustled Kat and one of the twins into the living room entryway. Harriet pulled Mercedes, holding the second baby, towards the exit to the kitchen.

The TV audio crackled. "Well, folks, that was the greatest open in the history of television, bar none," the announcer's shaky voice broke.

Looking out her sister's window, Harriet saw a wave of water coming down the block. After a moment of confusion, she realized that what she was seeing was the contents of an above ground pool.

It took twenty minutes before the networks resumed coverage of the quake. The Goodyear blimp, which had been located over Candlestick Park for the game, relayed startling images of the damage. The Nimitz Freeway had collapsed. A section of the upper deck of the Bay Bridge had fallen onto the roadway below.

"Holy shit," Mike kept saying. "That was a big one."

No one in the stadium had been injured.

Harriet tried to call the dojo, concerned about Eddie, but the telephone lines were down. At six p.m. the house's power went out.

In the resulting darkness, Mercedes and Kat put the babies to bed.

Mike and Harriet sat side by side in the dark living room. Harriet remembered Bobby Hopkins describing his junior high school science teacher's demonstration of the effect of an earthquake on the unstable fill used to expand buildable land around the bay. Re-creating the Santa Cruz mountains with a shovel-full of dirt and the Pacific shoreline with a scoop of sand, the teacher shook the model with as much agitation as he could muster. The simulation of the San Francisco Bay Area dissolved into a swirling tornado of water, dirt, and sand. The teacher's lesson: "This would be the effect of an 8.0 earthquake."

She worried about the fill under her sister's house. She worried that the pavement of the local highways had buckled as it sometimes did. She wished that her nephew would walk in the door with that arrogant grin of his and say, "Turn on the lights already." But without the TV, the only sound she heard was the babies crying themselves to sleep.

"Hold on," Mike said, disappearing into the darkened garage. He re-emerged with a flashlight and a transistor radio.

"The epicenter of the quake was in Santa Cruz," he reported. "1.4 million people are without power."

They listened to updates on the radio all evening. Buildings had collapsed, houses moved off their foundations. By the time the first mortality reports began to come in, Mike had finished off the beer and Harriet the nachos. Kat used the flashlight to put together a scavenged supper from the dead refrigerator—cheese and leftover macaroni. Mercedes ate melting ice cream directly from the container.

Eddie didn't arrive until 10 p.m. In the candlelight, he looked pale, almost ghostly, as he stumbled into the room.

"Are you drunk?" Mike asked. Eddie never drank.

"I am so relieved to see you," Harriet gave her nephew a hug before she smelled the liquor on his breath."

"Where have you been?" Kat asked. "We've been worried sick."

"The roads are a mess. Roadblocks everywhere. I hung out in McCarthy's until I could get through." Eddie flopped down on the couch and put his head in his hands. "What a mess," he said.

If there had been electricity, Harriet would have made him a cup of coffee. Instead, she asked him if the dojo was alright.

"It's still standing," he answered, enigmatically. His usual bravado seemed to have been shaken by the quake. Sitting in the dark, she waited for him to say something more, but he clearly did not want to talk.

Kat distributed a pile of blankets. Harriet and Mercedes made beds on the living room couches. Eddie headed into his bedroom, shutting the door behind him with a dismissive click.

By morning, power had been restored. The Loma Prieta Earthquake caused $6 billion dollars in damage, the morning news reported.

Game three of the series was not played until ten days later. The A's swept the Giants, four games to none.

By then, Harriet couldn't have cared less.

***

"I, for one, do not believe a word of it. Eddie would never hurt a child," Harriet poured Kat another cup of coffee. "Sure, he believes in discipline. He got that from Dad. But I've watched him with his students. His gentleness is remarkable. In aikido, the Sensei sometimes uses the bamboo poles to hold a student's attention. A light tap here, a nudge there. Believe me, Eddie's students have blossomed under his instruction." Harriet had been rehearsing this argument for days.

If only she could convince herself. In the earlier morning hours, as she stared up at her bedroom ceiling, she pictured Eddie raising that bamboo pole. Where there had once been bruises on her arms and thighs from repeated falls, she felt nerve endings tingle, the visceral memory of injuries she had clearly inflicted on herself.

Her sister was more receptive to this explanation than the lawyers who had been hired by Eddie's students' parents. In the deposition, they had responded with disbelief and obvious suspicion. The journalists who had knocked on their door with pens poised to break the story had written down her words without probing further.

After the door closed, Harriet thought of all the questions they had not asked, and that she could not answer.

"Is this man capable of hurting others?"

"Are you confident that no child was injured?"

"Why are there weapons on the wall if they are not intended to be used?"

"Who determines the line between discipline and violence?"

Eddie refused to speak up in his own defense. He was too angry to be of much use. Harriet was afraid that if he addressed the charges, it would only make matters worse.

"Where do you think the parents came up with this malarkey?" Kat lit a cigarette. Since the lawsuit became common knowledge, she had started smoking again, although usually not around the twins who were busy studying their feet as they wiggled restlessly in the car seats she had deposited in Harriet's entryway when she arrived.

Harriet held her hands open. "Who knows? The children Eddie teaches are not the kids of military men. You know the parents. Most of them are loaded; they made their money on multi-billion-dollar computer startups. They don't like their children to be touched. I have to deal with them all the time. They don't respect an instructor's authority." With Kat hanging on her every word, her arguments seemed irrefutable.

Sunday's *San Jose Mercury News* had called the lawsuit a nuisance, but not until reiterating the parents' accusations of intentional and repeated child abuse. The local reporter repeated the parents' claim that Eddie had struck his students, threatened them with dangerous weapons. The story had been picked up by local news stations, repeated in the *Palo Alto Times* and reported in headlines in the *San Francisco Chronicle*.

"It's outrageous," Kat kept her voice low but her fury filled every word. "Eddie could lose his livelihood. It's bad enough that enrollment at the dojo has already plummeted. If he can't make the mortgage payments, the dojo will go into foreclosure."

"Kat, no one knows that better than me. Remember, I keep the books."

Harriet knew why Kat was sitting in her kitchen. It wasn't for sympathy. Mike and Kat had spent all of their small inheritance from Joe on the down payment for their new house. Now that Kat was staying home with the twins, they had nothing to spare. Making ends meet was a struggle. They depended on Eddie's success.

Kat had made it clear that she resented her father's decision to leave the family home on Picaflor Court to Harriet. It came out in small ways, her insistence that Thanksgiving dinner be held at Harriet's which was, after all, "the family home," her refusal to claim boxes which Harriet had labeled "Kat's memorabilia" and had placed in the hall closet for her sister to pick up, her frequent references to Harriet "rattling around in that big old house." Kat told Kevin that Mercedes' contributions to Harriet's household account should have been split among the siblings, a comment which he laughed off, but which Eddie repeated to Harriet when Mercedes complained to him.

Now Kat expected Harriet to rescue Eddie. "I wish Dad were here," she said. "He would have known how to handle this."

Harriet knew what her sister meant. Their father had always come to Kat's rescue, usually with Harriet's assistance.

"The lawyer thinks that Eddie should settle the case without admitting guilt. Make the suit go away," Kat lit another cigarette and held it between two fingers, her nails polished blood red. "He suggested that Eddie move the weapons out of the Dojo to demonstrate his willingness to address the parents' concerns.

"Five hundred thousand dollars," Kat exhaled, "and the whole thing could go away. Where the hell is he supposed to get that kind of money?" Harriet knew that it was not a coincidence that her sister followed her comment with a long look at the familiar room around her, the kitchen where her family had gathered over the years.

"Harriet, I know I can depend on you." Kat's comment hung there like the smoke from her cigarette. She knew the ghost it summoned. Joe would have wanted Harriet to give her nephew the money he needed to salvage his future. The only way she could do this was to sell the over-mortgaged house. Harriet understood but her stomach, clenched in a selfish knot, resisted the suggestion.

Her father would expect her to come to Eddie's rescue. He would insist that the house, her financial security, the life she had cobbled together should not factor into the equation. He would be as oblivious to the sacrifices that his expectation required as Kat was now.

Kat extinguished her cigarette in the saucer, bringing the conversation to an end. She carried her dirty coffee cup to the sink for Harriet to clean. "I've gotta go. Think about it."

When Kat picked up one of the car seats to cart the sleeping twin to her Camaro, Harriet automatically followed her with the other seat, careful not to jostle the sleeping baby. Side by side, they clicked the seats into the back of the car.

"Can you babysit tonight?" Kat paused before getting into the driver's seat. "Mike and I desperately need a night out. This whole thing is driving us crazy."

Of course, Kat knew that Harriet was available. Until the case was settled, Eddie had cut back the hours that the dojo was open.

After starting the car's ignition, Kat rolled down the window. "Sweetie, if you sold the house, you would always be welcome to live with us," she said it before pulling away from the curve. "I could use your help with the kids. You know that we have always counted on you," Again, Harriet heard the echo of her father's words.

Watching her sister turn the familiar corner, Harriet stood in the empty driveway, in front of the empty house on the block she hardly recognized, in a town where, her sister had just reminded her, she no longer belonged.

✳✳✳

"I believe in his innocence," Harriet said again, this time to Mercedes as they sat together in the living room where Eddie had so often played.

"I never forgave Hiroko for questioning my actions. I can remember every angry word she said when she dragged me from Bobby's house. It was the worst night of my life." Harriet described the incident to Mercedes. Talking about Hiroko's accusations reawakened an overwhelming sense of helplessness, an almost physical paralysis. "It's terrible to be accused of something you did not do. I don't ever want Eddie to feel hopeless like that."

Mercedes nodded. "That's not really Eddie's thing. That boy has more confidence than most men I know."

"Maybe, but I have to give Eddie a chance."

"But, Hon, what are you going to do?"

Trust Mercedes to get to the bottom of things. All afternoon, Harriet had been trying to imagine where she would go if she were forced to sell the house. Would she continue to work at Eddie's Dojo? Would she accept Kat's offer and babysit the twins? Both prospects filled her with dread. It was too much for them to ask.

"I have no idea. Outside this house..." How could she explain? First Max, then the Dojo. One by one, she felt like she was being asked to give up pieces of herself. A leg here, an arm there, one day there would be nothing left. The story of her life. Maybe it should just end here.

"Kat has no right to pin this on you."

"Kat thinks only of Kat. It's an old story."

"It doesn't have to be yours."

Mercedes was right. No one was accusing her of wrongdoing. Why should she have to pay? She could just say "no" and let her sister suffer the consequences for once.

But then what?

Even harder to imagine than giving up the house, was walking away from her family. If she didn't provide the funds for Eddie's settlement, Kat would never forgive her. Kevin and Joey would not be there to defend her. Joe, already a persistent voice in her head, would haunt her forever.

She had everything to lose. Kat knew that.

"It's a matter of family," she told Mercedes. "Joe left me the house with the caveat that he knew I would look after the family. I don't see that I have a choice."

"There must be an easier way."

They sat in silence. There was nothing more to say.

"I'm sorry to put you out on the street," Harriet said, avoiding Mercedes eyes, refusing to accept her sympathy.

"Your brother will have to invite me along with him on the road. It's about time he made a commitment," Mercedes said, getting up to give Harriet a hug.

"Who will teach me to dance when you go?" Harriet smiled, swallowing tears, choking back the rage that threatened to replace the helplessness that had overtaken her earlier. She had made her decision, now she would have to figure out how to live with it.

The real estate agent assured Harriet that sales were brisk, and chances were, the house would sell for more than the asking price. It had to. After her father's many gifts, there was barely enough equity left. To provide the funds her nephew needed, she had to sell the house. Eddie expected this. They all did.

But when the agent pounded the For-Sale sign outside the kitchen window, Harriet shut the Venetian blinds. She couldn't look at the sign, not yet.

***

Bobby's new house had more than enough room for Patty.

"Take the west wing," Bobby told Patty when she arrived, suitcases in hand. His bedroom faced east. He liked the morning sun.

The house had six bedrooms and eight bathrooms. The post-modern style did not take away from the scenic beauty of the foothills that surrounded it. The swimming pool and koi pond had been designed to blend with the surroundings.

Bobby proudly showed his sister the European professional chef's kitchen. Natural light flowed in through the floor-to-ceiling windows of the living room. From the wraparound terrace, she could survey the entire valley.

"You would think this view would give us some perspective," Patty said. Bobby was barbecuing chicken for a half dozen kids that had just arrived in a school bus, the most recent winners of the Hopkins' Prize. Soon after Bobby had completed his education credits, he had initiated the prize to recognize local students who excelled in the innovative use of computers in the fields of business, art, and music. He had provided the initial funding for the nonprofit foundation that awarded the prize. The winners' barbecue was his latest inspiration.

"Perspective is a hard thing to come by, sis. I should know."

The high school kids, awed to be in the home of a celebrity, sat on the brick wall trying to pick out their houses below. Bobby showed them the high school which was easy to spot. The highway ran right behind it.

Bobby was happy that his sister had accepted his offer and agreed to move in with him. Sharon had another year before she would complete her doctoral program at the University of Chicago. They took every opportunity to use the hot-off-the-press Seed Link software to e-mail one another, but he missed her company in the cavernous house.

Patty could easily have purchased a place of her own. The Cupertino law firm that she had joined when she returned to the Valley was thriving. The senior partners had been delighted when Patty had asked the firm to provide counsel to several of Bobby's philanthropic foundations. Bobby served on their Board of Directors but, after his experience at the Seed, he had sworn off management leaving plenty of administrative tasks to be done so the accounts had proved lucrative. His sister was happy at the firm, enjoyed the enthusiasm of the young partners who were filled with the same positive energy that was causing companies to spring up all over the Valley. Creativity, not greed, was their bottom line, a refreshing change from the competition of New York, she told him. It had taken awhile but Bobby had finally convinced her that he was not a slave to his wealth. Lately, he had been substituting at the local high school; he particularly liked teaching math and science.

"Guess who's selling her house?" Patty asked him now.

Bobby answered. "Haven't got a clue."

"I was handing out cases to the junior associates today, and I saw the closing for the Jacksons' house in the pile to be assigned.

"There goes that neighborhood."

"Bobby, that's not fair."

"Just kidding. You know there was a time that I had a thing for Harriet."

"Poor thing. I heard her Dad died in a plane crash."

"That family never did have much luck."

"I volunteered to handle the closing. There is an associated lawsuit that is a bit tricky. You should have heard how surprised Harriet was when I called to tell her I would be representing her. I don't think that selling the house was her idea. The family needs the proceeds to settle the lawsuit against her nephew. Harriet sounded a thousand years old."

The students, settling in, began to horse around on the sloping front lawn. They reminded Bobby of his friends when they had been charter members of the Foothill Electronics Club. You could almost see the ideas swirling around their brilliant minds. What they lacked in coordination they made up for in enthusiasm.

Bobby sent a Frisbee flying in a blond kid's direction.

"Give Harriet my best. I really do hope things work out for her. Do you think her mother will be there? That woman hated me."

"Her mother disappeared a long time ago. Mom thinks maybe she went back to Japan. Joey, the baby, lives there too; he's some sort of expert on Asia for the Rockefeller Foundation."

"The Jacksons never did seem like they really belonged in the Valley."

The chicken skin was already turning brown. Bobby's housekeeper placed heaping bowls of salad on the redwood picnic tables.

"Dinner's on," Bobby called out. For the rest of the evening, he was in his glory, surrounded by students whose questions never seemed to end.

Bobby didn't notice when his sister went to bed. He was engrossed in showing the students his model of the Seed I which he kept in a display case in the pool room. At midnight, he joined the students splashing around in the pool, playing Marco Polo by moonlight.

1990

"Harriet, it's about time," Kat answered the phone after one ring. Harriet could hear her sister blowing out smoke, exhaling like a dragon ready to strike. "What the fuck is going on?"

In the background, Harriet heard Mike saying "Tell her the money never arrived. The whole deal is about to fall through." She listened for Eddie's baritone voice, but his parents had taken the lead on this one.

"Eddie never picked me up after the closing," Harriet said. Start with the easy part, Patty had advised her. "He left me standing there on the curb. Kat, I feel like a homeless lady."

"Maybe he had more important things on his mind," Kat said. "Like his reputation, his livelihood." Harriet had never heard her sister so angry. "I can't believe that you would withhold his money because you're pissed."

"It's not that," Harriet said, deciding not to point out that the money was hers, not her nephew's. "Standing on that corner, I felt invisible. You and Mike have each other. Kevin has Mercedes, Eddie has his dojo. But I have nothing."

"A hell of a time for you to start feeling sorry for yourself. Dad must be turning in his grave."

Of course, Joe would come into it.

"Don't do that."

"Don't do what? Remind you of your responsibilities to this family?"

Closing her eyes, Harriet pictured the gas station explosion again, this time feeling the flames in every muscle of her body. Molten lava in her veins boiling like underground fuel, her sister's words like a careless match.

"Never, never, have I forgotten my responsibilities to our family and you know it. Hell, Kat, I practically raised you and your son too. Did it ever occur to you that I am entitled to a life of my own?"

"Who are you?" Kat screamed into the phone. "And why, all of a sudden, now?"

"It's not his money." Harriet's heart was pounding. Her hands were clammy as she clutched the phone. "Dad left the house to me. I earned it."

"Bullshit. That house belongs to all of us."

Harriet reminded her. "It was mine as much as the gas station belongs to you and Mike. For once in your life, appreciate what Dad did for you and what it cost me. The proceeds from the house are the only assets I have."

The line was quiet now.

"And, Kat, I really need that money."

"Harriet, honey," her sister's voice softened. Harriet could practically hear her sister thinking, trying to come up with a more persuasive argument, "I told you we would help you out. The twins have been waiting all day for their Auntie Harriet to arrive. They are so excited that you are moving in with us."

"Kat, listen to me. I'm not going to raise your children."

Another match lit, she heard her sister inhale, and waited for what came next.

"You selfish bitch." And that was that.

A loud clonk, she could hear the phone receiver being thrown. Voices in the background arguing. Kat's angry voice, Mike's steady response, and then Eddie's apologetic voice on the phone.

"I'm sorry, Harry," he said, obviously coached. "I didn't mean to leave you there. I was just so relieved. I should never have left you standing on the corner. Please believe me."

"Eddie..." Harriet's resolve faded at the sound of her nephew's plea. "I do believe you. I believe in your innocence." She said the words that she had always wanted to hear. "But the time has come for you to prove that you didn't do anything wrong, not to slink away with a settlement which would never really clear your name. Believe me, these things are hard to shake. They follow you through life."

"We had an agreement." She could hear the little boy in the man's quavering voice.

"I'm sorry, sweetie, it was an agreement I couldn't live with. I'm not going to give you the money. I'm not going to change my mind."

"Mom's ballistic."

"Talk to her. Tell her that you can defend yourself. Tell her that you did nothing wrong."

Harriet waited for her nephew. She needed him to say the words.

"Shit, this is such a mess. Harry, you know how much the dojo means to me. We built it together. You are walking out on me, on all of us."

"Eddie, they have photos."

"What are you talking about?"

"Photos of the kids. Bruises. They say you hurt their children."

"Harriet, you know me. You know that isn't true."

Harriet said nothing.

"Harriet? You can't really be asking me if their ridiculous accusations are true." He was furious. Even over the phone, Harriet felt his righteous indignation. The fight that surged through him, the strength that she had lacked when she needed it.

"Save the dojo. Fight for it. We'll both be better off if you do." Harriet had never felt more confident. "This is the right thing for both of us."

"Mom will never forgive you."

"We're family, Eddie. She has no choice."

"Good luck with that. I guess that means you're quitting?"

Harriet didn't need to answer.

"Shit."

"Eddie, think about it. I never applied for the job."

Her hands were steady now. Maybe it was the mountain air. A great weight had been lifted from her shoulders.

"Good luck, Kiddo. You're going to be okay. Fight like hell for what you believe in."

"God, Harry."

She was about to hang up when he said, "You too."

"Thanks, Sweetie."

She could only imagine the scene that took place in Kat's living room after Eddie hung up the phone.

***

Looking down from the hillside, Harriet felt she had traveled a great distance. Maybe the wine had gone to her head. Her house was no longer her home but simply one of a thousand dots of light flickering below in the smog of the valley. Everything appeared clearer up here.

"I remember your dad. He was gorgeous, always flying off somewhere exotic. My dad was such a nerd in comparison." Patty had joined Harriet out on the terrace. The two women looked down on the sub-divisions below as Patty opened a bottle of Beaulieu Vineyard Cabernet. She had helped herself to a bottle, a few bottles, from Bobby's wine cellar. Harriet sipped the expensive wine gingerly.

"My dad flew phantom RC4F reconnaissance planes in Vietnam," Harriet remembered her father's pride when he described his mission, the reverence of his fellow officers at the base. Her dad, everyone told her, was a hero.

"Shit." Patty poured herself another glass.

"I miss him though."

"I mean, shit. You do know the role of naval aircraft in the Vietnam war, right?" Patty hadn't gone to college in the '70s without raging a lot about the horrors of the Vietnam War.

"They provided guidance to the Vietnamese Army," Harriet replied.

Patty snorted "Guidance, sure, and they dumped about 400,000 tons of napalm."

Harriet had no idea what Patty was talking about.

"The US Navy dropped napalm on everything: troops, tanks, buildings, jungle villages, even innocent civilians." Once she got going, the former activist couldn't stop herself. "Napalm sticks to people. It causes excruciating pain, burns, unconsciousness, and even death."

The color drained from Harriet's face. "He never said..." She chewed on her hair, squinted in the darkness. "Next thing I know you are going to tell me that my mom was a spy."

"That would be hard to imagine. I always thought of your mom as some sort of prisoner.

Harriet felt the ties that bound her to her family fraying. Ripped from their moorings, collateral damage from the earthquake. "You must think that I'm incredibly naïve."

But even earthquakes have explanations, faults underground that store up energy that sooner or later must be released.

"Don't sweat it, Sweetie. Every family has its things."

Harriet disagreed. "Except yours. The perfect Hopkins. We called your family the Glasses, you know. Brains, with your perfect house and your perfect yard with its perfect rose bushes and your brilliant brother who couldn't stand to steal and parents who were always there when you needed them.

"And even when we didn't." Patty didn't bother arguing. "Honey, don't fool yourself." What was the point? Anyhow, they both could hear her brilliant brother's BMW coming up the driveway now.

***

"I don't think we've met," Bobby said when he entered the room, "you must be my sister's new girlfriend."

Harriet stared at him in confusion, this chunky middle-aged man who had given the cook dinner instructions as he passed through his spectacular living room.

"Look again, Bro," Patty said. "You know Harriet."

Bobby did a second take and laughed. "Hello, Harriet, I hear you've sold your house."

She could feel him looking her over. In her intoxication, she had no idea what he might be seeing.

"My bad. You probably don't even know that my sister is a lesbian now."

"A...?" Tonight, nothing was as it seemed.

"Yeah, that's what I thought."

"Patty, really?"

Bobby winked at his sister. "We call her a lipstick lesbian, all cleaned up and ready for prime time, but believe me when I tell you my sister has her surprises."

"I guess so," Harriet was flustered, but it made the uncomfortable situation easier, talking about Patty. "I once drove Patty, you know, to the Greyhound Station. I believe

252

she was running away." Without Patty standing there with her hand on her hip, it would have been so much harder to think of something to say to her brother, the brilliant founder of Seed, recipient of everything golden in the Valley.

"Mind if I join you?" Bobby poured himself a glass of the Cabernet. "I see you've raided my wine cellar."

"We're celebrating the sale of Harriet's house."

"To Harriet, then," Bobby said, holding up his glass with an impish grin.

"To Harriet," Patty echoed, smiling.

"What's next?" Bobby asked Harriet.

"Well, I'm homeless," Harriet thought a moment and then said "I'm thinking of visiting my mother in Japan. And then maybe buying a house on the beach, some place far away from this Valley." She said it before she had thought it out, but when she said it, it sounded like a plan.

Dinner miraculously appeared in the kitchen, tacos, rice and beans, and a fresh avocado salad. After the housekeeper had cleared their plates, Patty excused herself to check in with the office. Bobby described his day to Harriet. He was teaching math at the junior high school. Harriet reminded him of the evenings so long ago when he used to tutor her in algebra.

"I'm a decent bookkeeper now," she said. "No thanks to you."

"And I'm a decent teacher, I think," he said. "Would you like some chocolate?"

Bobby led her to a chilled cabinet where he maintained his stash. Nothing but the best, imported chocolates from around the world. Harriet chose a dark chocolate. "I ordered those directly from Henri Le Roux in Paris," Bobby told her. "Their caramel filling and pates de fruit are incomparable." His French accent impressed her.

"Kevin's girlfriend, Mercedes, has been teaching me to dance. Do you know how to salsa?"

"No, but I've always wanted to learn."

By the time Patty returned, the audio system was cranked up, speakers blaring Shakira throughout the house. Harriet patiently instructed Bobby how to salsa: "Start with your feet together. Hold on the first beat. On the second step forward with your left foot. On the third, rock back with your right. On the fourth, step back with your left."

Bobby struggled to follow the beat. Harriet was forced to lead. Unlike, Mercedes, Bobby had a lousy sense of rhythm, but Harriet didn't mind. She felt as carefree as Kat in her silver cocktail dress and matching stilettos. When Bobby stepped on her foot for the third time, she giggled. "Steps are the easy part," she said. "Dancing with a partner, now that's tricky."

"Don't I know it," Bobby said.

The two former neighbors moved together in the darkness. After a while, their movements became more graceful, their hips swaying in unison. They held each other with a light touch, honoring the memory of the people they had once wanted to be.

In the valley below, cars continued to jockey for position and lights burned in the windows of office buildings where programmers were hard at work creating worlds that the original inhabitants of Silicon Valley could never have imagined.

About the Author

Raised in Seattle and the Santa Clara Valley of California, Kathryn Holzman left the west coast of the US seeking adventure in the Big Apple where she met her husband at a poetry reading. After attending Stanford University and NYU, she chose Health Care Administration as a career, working with public inebriates, dentists, urologists, and cardiologists. When the right side of her brain rebelled against endless databases and balance sheets, she moved to New England with her husband, now a digital artist. Both flourish in the lush beauty of Vermont and the creative communities of New England.

* 9 7 9 8 9 8 7 2 2 1 7 4 7 *